BRUXA
The Secret Within

ISBN: 1463704275
ISBN-13: 9781463704278

Library of Congress Control Number:
2011912009
CreateSpace, North Charleston, SC

ACKNOWLEDGMENTS

Without the support and help from friends and family, none of this would be possible.

This being my first novel I have a lot of thanking to do, so if I have forgotten anybody I apologize. I want to thank Teresa, Deny, Rachelle, Rute, Kris, Nicola, and Scott for being there in the painful start. I want to express my gratitude to the "CreateSpace Team" especially Jenny.L for always answering my distress calls. To all the editors who have helped me along the way, and a special thanks to my tough critic group Kelly, Michelle, and Amanda I love you guys.

A special shout out for the award winning team at Donato's, and all my clients for believing in me. I want to thank Nadine, Tiffany, and Ashley for keeping me strong and Brooke London for all her amazing advice. I am beyond grateful for my husband and son for putting up with my writing affair.

TABLE OF CONTENTS

This book is dedicated to all my Familia and to my son Matteo always remember your roots and no matter what life brings you, know that I will always love you.

BRUXA
The Secret Within

A Novel by

A.F. Costa

Chapter 1

WATCHER

"I promise this time we'll stay until your graduation," my mother Sonia whispered, as my eyes fell from her frown to the dark trench coat that hugged her delicate body, giving her the strong facade she needed. She tried desperately to maintain her composure as she continued. "I love you, Gabriella; please be careful and listen to your godmother Maria."

With a gentle hand she reached forward to sweep the hair off my face. Her dark eyes misting a bit as she looked at me to excuse her emotion with, "I can't help if I love you Gabriella — I'm your mother, and this is the first time we're separating." Then she recovered by giving me her famous affectionate slap on the arm, something she did when she felt apprehensive.

"I love you, too," I said. "I'm seventeen years old. I'm not a little girl anymore; I can take care of myself." I relented with a sigh and hugged her tight. "It's only going to be a few weeks until you join me there. And besides I think I can manage in your absence, it's you missy, that had better keep out of trouble." I smirked, trying to lighten the mood.

I glanced back to wave goodbye before passing through the security gates. I took a second look, admiring how beautiful my mother was. Her lush black hair cascaded over her shoulders; her flawless olive skin framed her astonishing dark eyes that radiated so much love and compassion. I could see them welled up with tears as she waved back to me.

As I stood at the gate waiting to board the red-eye flight, a haunting chill brushed by me like an icy breeze, forcing the tiny hairs on my neck to stand up. I sensed something deviant lurking nearby. Maintaining my composure, mentally canvassing the area around me, and opening my mind, I channeled into the thoughts of all unsuspecting people nearby.

Unable to detect anything out of the ordinary, my attention strayed to a loving father who cradled his sleeping daughter's tiny body in his arms. Envious, I looked away, wishing I still had my father. Ten years had passed since his death, and nothing had been right since.

"Gypsy" is one word that described my mother Sonia, as she dragged me with her from one city to the next, experiencing all that North America had to offer. I boarded the plane with mixed emotions; this new adventure to Gloucester, Massachusetts did not surprise me, it was the fact of me actually attending public high school that had me on edge.

I settled into my seat, pulled out my iPod and quickly put on my headphones. I turned up the volume as the, "silversun—pickups," drowned out the passengers and their thoughts, allowing the memories of my godmother Maria to fill my mind.

It had been years since I last saw Maria. Thank God for the Internet; we had at least been able to keep in contact. I giggled to myself, letting childhood rituals play out in my mind. Her white dress whirling outward as she danced, while the white cigar smoke swirled around, until the two merged into one. She is an Umbanda priestess, from an Afro-Brazilian religion that practices only white magic.

Reality kicked in and a wave of dread shot through me when the pilot announced our arrival in

BRUXA

Boston. Excited that I would finally be able to leave the confinements of my private Catholic boarding school for girls and live a somewhat normal life. The thought of public high school terrified me — especially with the first month of school already in session; I would be the obvious new girl.

It was my mother's attempt to introduce me to the real world. Until now, my whole existence had centered on strong religious beliefs and the art of magic. Born telepathic with the ability to channel and read thoughts, I had learned to control my gift with little stress but struggled with the idea of fitting in with others my age.

Excitement took over as the plane landed; knowing my god mother Maria was waiting for me. I was eager to see her. She had gone back to Brazil a year after my father's death, I hadn't seen her since. I grabbed my bags and practically ran to her when I exited the baggage claim. I instantly recognized the same crazy, frizzy hair she always twisted back into a rolled bun.

"Oh my lord, I've missed you so much!" Maria roared ecstatically in her thick Brazilian accent. "I can't believe how grownup you are!" She released her grip on me and took a step back to examine me. "You've become such a beautiful creature, and you look so much like your mother. Your eyes are definitely your father's."

"I've missed you, too!" I exclaimed. "I'm so glad to finally see you again." I wrapped my arms around her. She was just as I remembered her, right down to the warm hazel eyes and the beautiful full figure she carried so elegantly.

Maria filled me in as we drove out of Boston, talking about her week here and informed me that the movers had brought my things a few days earlier and that she set up my room. We talked so much that the drive didn't seem long. I was surprised as we passed the welcome sign for Gloucester. I felt anxious again as we turned down a long, winding side road. My catlike eyes allowed me too easily probe in the darkness as we drove up to an open set of massive iron gates.

"Welcome home, Gabriella." Maria turned to give me a warm smile as we entered the property. I stared through the car window while we pulled up in front of the house—more a grand mansion than a mere house. Overexcited, I flung open the car door before Maria could put the car into park and leaped out, eager to get a good look at our new residence.

The old world charm of the architecture blew me away. I stood there staring, while my mouth dropped open in disbelief. "Are you kidding me?" I squealed. I turned to let my eyes travel over the

Victorian embellishments that gave charm to the brick mansion, the stone tower rising toward the heavens, the grand stone pillars supporting the roof of the wraparound porch. The house was perfectly preserved from the ravages of time.

"Oh my God, I love this place! It's so mystical! Is that the waterfront?" I howled with enthusiasm as I ran toward the back of the house. I rounded the corner, tasting the salty ocean air. I stood at the edge of the yard, gazing at the moon's reflection dancing on the dark, vast body of water. Then I spun around like a little girl, pulling in the moon's light.

"Crazy child, get back here and help this old woman!" Maria yelled, her tone rich with amusement, shaking her head at my foolishness.

The home felt so familiar, welcoming me into its prestigious halls as if it had been waiting for me. I tossed my bags down in the foyer, my mouth parting in wonder at the elaborate interior, the lavish decor, like an enchanted fairytale mansion. Whoever had built this home had spared no expense in details.

I trailed my hands across the walls, feeling for imprints left behind by previous family occupants. Strangely, I did not feel anything. I thought for sure this home would have secret stories to tell. Maria must have done an excellent job in cleansing this home of unwanted energies.

Maria guided me through a brief tour of the home; there were too many rooms for me to truly process. The study, on the other hand, was memorable in its astoundingly rich detail and the fact that it sat in the round tower of the home. Bookshelves soared between tall, narrow windows to a domed ceiling twenty feet above. The plaster painted ceiling displaying fresco artwork that depicted angels flying in clouds. The finely detailed images were so life like; it was as if the angel's eyes were actually gazing down on those in the room below.

Maria led me down the hall in the west wing and stopped at the last old oak door. I knew this was my room even before she threw the door open, unprepared for the luxury within. I felt like a princess as I stepped into the huge room and wandered around, peering into the en suite washroom running my fingers along the fireplace's marble mantel. Similar to my mother's room in the east wing, which Maria had shown me before, this one was mine.

I settled languorously on the cushions in the bay window and lifted back the curtains, to reveal an amazing view. The moon's reflection dancing across the water, highlighted an abandon lighthouse further down the bay. Smiling in delight, I leaned back and closed my eyes, opening myself to absorb the details of the house! I loved this home already. I felt a familiar welcoming, as if it had been waiting for me all along.

"Come, child," Maria urged. "Get to bed. Tomorrow is going to be a busy day."

I rose, crossed the room, and threw my jet-lagged body onto my bed, giggling as I sank into the thick featherbed and the mountain of pillows.

"Try to get some sleep, child," Maria said, smiling at my giddiness. "Tomorrow you can explore more, and we'll have to get you ready for school on Monday."

****

I woke to the grey light of an overcast morning. Immediately whipping off the bed sheets, I jumped out of bed, not sure of the time and too wound up to actually care. Undiscouraged by the gloom and the possibility of rain it suggested, I washed and dressed hastily, then flew down the stairs, anxious to explore.

Swinging open the back door, I inhaled the cool breeze, allowing it to run through me, filling my senses with its freedom. I followed the cobblestone path toward the dock, my heart leaping with the waves as they washed in and out. I stood there taking it all in, scanning the area. My eyes locked onto a wooded area behind me. On impulse, I turned and followed a path that would lead me into a fog-wrapped depth.

The wind whispered through the branches and rustled the loose leaves, spiraling toward the ground. Tilting my head back, I closed my eyes and let the cool wind dance around me as instinct guided me. My fingertips slid across the rough bark of each trunk as I passed, searching for a story. The sweet damp woodland air filled my senses with a peaceful calm.

Suddenly my heart started to race, and a foreign burning sensation pulsed within my veins, stinging like liquid fire. At the same moment, everything fell silent.

My eyes flew wide open to scan my surroundings. I took my racing heart as a warning, the burning sensation had a familiarity that bred unease — these instances stronger, more potent then I ever remember. I looked around frantically, to see nothing; I only felt the weight of intense scrutiny — eyes watching me from a distance.

Aware I knew of its presence, it vanished just as quickly as it appeared. The burning sensation faded, leaving me only with the cool mist in the air. The wind returned to hiss through the leaves as the strange sensation evaporated completely. Apprehensive, I turned myself around and made my way back to the house.

Maria stood there waiting impatiently at the back door. She shook her head when she saw me coming from the direction of the woods. "Come and get yourself organized, child," she called, waving for me to come back to the house. "You have a lot to do today to be ready for school tomorrow!" she yelled out.

Approaching Maria, wanting to tell her what had just happened in the woods, I became tongue-tied. It had been years since I last saw her, and I didn't want to dampen our reunion.

I ran back upstairs to my room and started unpacking my things. I tried stirring my thoughts away as I worked, but I couldn't stop thinking about how compelling the presence felt, as if it looked right through my soul. I should have been more scared, but instead it intrigued me how it flared up something inside of me, that some how felt so familiar yet foreign.

I pulled out an old picture of my father and mother from my suitcase. My mind drifted as I ran my fingers over my father's face, wishing he was still here, and admiring my mother's loyal soul striving to forever preserve their love. I could not blame her, looking into those intense, golden topaz eyes fringed in thick, dark lashes that stood out against his velvety, porcelain-smooth skin. He possessed a dark and mysterious look, but carried the heart of an angel. He was not of Bruxa blood like my mother, her family forbade their love, and they fled from Portugal to a remote part of the Canadian Rockies where they secretly got married and had me.

My mother found my catlike eyes and my mouth so similar to my father's, a constant reminder of him. This worked in my favor whenever she got mad—I just had to look at her. I sighed, wondering what life would have been like if he lived.

My mother had been fortunate; he came from old money, leaving behind real estate everywhere. Fixing up and selling properties is the reason we moved around a lot. I never understood why he chose so many random places in Canada and the United States, even Europe; though my mother refused to ever go back.

It took much of the day to organize my room the way I wanted it. In between unpacking, I snuck off here and there, exploring in short bursts. When nightfall came, I threw myself on the bed. Exhausted, I instantly fell asleep.

I bolted upright when my alarm went off, and then jumped out of bed in a burst of panic. Attending an all girl's private schools with uniforms. I never had to worry about fitting in surrounded by nuns and other girls. I might have been sheltered but I wasn't naive to the differences between girls and boys whenever the two mingled. I prayed no one would notice me I hated feeling like I was center-stage with people staring and, worst of all, hearing their curious thoughts. I hated my gifts at times (though they definitely had advantages). Now I was thrust into a situation without the safe anonymity of a uniform to hide behind.

I must have tried on at least five different outfits, second-guessing each one. Finally, I tugged on my jeans and a hoodie, hoping to blend in with the rest of the students. I vigorously brushed my thick mane in a foolish attempt to add volume to naturally straight hair made flatter by its own weight — it fell down my back in a dark curtain. I contemplated the makeup my mother had bought me a year ago, and then pushed it aside. Who was I kidding?

Maria did not say one word while I ate breakfast, but she had one order: for me to relax and enjoy my first day. I grabbed the keys grateful my mother had sent down our cars a few days prior to the move. My mother said she would manage without a car for the few weeks while she stayed back in Toronto organizing the final deal of the house sale.

I felt totally unnerved as I pulled into the school parking lot, though some relief crept in when I saw it was half-empty — less chance of encounters. I got out, my head lowered in an attempt to go undetected as I approached the school entrance. My sweaty palms pulled open the front doors; anxiously I entered the school.

I took a deep breath as I entered the office, reassuring myself to be positive. I stopped just inside and glanced at the woman with short, mousy hair bent over the front desk. I didn't have to read her mind; I knew she was the school secretary.

"Hi," I said as she looked up. "My name is Gabriella, Gabby for short, uh…Fragoso. I'm here to get…my schedule." My face flushed and my nerves flat-lining, I glanced wistfully over my shoulder at the door hoping no one heard how nervous I sounded.

"Welcome to Gloucester High," the woman replied with a warm smile. Her cheerfulness was refreshing. "I'm Mrs. Gaston. You'll love it here," she added, no doubt noticing the panic in my eyes. "Here you go." she held out a piece of paper. "Oh, Gabber — I mean Gabby!" she said as I turned to go, and chuckled self-consciously at her slip. "You will need this map as well. Give me a second… let me highlight where your rooms are."

I waited, flattered by her thoughts about me as she worked. She liked my appearance; given my previous academic record, she was surprised I was even attending grade eleven when clearly my education was at college level. "Here you go." she said with a smile, ending my mental eavesdropping.

"Thank you," I said politely, reinforcing her opinion of me.

Horrified, all of my teachers made me stand up in front of the class as they introduced me. Emotionally exhausted by everyone's curiosity, I watched the minutes pass in my last class before lunch, waiting for the bell to ring. When it did, I felt the wondering minds all around me as I rose from my desk. Hoping to make a clean getaway, a group of my classmates surrounded me like a pack of wolves.

"Hi Gabby, I'm Cindy!" A beautiful blonde Barbie doll chirped. She introduced the others with her one by one. "This is Allison, Ana, Rayne, and Ashley. You're welcome to join us for lunch." Not giving me a chance to respond, she linked her arm with mine and pulled me out of the classroom, assuming we were instantly friends.

Cindy reminded me of the Energizer Bunny; she never stopped. As we all sat around a table in the cafeteria, she told me everything I needed to know about the school and its students. I couldn't even get a word in, amazed that one person could talk so much and still breathe at the same time. Finally, I tuned her out.

"How are you enjoying Gloucester?" The dark haired girl, Ana asked, interrupting Cindy. Her features were similar to mine. Scanning her mind, I sensed strong Italian family values that conflicted with her adventurous side, this intrigued me.

"Actually, it's starting to grow on me." I said, her interest relaxing me — until I felt everyone's curiosity flooding my mind. Their mental voices mingled together cranking my head to drop the unwanted frequency buzzing in my head. .

A boy stepped up to the table, a late bloomer who still wore his adolescence comfortably. "Hi beautiful," he said, his eyes on mine. "I'm Forest and I'll be at your beck and call." He bowed dramatically, while grabbing my hand and kissed it. I sensed a compassionate class joker who had a real flare for drama.

Rayne laughed, shaking his head at him. "You're brave, Forest."

Of course, Cindy was whispering everything I needed know about Forest, in school and out. However, with Forest's arrival my anxiety seemed to vanish. Normally I hated attention; I realized, with a selfish thrill, that I was starting to enjoy it.

BRUXA

"Gabby, you can follow me to our next class," said Allison, the prettiest girl in the group. She regarded me with her big blue eyes, reflecting off her flawless caramel skin. Right away, I sensed her honesty and felt a strong connection to her. I followed her to history class knowing she would be the one person I could trust.

As the school day came to the end, I gathered my things and made a mad dash to my car, hoping to avoid another gathering of curious students. Just as I started my car, a strong urge forced me to look up. My mouth dropped, as if an angel had descended in front of my car. I couldn't help but gawk at the most beautiful boy I had ever seen. Sunlight glinted off his golden brown hair, which framed his strong, alluring face. He looked excessively fashionable to be a jock, even though he had the build and height of one.

When his big brown eyes met mine, I ducked my head in embarrassment, hiding my sudden blush behind my hair. All I could think of was how amazing he was. Wow, just amazing. The way my cheeks burned, I knew my face was beyond beet red. How could I look up, with that telltale signal of my interest? Pretending not to notice him, I put my car into drive and pulled away.

The whole drive home, I could not stop thinking about those big brown eyes, that perfectly molded body, his lush, rich, golden brown hair. It was unbelievable that God had created such perfection and placed it right in front of me. I giggled, feeling foolish. When I arrived home, I jumped out of the car and ran inside, eager to tell Maria about him.

"Hello Maria!" I shouted as I burst through the front door. "I'm home... hello...where are you?" I concluded from her lack of response that she must have gone out. I was disappointed to find I had no one, I could release all the emotions I had felt today. I wandered into the kitchen and found the note she had left on the refrigerator: Gabby, food is in microwave. I had to run out for a few hours. Love Maria.

I grabbed my homework and went out to the dock so I could enjoy the calm of Mother Earth while I worked. The cutest black Lab puppy easily distracted my attention as it scampered along the rocky shore. I watched it for a few moments and looked around for its owner, seeing nobody in sight. I put down my book and knelt down to invite it over, it ran eagerly into my arms. I laughed as it enthusiastically licked my face. "You are the cutest thing." I told it, lifting it up. "You're as cute as the boy I saw at school." I felt my cheeks become warm again, feeling ridiculous for telling a dog about the boy. At least I got the chance to release my enthusiasm.

I cradled the puppy in my arms, scratching its head while I backtracked along the trail it had followed along the shore, hoping to find its owner. It licked the whole side of my face again, then squirmed out of my arms and took off.

"Hey!" I called and ran after it losing it in the wooded area. I hope it makes it home safe, I thought. It must be one of the neighbor's dogs. With our property being at least twenty acres, I haven't had the chance to meet any of them yet.

I returned to the dock to retrieve my books and stood there for a moment, enjoying the ocean breeze against my face as I thought about my new life here and the challenges yet to come.

"Gabriella, come give this old lady a hand!" Maria yelled from the back door, breaking me out of my trance. I ran up to help her finish unloading the bags from the car trunk. "Are you going to tell me about your first day?" Maria asked, smiling and lifting one eyebrow as if she already knew what to expect.

"It was great!" I exclaimed. "Everyone was friendly, and —" I felt my stomach tingle as I thought about the boy. "Oh Maria, I saw the cutest boy! We didn't talk, our eyes met for a quick second." I flushed, hearing how foolish I sounded. After all, I was seventeen years old, not twelve.

****

I got up earlier than normal the next morning to spend extra time on myself. I practiced different expressions in the mirror as I put on mascara, in case I had the opportunity to talk to him. I was amazed how catchy this teenage hormone thing was. I shook my head, feeling like an idiot. All this effort, when all I had to do was focus into his thoughts to see my chances. Now I understood how stray thoughts could cloud one's perspective.

Cindy and her whole group approached me as soon as I got out of my car at the school. "Hey, Gabby," she said, "how was your drive?" Before I could answer, she continued. "I'm upset — it's calling for rain. I was hoping to eat outside today, because you know everyone's curious about you, especially the boys."

Rayne laughed. "She's not a prize to parade around," he told her.

"Gabby, I think you're in my first class today," Ashley interrupted, much to my relief. "English with Mr. North?"

I nodded. "Can you tell me what to expect in his class, to better prepare for the year?" I was eager to change the subject. "I'll see you all later, at lunch." I said over my shoulder as I walked away with Ashley.

The morning was overwhelming, although I had to admit that I liked being on the A list. My confidence bloomed, even though I read resentment in many of the girls' thoughts, and some of the boys' thoughts disturbed me. Rayne was a great guy, I decided after a glimpse of his thoughts. He's in love with Ashley and she feels the same way about him, but both are too scared to admit it to the other. As for Cindy, her heart was in the right place, even though she came on too strong. I didn't see my mystery boy, and wondered if he was one of the curious ones.

I was sitting at my desk, doodling on a piece of paper as my stomach growled, waiting for the lunch bell to ring, suddenly out of nowhere two heads poked into the classroom from the hallway and quickly scanned our room. They looked older, probably in the graduating class, and they had "troublemaker" written all over them. Their eyes stopped on me, they pointed and snickered until Mrs. Vito closed the door on them. I heard their expressed amusement as they walked away and it troubled me — why were they laughing and looking at me? More importantly, why had I been unable to read them? The event dampened my emotions, so much that I didn't even hear the bell ring.

"Are you coming, Gabby?" Allison asked, waving her hand in front of my face to break me out of my daze.

"Um, yeah..." I muttered in confusion, while I gathered my stuff, not looking at her. I felt humiliated, even though Allison wasn't the cause.

"Are you okay?" Allison's bright blue eyes peered at me as she asked concerned.

"Yeah, I'm just tired. Thanks for asking." I forced a smile.

I followed Allison through the crowded hallways to a packed cafeteria. There seemed to be twice as many people there than yesterday, probably because of all the rain. My head started spinning; there were too many people, too many thoughts. When we sat down, I closed my eyes for a moment and tuned everything out. I stared hard at Cindy, trying to focus only on her as she gave me the dirt on everyone in the cavernous room.

"And that's the rat pack, "Cindy said, pointing over my shoulder. "The twins Scott and David Graver, Paul Dacicco, and Joey Davale." Cindy blushed and smirked sheepishly. I did not need to read her thoughts to know what she thought of them.

I looked over my shoulder, and my heart and mind froze — it's him! I jerked my head back to stare at the tabletop, taking a second look. The two goofing off were the same two I had seen peeking into my classroom; I guess those were the twins. Not wanting to be caught spying over my shoulder, I turned right around and stared boldly. They all looked as if they did not belong here; they were too edgy, their attire too fashionable, their hairstyles too perfect for this small city school.

"Those are the gods of the school." Cindy continued, leaning way over the table to whisper loudly near my ear. I tried to guess which name belonged to the god I had seen yesterday in the parking lot. "They're a very tight-knit bunch, been that way since grade school. Their families are the same. The twins Scott and David always cause trouble. Paul is nice, and a know-it-all. And…"she paused to sigh, "Joey. The sexiest guy alive in Gloucester; way too focused on his schoolwork though. He also gets around—not at all the commitment kind." She sighed again. "What a waste."

Joey, I repeated in my head, and heaved my own mental sigh.

Allison put on a mock frown. "Why do they keep looking at us and giggling at Joey?" She looked at me and cracked a big smile. She had a secret crush on the cute, dark-haired one—Paul. He reminded me of a European soccer player with his dark, wavy, unkempt hair and huge brown eyes. I had to agree with her secret assessment of him: *adorable*.

"I wouldn't start thinking anything!" I said aggravated that they were laughing at me, unable to read any of them, bothered me more.

Rayne overheard our conversation and slid into the empty chair next to me. "Do you not know how beautiful you are, Gabby?" Rayne said seriously, regarding me with those deep blue eyes of his. "Every guy I know thinks the same."

"Thanks, Rayne." I bit my lip as I felt my cheeks burn. I had no experience with the male gender. It was strange to think of myself, little Ms. Plain Jane as desirable. I did feel a surge of hope with Rayne's statement — maybe I did have a chance with Joey.

With fifteen minutes left of the lunch period, I found courage and walked by him, throwing him a smile as he glanced up at me. He turned his head quickly away, with no response. Unable to read his thoughts, I kept on walking, in an attempt to hide my painful embarrassment. Did he find me that repulsive that he would turn his head? Was this the reason his friends kept laughing at me and even worse, going out of their way to make fun of me in my own class? My throat closed and I held back tears.

I escaped to the girls' washroom and hid in a small bathroom stall until I could gain control of my tears. I felt so humiliated, an emotion I didn't feel often. I never cared if people liked me or not, never felt insulted. But now... Taking a deep breath, I pushed my bruised pride to the back of my mind and found my composure again. *I am the master of hiding emotions*, I reminded myself sternly. *No one is able to read me, not even my mother*. Head high, I strode out of the washroom and returned to the cafeteria

"Allison, the bell is going to ring soon; do you want to get a head start with me to Social class?" I said loudly, smiling at her as I walked past Joey and his rat pack as if they didn't exist. Then, as she stood nodding, I threw over my shoulder as we walked away, "I'll see you guys later."

The drive home from school felt like forever. The rain was coming down hard, forcing me to drive carefully. This gave me extra time to think about how stupid I was for thinking Joey would be interested in a five-foot three tree-hugger who couldn't even apply mascara properly. *Guys like Joey have beautiful well put-together girls throwing themselves at them*, I lectured myself. *One thing for sure*, I thought with the firmness of wounded pride, *I will never change who I am for some guy*.

The rain had slowed to a drizzle by the time I pulled up in front of the house. I ran quickly inside.

"Maria, I'm going to go for a walk." I called out, "I'll be back soon." I kicked off my shoes, pulled on my rubber boots, and swung my raincoat over my shoulders.

"Gabby, you're crazy." she protested, stepping into the kitchen doorway. "Dinner will be ready in a couple of hours. Be careful!" She added when she saw me already dressed in my rain gear.

Unlike most people, I have always loved the rain but then again; I am not like most people. My father always made time to play with me when it rained. There was something magical about a shower, as if God is cleansing the earth of its sorrow and pain.

I stood on the dock's edge and stared out into the bay, as the white waves moved across the grey ocean and crashed against the rocks. The rain seeped down the outside of my raincoat, and I imagined it washing away today's worries. It seemed to help; curiosity replaced my wounded pride as I turned my body and proceeded toward the woods, deciding to test fate again.

I stepped into the trees with a sense of freedom; I found calmness in the patter of each drop dancing its way from leaf to branch to needle to twig, as it made it way down to the ground. Captivated by the serenity, I tilted my head back and closed my eyes, allowing the rain to splatter onto my face, inhaling the smell of damp tree bark and wet earth as the birds sang to one another overhead.

My head snapped down as my heart suddenly thumped into overdrive, and that strange burning flowed through my veins. Everything seemed to stand still. Again, I sensed those intense, inquisitive eyes. I opened my eyes and looked around, wanting it to know I knew of its presence. This time it did not scurry away I felt its curiosity as it probed me, more deeply this time, as if it had a desire to know me.

As if we both have the same eternal desire to know one another, my mind supplied. Spellbound by its energy, I channeled deep into my thoughts, wanting to feel its emotions. I sensed it approach from behind — and then it was gone again.

A growling Rottweiler charged at me, appearing out of nowhere. I froze, unsure if it was about to attack me. The anger in its eyes seemed directed right at me. Then it stopped several feet away and approached slowly, sniffing all around me. I held my hand out, releasing some energy at the same time, to shield myself. It sat down in front of me as if it were observing my power and my failed attempt to control its mind. When I held my hand out in a friendly manner, it rose and trotted away disappearing into the underbrush. Confused and afraid, I didn't waste time getting back home.

"Maria!" I screamed as I burst into the kitchen, dripping rainwater I stopped on the threshold, seeing her seated comfortable at the table.

"What is wrong with you, child?" she exclaimed mildly, scrutinizing my face before her eyes fell to the puddle forming below me. "Go get changed, and we'll talk." she instructed me.

Her calmness helped calm me. I shrugged out of my raincoat, kicked off my boots, and ran upstairs to change into dry clothes. I actually felt refreshed and warm as I made my way back to the kitchen. She sat a bowl of soup and fresh bread out for me. I sat down and lifted the spoon.

"Are you going to tell me what's going on?" Maria asked, sounding surprised that my seeming panic had given away so easily to hunger.

I sighed. "Sorry. I needed to process a bit. All my senses are having a hard time adjusting here, grasping the concept of strange things and new people." I ended up telling her about my whole day as I ate. When I had finished both account and soup, I moved my bowl aside and rested my forehead on my folded arms on the table. "I feel this unusual bond with this strange presence I feel no evil in it.

But it's persistent. As for Joey, he offended whatever little ego I had," I whined, lifting my head.

"Gabby, I think that you may scare him," Maria assured me gently. "You're a beautiful, mystical creature with the purest soul." She said nothing of my visitor in the woods. "You aren't the same as most people, Gabby; don't forget: they are the lambs. You're of Bruxa blood, able to see what they can't." Maria regarded me with compassion, "You mustn't get carried away with nonsense, or boys. Always be true to your heart, follow your instincts—after all, you aren't one of them." Smiling, she rose and came to wrap her loving arms around me.

Chapter 2

COLLISION

Finally, Friday! I was ecstatic to leave school behind for the weekend as the day ended. Gathering my things from my locker and slamming the door shut, I sensed Allison approaching from behind.

"Hey, Gabby," she said, leaning on the locker next to mine to regard me with her intense blue eyes. "I'm glad I caught you before you left. We are going into the city tomorrow night, and we would love for you to join us. So, what do you say?" Allison continued to gaze at me, waiting on my answer.

I grimaced with uncertainty. "I'd love to go but I have to ask my godmother before I can give you an answer."

BRUXA

Allison shrugged good-naturedly. "Well, here's my cell number, anyways. Call and let me know." She pulled one of my notebooks from my bag and wrote her number on a blank page. She assumed right that I didn't have a cell phone I think the fact I 'm the only one who isn't texting during class was a giveaway. "Call me before two o'clock to let me know." Smiling and giggling, she waved goodbye and walked away.

I walked in the opposite direction, with my head down, jamming the notebook back into my bag. As I turned the corner, I ran right into Joey, who seemed to have been walking backward. His attention on a friend behind him, he turned around only when he reached the corner. A powerful jolt of energy went off as we collided, knocking us both off our feet. My books exploded from my bag and slid over the floor in all directions.

We both stared at each other in an awkward silence for several seconds. I recovered first, scrambling to my feet and stooping to gather the contents of my bag, anxious to leave before he said anything to bruise my already wounded ego. He sat back as if immobilized by shock, watching me. From the corner of my eye, I saw his face turn a pale grey. *Oh my God, the boy who hates me knows I am a freak!* I thought in mounting horror, and snatched up the last two books and fled without looking back. *How could I be so reckless with my powers?* I scolded myself as I raced out.

I reached the safety of my car, jumped in, and locked the doors. Only then did I relax enough to exhale. Joey came out of the school, looking distraught; his friends ran to his side. Mortified, afraid of being confronted, I jammed my key in the ignition, threw the car into gear, and took off. I never wanted to see him again.

My heart raced, I clutched the steering wheel so tight I was surprised it didn't come off in my hands. I struggled to make sense of what had just happened, hoping he would only think of it as a freak accident and nothing else. "Oh my God." I moaned as my panic only grew praying God would hear my call.

I had to pry my fingers off the steering wheel when I arrived home. I dropped my head resting it on the warm plastic in frustration—only one week, and I had managed to slip with my powers. As my self-blame eased its influence once, I heard samba music. The exotic, intoxicating sound embraced my mind, and I felt my shoulders relax.

Following the music to the backyard, I found Maria dancing around a fire she'd embedded in the lawn, her white dress whirling as she moved in expression of the music and smoke dancing around her. The sight brought back childhood memories as excitement outweighed my stress. The cigar smoke she blew around took away my bad energy, as I felt my body sway to the music, amazed at its power to change my mood.

I ran inside, tossed my bag onto my bed, and changed quickly. I rushed back outside, eager to participate in her ritual and free myself of my worries. We danced around the fire, two free spirits with no worries, no worldly concerns. She was preparing and cleansing the earth for the new life cycle to come, not just burning the dead yard waste. We laughed and sang for hours, I felt free and alive again as my body synced with the music.

When I stopped to drink some water, I noticed that same Rottweiler, sitting on the beach, watching us with curiosity. I ignored the dog and we carried on for another hour, until both of us were hungry and tired we called it a night and ordered pizza.

As we waited for the food to arrive, we both changed into warmer clothes, carried the pizza back to the backyard to eat it by firelight. I got up the nerve to face my fears from earlier in the day.

"Maria, I have something I have to tell you," I began, setting down my piece of pizza to concentrate on what I was saying. "Today in school I bumped into Joey. My shield must have been up or something, because I didn't notice that he was there until we walked into one another. The force of the collision knocked us both down — the force, not the impact," I clarified. "I'm scared he'll tell everyone that I'm a freak."

Maria smiled as if it were no big deal. "Gabby, you have nothing to worry about, trust me."

I didn't think it could be dismissed that simply. I shrugged and said, "I guess we'll have to wait and see. Oh, by the way — do you think I can go out tomorrow night with some girls from school? Please!" I added with my winning smile and hopeful, puppy-dog eyes.

My attempt to wheedle an immediate answer from her didn't work. "I'd have to talk to your mother first," Maria said. "She'll be calling in the morning, so you can ask her yourself."

Satisfied with that, I stood, gathered some of the remainders of our pizza dinner, and leaned over to kiss her forehead. "Good night, Maria. Thanks for tonight — it was just what I needed."

I looked back on my way to the house. As if it had seen all it needed to, the Rottweiler stood and trotted off into the night. Normally I understood and got along with animals, but this dog seemed threatened by me and untrusting, which I found disturbing. It was not at all like animal behavior, but more human like. Maybe a lost human soul had possessed this poor dog. I decided that tomorrow I would find the underlying cause of this weird dog situation. Right now, I needed to sleep.

My body felt a bit feverish and a little woozy as I made my way to my room. I opened the window to let in the cool night breeze before crawling into bed. Instantly I found myself lying motionless on the bed, unsure if I was dreaming or awake. The room was dark; I sensed a brightening that slowly grew into a faint glow. The light shifted into the figure of a man standing over me, and I faintly heard the sound of indrawn breath. A cold hand stroked my cheek. I sat up abruptly, breaking free of the dream, or the vision, or whatever it was. I looked around, wide-eyed — relieved to be alone.

Still feeling unsettled, I rose and walked over to close my window, then dashed back to the bed and burrowed under the duvet.

****

I dragged myself out of bed the next morning loathing leaving the comfort of my bed. I threw on a sweat suit and twisted my hair back into a messy bun. Who cared what I looked like? I had only planned to jog over to the neighboring house, about a mile away.

Breathless and sweaty, I made my way up to hit the doorbell, waiting impatiently for someone to answer. When it seemed I had waited too long, I turned to walk away. Turning back, I heard a voice behind, "Yes, may I help you?"

I turned around and my heart jumped into my throat. *Joey!* I struggled to control my emotions by acting as if I had never seen him before. Out of all days, he could have seen me; it had to be on a day when I looked like this! I wanted to curl up and die.

"Hi, I'm your new neighbor," I stammered, "I don't know if you can help me or not. You see, I keep finding dogs wandering around our property, and I wondered if they happened to be your dogs, or if they're just strays." I furiously fidgeted with my hands, shoving them behind my back, and felt the betraying flush in my cheeks as I thought about the day before. I realized, *He turned a shade paler when I turned around.*

"Oh yeah, sometimes my cousin comes by with his Rottie and Lab. Are they a problem?" His voice was smooth, and he had a better grip on his facial expression than I did, I noted ruefully.

"I'm sorry, do you mind asking him to keep them off our property? They're beautiful dogs, but a few days ago I had an encounter with the Rottie and he seemed a bit aggressive." I shrugged sheepishly. *Now he really thinks I am a freak.*

He stiffened. "I'll be sure to tell him. You won't have to worry anymore." He sounded offended, and his gaze shifted to a point somewhere off over my right shoulder.

"Thank you, I do appreciate that." I said sincerely, then pressed my lips together, trying desperately to keep my cool.

"All right. If you don't mind, I've got to finish my project," he said coldly and closed the door on me as if saying, "Get lost, freak."

I rolled my eyes. *I would love to knock him square in the nose,* I thought. *What a jerk! Who does he think he is?* Worst of all I had actually taken an interest in my repulsive, rude, jerk neighbor. What could possibly be worse? *My mother inviting his family over,* my mind supplied. I cringed. Definitely, I would die if I had to be in the same room with him.

As soon as I got home, I heard Maria saying, "She's walking in right now." She passed me the phone and mouthed, "Your mother."

"Hi, Mom, how are things?" I said brightly. "Are you going to be much longer? I miss you so much." She asked me how school was. "It's all right, they're doing work I did two years ago so I'm flying through everything." I hesitated. "Ah, Mom, a girl from my class asked me to go out tonight. Is that okay?" I had no idea what her response would be. Never have I gone out with friends.

She sighed, putting a wealth of worry into that simple exhalation, and I waited anxiously for her response. "Um...yes. However, Gabriella, be careful. Stay with your friend, no wandering around, and be home before eleven. Please, don't do anything stupid." she made another heavy sigh. "Well, I trust you."

"Thanks, Mom—I love you, too." I hung up the phone before she could change her mind and hugged Maria before eagerly dialing Allison's number.

Allison said she would meet me at my house and we would join up with Ashley and Cindy at the theater by 7:30 to catch an early movie, and then go to this coffee house called Jazz. "It's the new hot spot," she told me. I was ecstatic and nervous; this is my first night out with girlfriends— actually my first night out *ever*.

I dashed up to my bedroom to find something to wear. An hour later, not having the faintest idea what to wear or how to put myself together, I called Allison with my crisis. She didn't hesitate. "I'll be there ASAP," she said matter-of-factly and hung up.

I heard the doorbell ring while drying myself off after my shower. Throwing on a tracksuit, I rushed downstairs to greet her. Maria beat me to the door; I heard her welcoming Allison inside.

"Hi Gabby," Allison said, kicking off her shoes. She grinned with anticipation, definitely in her element, beyond excited to dress me up.

I paused, remembering my manners. "Allison, this is Maria, my godmother."

They smiled and shook hands. "It's nice to meet you, Allison," Maria said, surreptitiously eyeballing her.

"It's nice to meet you, too." She looked around and added in awe, "Wow, your house is beautiful!"

"Thanks; we're still waiting for some of our furniture—and my mother's touch," I said, grabbing her elbow and guided her upstairs to my room.

Allison stopped in front of my closet and folded her arms. "All right, Gabby, show me what we have to work with."

I opened the closet doors. "There's not much, mostly casual stuff. I've never gone out much; I've worn school uniforms my whole life, or lounging clothes," I muttered, looking away in embarrassment.

Allison approached the closet and put her hand on her hip. She pressed her lips together and gave me a firm look, "How long will it take you to dry your hair?" she questioned.

"About half an hour." I replied, lifting a hand to my mane of long hair.

"Good, because we're going shopping," she announced. "You'll have to hurry up we only have a few hours before we have to meet the others." Her eyes strayed back to the closet. "Trust me; you're going to need a few hours."

I felt both anxious and excited as we entered the mall. Allison was beyond thrilled to be my fashion coach, especially when she learned that I had a thousand-dollar limit on my credit card. She dragged me from one store to the next, and almost everything she picked out looked good and felt comfortable — she had a natural knack for selecting clothes. I wore my favorite outfit right out of the store, and I embarked on Allison's true passion — shoes. Unable to relate to her passion, I had to give her credit; she found the perfect shoes and boots for me.

"Now, to finish your new look, you are going to need the right makeup," she insisted, studying my face critically. "You don't need a lot, just the basic eyeliner, mascara, gloss, and a great bronzer." She guided me to her favorite cosmetics store.

"Very natural, please," I told the cosmetician nervously. "I don't wear makeup and I don't want to look plastered up."

The woman laughed. "Don't worry; I've got the perfect look for you." She showed me how to use liner, how to apply mascara, and how to brighten my features.

I was relieved when she finished, seeing that I did not look plastered. "Thank you, I love it." I smiled at the woman, who had just de-virginised my face.

"I love it," Allison gushed after standing back to study me. "You were stunning before — wow, you look amazing now!"

"Thanks, Allison, you're the best." I gave her a hug of appreciation. This was my first girl experience, and I loved it.

Allison checked her watch. "We have to get going, we don't have much time." She helped me gather up my bags, and we hustled back to my car.

Cindy and Ashley stood outside the theater as we arrived. "Oh my God, Gabby, you look amazing!" Ashley squealed when we ran up to them. "I love this look on you," she clapped her hands in excitement.

"Thanks to the fashion expert Allison," I said, smiling at Allison as she took a bow.

"Allison, great job!" Cindy smiled her approval. "Gabby, you look hot! I love the boots."

"Okay guys, we'd better get our tickets," Allison said, moving toward the entrance.

"Sorry guys, the movie is sold out." Ashley told us with a shrug. "That's why we're out here waiting for you both. We still can go to Jazz and get something to eat and hang out."

Standing outside of Jazz, I stared inside, blown away by how chic the place looked and beyond thankful for Allison's fashion acumen. It only got better as we walked in. A cross between a coffee lounge and a glamorous martini bar, the place was dimly illuminated to highlight the light coming from candles on every table, giving it a mysterious yet calm atmosphere. We sat up front by a mini stage, ordered some appetizers and lattés, and gawked at the place while we waited for our food to arrive. Cindy filled us in on the latest gossip, falling silent when the server brought our food. I looked around; the place started to fill up. *Maybe it was a good thing our movie sold out,* I thought.

"Oh my God — look whose coming and sitting down beside our table!" Cindy hissed in excitement, and we all turned to look.

I choked on the piece of biscotti I just bit into. *Great,* I thought sourly, *just as I starting to enjoy my night, the whole rat pack had to waltz in.* Two gorgeous girls came in with them. I was certain one had to be with Joey.

"Are you all right, Gabby?" Allison asked as I cleared my throat.

I nodded yes, as my blood boiled with annoyance. This boy is my curse! What had I done to deserve the constant torture of bumping into him?

The lights dimmed and the piped music stopped as the host stepped onto the stage. "Good evening, everyone thanks for coming. We have special guest performing tonight. Let's give a big round of applause to Alvero."

The lighting dimmed further as the applause died down. Head bowed over his guitar, Alvero fingers stroked graceful over the strings, coaxing forth a melody, and the whole place fell silent. As he began to sing, the spotlight slowly brightened. His passion and the angelic tune captivated everyone. He lifted his head up slowly into the spotlight, and I gasped — actually, every woman in there gasped, the sound rippling toward the back of the room like a domino effect.

Absolute perfection. He was the most gorgeous thing I had ever seen. He had full, astonishingly pink lush lips, porcelain skin, and alluring turquoise eyes, startling beneath the rich espresso of his hair.

A cross between a young Elvis and James Dean, he had that sexy rebel appeal down pat.

An unnerving sensation erupted as our eyes met, and my heart raced, sending my blood pulsing uncomfortably to my extremities. A burning ache filled my veins as I felt it slowly suffocating me. Like something inside me wanted to take over—I had to get out before I lost control. "I'll be right back," I yelled over the music and sprang to my feet.

I rushed out to the patio doors and stood outside, eyes closed, gulping in deep breaths of air. Lifting my hands to cover my face, I chanted a prayer until my breathing calmed and my heart eased. I felt myself slowly return to normal.

"You'll be okay, Gabriella." a soft voice whispered behind me.

I turned to find nobody there. Confused and frightened by what had happened, I knew I had to leave. This was my cue to go home. I went back inside.

The beautiful Alvero had finished his first set and was nowhere in sight. His unnerving presence had been replaced by something even more disturbing—Paul and Joey sitting at our table, chatting and laughing away with my new friends. I felt sick to my stomach the beautiful girls were still sitting at the other table with Scott and David, the twins.

I approached our table, holding my stomach. "I'm sorry, guys, something I ate didn't quit agree with me. I have to leave."

"No problem, Gabby. I hope you feel better soon." Allison peered at me with concern, and then asked, "Do you think it would be okay if Paul and Joey caught a ride with us too?" She smiled and whispered something too low for me to hear, and winked at me.

Torn between my pride and doing the right thing, I knew how much she liked Paul. If only she knew how much I despised Joey! "Yeah," I heard myself saying, "If they don't mind leaving soon." I didn't even look at Joey.

"Thank you, Gabriella," Joey's friend said, stood up to shake my hand, "By the way, I'm Paul. I appreciate it. Since you and Joey are neighbors, you can just drop me off with him." He glanced back at the other table and smirked. "I don't think the twins will be going home anytime soon, and unfortunately we came with them."

Allison and I hugged Ashley and Cindy goodnight as we left Jazz with Paul and Joey. Allison jumped into the backseat with Paul right way. Clenching my teeth, I waved at the passenger seat in resignation.

"Thank you." Joey said with a grimace, obviously disliking me as much as I disliked him.

"Don't worry, it's no problem." I said through my teeth.

Paul and Allison savored each other's company, laughing and talking the whole ride home. I tried to tap into Paul's thoughts. I found it strange—I was unable to read any of the rat pack boys. Allison was a different matter. She was wholly awestruck by Paul and hoped he felt the same about her. At least he seemed to.

"You have a nice hair color." Joey commented unexpectedly and completely took me off guard.

It was such an odd comment that I wasn't sure if I had mistaken what he had said. "I'm sorry; I don't think I heard you."

"You have a nice hair color." he said louder pointing to my hair.

Apparently not. "Um…thanks." I had no idea how to respond to his odd compliment. We both remained silent until I pulled up to his house.

"Well, I hope you feel better tomorrow." Joey said as he got out of the car. He actually sounded concerned.

They both said thank you and waved goodbye as we drove away. Thank God, that was over! Nice hair color—why on earth would he comment on my hair color? I barely heard Allison saying how this was one of the best times she'd ever had, and that they had exchanged numbers.

"He's going to call me tomorrow," she chirped, on a natural high. She looked at me. "So, did you have fun tonight?"

"You can say it was quite the experience." I said wryly smiled, pretending to be just as thrilled as she was.

"I think Joey might like you," she decided. "I've never seen him so timid — I couldn't help but notice. While you were gone he was talking and telling jokes, when you returned he froze as if he were in awe of you." Her eyes widened at her outrageous theory.

If you only knew, I thought. *He was truly awestruck by me yesterday afternoon.* "Yeah, I don't think so," I said aloud," we had a few bad run-ins with each other. This morning he practically slammed the door in my face about some dumb property issue."

She looked interested. "What happened?"

"I'm sorry, Allison, I'd rather not talk about it, I'm still trying to forget." I looked away, feeling bad for lying to her. I hugged her good night, wished her good luck on that phone call, and watched her leave. feeling drained and wanting only to hide myself in my bed. I realized sadly that I would never be able to talk to her about my true feelings. What would I tell her? That I am telepathic, see strange things, and am slowly learning to manipulate matter with my mind? That I come from a bloodline of secret witches known as the Bruxa, who are good witches and believe in God, and if you revealed our secret, I'll have to silence you forever? It's not exactly something you tell someone you want to be friends with, unless you are completely brain-dead.

While washing up before crawling into bed, I stared at my reflection, consumed with confusion. What was becoming of me? I opened my mind, trying to understand my reaction to Alvero. What had come over me tonight? Besides the fact of him being incredibly gorgeous, I felt a strange hunger when our eyes met; an instinctive feeling crawling within my skin, as if something inside wanted to tear itself free. A familiar sensation haunted my memory, just shy of the conscious level, and I felt a deep fear. What lay beneath the surface of *me*?

Chapter 3

RUSH

I did not feel quite like myself the next morning. Sunday Mass was the last thing I wanted to attend, and the house felt empty with Maria gone. Determined to savor this opportunity of being alone, I brewed a pot of coffee, inhaling the aroma that awakened my senses. I walked out onto the deck, hands wrapped around the warm mug. I sipped its contents, enjoying the warmth flowing down my throat, while the chill morning breeze caressed my face and the backs of my hands.

I perched myself down on the deck step, taking in the same autumn air that rustled the branches of the grand oak tree, while pondering my life's purpose.

BRUXA

I watched the copper bronze leaves cascade to the ground. What was to become of me when I turned eighteen and had my coronation, the time when a Bruxa becomes one with their gifts?

Who am I, really? I wondered. *What is my purpose?* We believe in the Book of Spirits. Only those of Bruxa blood can read and interpret its mystical writings, understand its powers. The lambs are the ordinary people who see only with human eyes—they have no idea of the true spiritual world. Throughout the ages, humans had wanted our gifts and powers. Easily misguided and misled by their egos and lust for power, unknowingly they open wrong doors, doors that welcome evil, dark spirits. Bruxa have been forced into secret lives because of the lamb's desire for power that is beyond their grasp, and paying the price for those egos.

There are many different groups of witches, some seduced by the dark arts—often lambs whose eyes were open to the spiritual world. Unlike the others, Bruxa are born into this life along bloodlines passed from mother to child, the lineages going as far back as ancient Iberia—modern-day Portugal, Spain, Andorra, Aragon, and France. My mother and I are of the Malicus bloodline, the rarest line left, and the noble Brujeria bloodline. Most all Bruxa have influence, power, and money throughout modern Europe, South America, and parts of North America as well.

We kept to our own to protect our secret way of life. My mother had broken the rules with my father; it took a long time for her family to forgive her. My grandfather still refuses to have anything to do with us. I had been fortunate to have the opportunity to see my grandmother a few times. My gifts surprised her, since I am a half-breed and not had the proper training. She told me stories about our enemies, the Lampirs—the original vampire that hunted down the Malicus bloodline leaving me the last female born.

For hundreds of years we have been at war. They tried to destroy our kind by killing off the women, especially those of the Malicus line. After World War 11, a truce had been made, as humanity took a turn for the worst; both sides still carried a strong hatred for one another.

The phone rang, and I jumped up and ran back inside, abandoning my brooding thoughts.

"Hey, Mom!" I said after reading the caller display. She expressed surprise that I answered; she expected the machine to pick up. "No, I didn't go to church today. It's been a long week and I needed to think." We exchanged news and I finished with, "I can't wait until you come, you're going to love it here, — love you, too." Hanging up the phone, I realized how much I needed my mother. I love Maria, but I needed to find out the truth from my mother.

The call left me feeling a lot better. I ran upstairs, washed my confusion away with the last vestiges of sleep to enjoy the rest of my day. I decided to run out and get some munchies, watching a movie would be a great way to pass the time. Hopping into my car not having the faintest idea where I was going, but I knew I would find something down town.

I passed Joey's house and started thinking about our collision in the hallway on Friday. I figured it's not worth being angry with him, it's time to let go of my wounded pride. *What is the big deal?* I asked myself. *So what, he does not return the interest I had in him.* I think my inability to read him intrigued me more. His beautifully constructed face and amazing build were merely pleasant distractions.

I pulled into the first plaza I saw that it looked promising; I couldn't help noticing an eye-catching motorbike. As the sun glinted off satin chrome drawn in by its appeal, I parked right beside it, getting out of my car for a better look. Of course, it had to be a Harley Davidson. I had never been this close to admire such a beautiful bike before. I always had a passion for bikes — I found their suggestion of freedom alluring.

"Isn't she a beauty?"

The voice ripped my mind away from the infatuation. "Yeah, it's gorgeous." I breathed, then gasped when I looked over my shoulder to see Joey standing behind me. "Is this yours?" I blurted in shock.

"Actually, no. But it is a nice bike." He smirked and walked away, keying his cell phone.

I gaped after him, then remembered my mission and went into the convenience slash video store. I browsed the chick flicks row, noticing Joey peeking into the store several times. Finally, I grabbed a bag of chips and went to the counter to pay. There he was again! He was still on his phone, while he secretly watched me. I thought it was odd how our paths kept crossing, yet he had not mentioned our Friday collision. Could that be why he was watching me? Was he waiting for his chance to call me out as a freak?

I could not help looking his way as I exited the convenience slash video store. His solid frame leaned against the bike; they were a perfect match for one another. His eyes followed me as I walked to my car. I looked around to see if there was anybody behind me, but we were alone in the lot. He in fact was looking at me intently, as if trying to read my thoughts. Our eyes met and locked, and I felt suddenly shy and somehow ashamed; I ducked my head in a futile attempt to escape my emotions.

"Gabby." his voice cracked.

"Yes." I tried not to look up as my checks felt flush.

"You know, I…"He hesitated.

"I thought that wasn't your bike." I said, purposely trying to gain the upper hand in this awkward situation by catching him in a lie.

"I wasn't being completely dishonest," he replied. "It's not mine yet. It still belongs to my father." He laughed nervously.

Wow, he is human, and even capable of laughing.

"Would you be interested…in going for a quick ride?" he blurted timidly, his hand shooting up to run over his perfectly free falling haircut. He looked like a model posing for a *GQ* ad—picture perfect. "It's okay if you don't." he shrugged quickly, assuming I had no desire.

"Are you kidding? I would love to!" I impulsively blurted out. "There's a slight problem—I have no helmet."

"If you want, I can pick up another one from my house and meet you on the side road—after all, we are neighbors." He offered as he mounted the bike.

"That would be great, I'll meet you on the bend in the road between our two properties."

My head leaned back against the headrest. As I drove my car to the rendezvous point, I realized how eager and desperate I sounded. So what just happened? I wondered while pulling onto the shoulder of the road. All of a sudden, he's talking to me and taking me out for a ride. Okay, he is just being a nice, a good neighbor I sternly told myself not to think anymore of it than that.

I enjoyed the sunlight that streamed through the windshield as I waited restlessly for Joey. The cold fall day had warmed into a perfect Indian summer day; I emptied my mind of all irrational thoughts convincing myself to just enjoy this time, and moment. *Soon I will be enjoying it on a Harley,* my mind intruded. *What an opportunity! On a Harley. With him, it couldn't get much better than that.*

He pulled up behind my car, looking as eager as I felt. I sprang out of my car and, looking into his eyes as I approached him, all I could think was, *I have to be dreaming this.* Whatever is happening, I will embrace it and take it while I can. He handed me the helmet and I swung onto the back of the bike, knowing this was very real.

"Hold on tight, and pinch me to slow down." he said as he kick-started the bike.

"What do I hold onto?" I yelled over the roar of the engine.

"Hold onto my waist and move with me." he yelled back.

Ecstatic, I put my hands on his waist. His body felt strong and astonishing next to mine.

As we ripped along the road, the speed thrilled me, made me feel alive, almost high. The growl of the motor sank into my core and made my heart race with excitement and fear. I'd never felt so free. Our bodies moved in perfect harmony. Somehow, it felt natural, as if a magical thread held our bodies together. Pushing away all fears of another rejection, I concentrated on the moment, on letting go.

Slowing, Joey turned the bike down an old gravel road, and I realized we were on the way to the abandoned lighthouse. When he stopped in front of it, I felt a prickle of panic—what was his intention?

He parked the bike and pulled off his helmet, then twisted to look over his shoulder at me. "Are you alright?" he asked when he saw my expression.

"Uh, yeah…that was incredible. Um … but why are we stopping here?"

"I wanted to show you this place." He said, swinging off the bike and looking around with enthusiasm. He rested his hands on his hips and looked back at me. "Consider it a local tour. It's got an amazing view."

I busied myself taking my helmet off so I would not look so nervous. I was still trying to grasp the complete three-sixty he'd made in his opinion of me—first disgusted and now friendly. As I got off the bike, I thought maybe I should be scared. He seemed a little Jekyll and Hyde. However, I didn't care; all that mattered was this moment.

"I come here to think and get away from stresses in my life." He said with a conspiratorial smile before turning to lead the way to the edge of the rocky escarpment.

I stopped and gaped when the land draped into the ocean as the water foamed around rock escarpment, leaving a breathtaking view. "Wow, this place is amazing." I murmured dreamily. "It almost sounds as if the ocean is talking, and this cliff—it looks as if God sketched it with his own hands."

Joey grinned in satisfaction. "I know, it's beautiful here Come with me." He beckoned as I followed him to a boarded-up doorway in the side of the lighthouse. A few of boards were missing allowing us to squeeze through the gap.

Enough light seeped inside and I could see the never-ending stairs spiraling up the outer wall of the tower. Looking at them made my legs throb. I dropped my gaze, and we looked at each other apprehensively.

"I'll race you!" I shouted, and dashed toward the stairs. A shout to protest my head start, Joey followed me.

BRUXA

Halfway up I started breathing like a winded horse and my legs wobbled with every step, but I was determined to win, so I kept pushing myself up those stairs. I was pretty sure he felt the same way as I heard him pant from behind me.

I staggered onto the upper platform with as much bounce as I could muster and instantly turned to boast, "I beat you!" as he pushed himself up the last few steps. Then I looked around and my jaw dropped in amazement. The view went on forever; you could even see the whole city of Gloucester from here.

"Oh my God, it's beyond belief!" I yelled exuberantly. I went to the rail and looked over. I peered down the cliff at the ocean far below and across the landscape toward the horizon. I realized how tiny, how minute our presence is in this vast world, and I suddenly felt humble.

Joey came up beside me and bent over, bracing his hands on his legs while he caught his breath. Then he straightened and leaned against the rail beside me. "Isn't it crazy? Look over there — that's your property, and that's mine; with binoculars you can watch the action in our little city," he said excitedly, pointing out everything. Then he turned and looked deep into my eyes, as if searching for my soul. I felt his intense chocolate eyes melting into my thoughts; and for the first time I sensed a painful confusion lingering within him. "I feel at ease and my worries seem to evaporate when I come up here." He sighed with deep sadness as he looked away. "I become conscious of what life has to offer and there is still so much to discover and learn."

"I've seen this lighthouse from my bedroom window, and I've been curious about it." I smiled and strolled away, hoping to lighten the mood. I closed my eyes, and slid my hand along the cold cement wall, feeling the grooves and dents of age, the imprints of its many stories. "These walls have many secrets, and sad stories of loss, and memories of love. Yes, stories of love, pain, and loneliness." Caught up in the moment, I didn't pay any attention to what came out of my mouth.

"Gabby, you're an interesting girl," he said behind me not sounding surprised. "I find it refreshing that you're different from the others."

Realizing I had been musing aloud, I scrambled for a response. "Not necessarily different," I said lightly. "Maybe I just understand more—a lot more—than you know."

He grabbed my hand and I felt a spark almost like a jolt of energy. In that second, I saw into him. Scared and embarrassed, I pulled my hand away, feeling trapped. I couldn't think of anything to say.

"Gabriella, I hope I didn't offend you. We have a lot in common, and I know how hard it may be sometimes, especially for you. Truth be told, nobody's knocked me off my feet before—I never experienced that kind of energy." He tried to reassure me with chuckle.

"I have no idea what you're talking about." I said stiffly and looked way, feeling my protective walls crumble. I felt exposed, and annoyed as if Joey had misled me here to confront me, I wanted to run as far from him as possible. "I'm no different from any other girl. It must have been some freak accident." I looked at him so hard it became a glare.

"Gabriella, please—I don't mean you wrong trust me, we have a lot more in common then you think." He smiled as if suggesting I was overreacting.

"Just because I look at things a little deeper than others doesn't make me different." I retorted. "Maybe you're the different one." I shouldn't have said that, I was hurt, and I knew there would be no way he would ever understand. "I'm sorry, that was rude of me," I sighed, and looked down at my hands on the railing. "Oh great, it's already four o'clock! I have to go—if Maria, or worse my mother, knows I'm running around with a boy it will be the end of me." I blurted in panic. It didn't help that I felt beyond uncomfortable with where our conversation seemed to be going; I would have grasped for any excuse.

"I understand, Gabriella." he sounded disappointed.

Not saying another word to one another, I followed behind him as we returned back to his bike, getting back on the bike knowing deep down inside, I did not want this day to end this way. I knew now that trying to be normal was going to get more complicated. As I held onto him on the ride back, I felt pain and disappointment in him when we reached my car...

"Thank you so much for the ride." I said getting off the bike, I handed him back his extra helmet bowing my head as I walked to my car. I turned back to face him and gave him a quick wave goodbye before ducking into my car.

Moments later, I pulled into my driveway; parking my car I slammed the heel of my hand against the steering wheel. Why had I done that? My emotions had gotten the better of me, and I overreacted. He had shown interest in me, and I quickly put it to an end. I heaved a shuddering sigh. This week had been too overwhelming; everything seemed so surreal, and I felt so much uncertainty. Now I knew why my mother had protected me from the world. Things had been a lot simpler before I came here. In less than a year, I would celebrate my eighteenth birthday coronation; the time a Bruxa becomes one with their gifts. How am I going to manage if I thought this first step into the world is already rough?

I sat for a moment, collecting my composure and calming my emotions before I grabbed my stuff and walked to the house. Hoping to avoid Maria, I turned the doorknob slowly and pushed the door open only wide enough to peek inside, hoping she was not standing there waiting for me. My shoulders slumped in defeat. Sure enough, she was the first thing I saw coming in.

Maria stood with her arms folded across her chest, looking at me with one disapproving eyebrow raised. "Where were you, Gabby?"

"Getting a movie and junk," I blurted, smiling innocently and holding up the bag. "Want to join me?"

"Thanks, but no you go ahead and enjoy your movie; I'm in the middle of reading something." Maria snickered, as if she knew exactly what was going on in my teenage mind.

Chapter 4

REUNION

I managed to avoid seeing Joey and his rat pack all the following week, which was a big relief. Paul called Allison; they were going to the Halloween dance together. Rayne found the courage to ask Ashley. Cindy and Ana were going to be each other's date; after all they are B.F.F's. I could not be bothered because I was too busy, anticipating my mother's arrival next week and since her arrival would mean Maria's return to Brazil, I wanted to spend as much time with my godmother as possible. Plus, I figured the less involvement I had with people at school, the less chaos I would create; I liked it better that way.

BRUXA

I went to bed Friday night feeling happy that the weekend was here and slept like a baby. I woke late morning to wind soughing through the bare tree branches and a thick grey fog beyond my window. Maria was nowhere in sight when I went downstairs she must have gone out shopping, thinking I would be in bed for a few more hours. I tossed my jacket and boots on and went for a morning stroll.

The air against my face felt cool and moist, and the fog made everything seem almost transparent and mystical. The wind seemed to whisper my name. Making me feel alive and refreshed. Standing on the balls of my feet, I lifted my arms up with a sense of liberation and released all my tensions into the wind and the mist. I closed my eyes, listening to the wind as it continued to call my name. I was spellbound as it took over me.

A cold breath brushed the back of my neck and a chill ran down my spine. Sensing my phantom visitor from behind, my blood burned as the ache pulsed within my veins. The uncontrollable crawling sensation underneath my skin began again and then he whispered gently, "Just breathe and relax. Trust me." His fingers slid up my arms lifting them above my head. His touch sent a jolt of energy that coursed through my body.

"You need to let go and feel the fire burning inside as you control each pulse." His words banished my fear and pain; I felt more control over what has been running through me. "Now breathe and own it. You're the puppet master controlling the strings." his voice tickled in my ear.

I opened my eyes and turned to see him, but he had vanished into the fog, leaving me feeling lost and overwhelmed with confusion. I fell to my knees as my protective walls caved in on me.

Off in the distance I heard somebody approaching "Gabriella, is that you?" Joey shouted in the distance, the fog muffling his voice. A moment later he emerged from the fog and ran up to help me to my feet. "You're freezing. Are you okay?" he inquired, his warm hands curling around my fingers.

I felt disoriented and held onto him. "Thanks," I mumbled.

He wrapped his jacket around me and rubbed my arms to warm me up.

"Where did you come from?" I asked, frowning in confusion.

"I noticed you from the road as I drove by you looked distraught so I pulled over. It's easy to get lost in this fog; please let me take you home," he insisted, turning me and walking me to his car. He opened the door for me and I got in, feeling a little ashamed of myself.

"Can I ask you a question?" I asked as he slid into the driver's seat. "How is it that you always show up at the right time?"

He looked at me with his intense brown eyes. "I don't know, maybe its fate. Or maybe it's because you're in front of my driveway entrance." He smirked, trying to divert my curiosity with an amusing answer.

"That's not what I asked you," I said, annoyed. "You confuse me — you hate me one moment, then you're my friend the next. You drive me crazy!" I knew I was making more of an ass of myself; but I had to voice my confusion.

He looked at me wide-eyed. "I've never hated you, and I don't mean to drive you crazy. I'm sorry if you feel that way about me."

He pulled up in front of my house, "Thanks Joey, I'm sorry it's just…you know what never mind, I'll see you later, thanks again for the ride." I rambled getting out of his car. I felt incredibly stupid watching him drive away. I wrapped my arms around the jacket he put around me — that I forgot to give back. Now I had to return it and make amends for my peculiar behavior.

I was surprised that Maria still hadn't come home, it felt like hours since I had left for my stroll. I glanced at the kitchen clock and was shocked to see that only an hour had passed. *What is wrong with me? I wondered with a flicker of fear. Who or what is that voice? It is not a sorcerer or witch; I know it is not human.* I gasped. Could it be a Lampir or a fallen one? No, I felt no evil within it. I knew I had to talk to Maria — she would tell me the truth or at least make sense of it. My mother always thinks I am unable to handle the truth, always sheltered me, but I could count on Maria not to hold back.

I sighed, thinking about my mother. While I yearned to have her here, everything with my mother is on a need-to-know basis — she never talks to me about anything serious or included me in any important decisions. I knew she loved me and wished me the world, but I am no longer that little girl waiting for her daddy to come home.

I heard the front door open and bolted out to greet Maria who just stood there, smiling. "Maria?"

"Surprise!" my mother shouted and jumped out from behind her.

"Mom!" I screamed, feeling a mixture of emotions as I hugged her tightly. While I was excited to see her, the confusion I had been trying to sort through still weighed heavily on my mind, that I couldn't fully enjoy the surprise.

BRUXA

"Isn't this house amazing?" Still smiling, my mother stepped back, taking in the houses as she looked around.

"Let me help you!" I exclaimed as I grabbed her bags. "I thought you had to stay another week!"

"Your mother wanted to surprise you, so I picked her up from the airport this morning." Maria was watching me I knew she saw the deep uncertainty behind my smile.

"Maria, I need to talk to you." I whispered as my mother ran forward to inspect the house.

"Child, I know you do. All I have to say is trust your instinct all will be shown to you." she winked, and walked away, leaving me more in the dark than before.

It had been a while since I saw my mother this happy. She seemed renewed, as if a light had switched on for her. I could not help but laugh and join her and Maria in their excitement.

My mother pulled out a bottle of wine and poured a glass for each of us for a toast. I thought of it as a bit strange. She wouldn't let me sip champagne, not even on News Years. "To a new beginning," my mother announced. "Wait one more thing—I have news! I am opening a holistic and spiritual healing shop in Boston, in this new posh area. Everything had been confirmed yesterday; we will be opening before Christmas." So that's why my mother is so wound up. She positively glowed with enthusiasm as we all raised our glasses to toast the shop's success.

"Congratulations, Sonia I'm happy for you." Maria hugged my mother.

"That's amazing! You're finally doing it." I squeezed her tight, knowing this had been her dream for a long time. She loved helping people and creating magical blends.

She and Maria celebrated all night long, drinking and laughing. I sat watching them, too consumed with my own worries to join in.

"Gabriella, you haven't told me about this boy." My mother peered at me with curious eyes.

I sighed. "There isn't much to say." I muttered, wanting to remove myself from this conversation.

"Oh, come on, it's your first crush! I would love to hear about it," she teased. She began to sway a bit. Never have I seen my mother intoxicated. Come to think of it, I had never seen her drink before.

"You know he is an extremely sexy young man." Maria joined in, and laughed.

"Maria! Not you, too!" I sank deeper into my chair, feeling like they had ganged up on me.

"Oh Gabby, you know it's time to find a husband." my mother giggled. "You have to make me a grandmother soon." She frowned in concentration as she poured herself and Maria another drink.

"Mom, that's not how things work anymore," I said in exasperation. "We're not living in Portugal a hundred years ago." I could not help but to laugh at how foolish they were acting.

"Sonia, let her at least kiss the boy first before choosing him for life!" Maria winked. "You know what they say!" She howled as my mother's eyes widened in disbelief. Then they both broke out in hysterical laughter.

"You both are cut off, I think its time to retire from the wine" I teased, shaking my head at them. I don't think my mother was drunk, but what ever she was I have never seen her like this.

"Come on," my mother drawled, "I just want to know if you like him or not. I won't stop until you tell me."

"Okay, I love to hate him," I exhaled, and left the kitchen before they said anything else.

I escaped to my room and sat on the window seat, gazing out into the dusk, preoccupied with all that had happened before Joey showed up. Who or what was this phantom visitor lurking in the shadows, why does he have that effect on me? It's too much to comprehend, whatever this shadow visitor is. Still, I found myself captivated; as if somehow he's a part of me, something that had been dormant, had now awakened. *No — reawakened,* and my heart started thumping secretly wanting to embrace the hidden energy and let it flow through my veins again.

Feeling as lost and ashamed as a child abandoned by her mother, I looked away from the window, and my eyes fell on Joey's jacket, hanging over my bedpost. I walked over to pick it up and cradle it, inhaling his scent, then laughed at how foolish I'd become since I first set eyes on him.

I loved disliking him, even though I knew I would take him anyway. There was something about his eyes I found alluring, that somehow pulled me in, plus those beautiful full lips! His smile engraved permanently in my mind. I curled up on my bed, arms around his jacket, and fell asleep imagining Joey holding me in his arms.

In my dream, I pushed through a dense fog, following a path nearly lost under the thick ground cover of mist. It led me to a mansion, forgotten or forsaken, for it seemed nature had reclaimed it. I entered the front foyer, where the air was cold and still and lit only by candles that did nothing to dispel the gloom. Then a gas lantern waiting on a side table lit up as if it had been placed there for me, I lifted it and walked down the dim hall, the lantern held aloft. Its light revealed amazing works of art that hung long-neglected on the walls, as if telling a story in time.

I found the first picture disturbing. An angel held a human, lying lifeless in its arms. I kept walking, passing other paintings but I hesitated in front of a picture of the Knights Templar at their burning. I remember studying the fall of the Templar's, and how they were falsely accused for witch craft and burnt to the stake, starting the inquisition. I shook my head in shame and moved on.

An uneasy feeling wrapped around me as my eye slid over to the next painting. A strong, masculine angel stood over a dark creature similar in appearance to the angel, clearly not blessed with the light of God. The angel held a scroll in one hand; his other rose, as if he were about to slay the demon angel. That's what he was about to do? I leaned closer — and the evil angel turned its head and looked at me.

I drew back with a gasp, tripping on my own feet as the lantern slipped through my grip. Not bothering to pick it up, I whirled and ran, driven by terror. The oil from the lantern burst into flames behind me. I was no longer able to feel my feet! I fell and scrambled along the cold floor as I got back up, struggling to escape the fire already blazing out of control behind me. Sobbing in frustration and fear, I finally pushed myself back to my feet and burst out of the mansion—into an open field.

A flock of dark-robed angels flew near, and then circled around me like crows. They threw back their cowls, all revealing their faces at once, all smirking flashing long sharp fangs, as if preparing to devour me. A rider on a white horse came out of nowhere, glowing too brightly for me to look upon him, and the dark angels shrank away in fear.

I gasped—and woke from my nightmare, covered in sweat. Trembling, I pushed myself out of bed and went into the washroom to wash my face in the hopes of washing away my fear.

I normally did not dream if I did, I never remembered them. So what was this? A warning? On the other hand, is it a glimpse of my inner self trying to come through? Whatever it meant, I had a hard time falling asleep again.

****

I felt sunlight burning against my exhausted eyelids and opened them to find my mother sitting on the edge of the bed, waiting for me to wake up.

"You are a beautiful creature, Gabriella," she said, stroking my hair away from my face.

BRUXA

I sat up, smiling sleepily. "Hey Mom," I moaned, still not fully awake.

"I missed you so much," she said. "I'm glad to be with you again." A line appeared briefly between her eyebrows. "I sense a great deal of confusion in you. Is there anything you want to tell me?" She smiled when I shook my head. "Okay. I will let you get ready. We will be waiting downstairs for you. I love you, Gabriella." She kissed me on the forehead, then rose and left my room.

I got up and stretched while looking out my window, enjoying the warmth of the sun. When my eyes touched on the lighthouse, I made a mental note that I had to apologize to Joey for my attitude the day before. Then I scrambled to get ready, knowing my mother was waiting for me. I wondered if she was planning our usual Sunday ritual. Mother insisted on focusing more on faith than craft.

I joined her and Maria in the kitchen, grabbing a fresh bun and some Portuguese cheese from the counter as my mother poured me a cup of coffee.

"I called and talked to your principal on Friday," she said as she set the mug on the table before me. "I told him you wouldn't be attending for a week. The movers should be here Tuesday morning, so we'll have some unpacking and arranging to do, to put some more life into this old home." She grinned and gave me a pat before walking away, sipping her own coffee.

Maria, seated across the table, stared at me for a while in silence. "I want you to promise me that no matter what, always trust in God," she said solemnly. "He will always be the light that guides you." She looked at me strangely, then got up to join my mother in the family room.

The way Maria had looked at me sent a chill of discomfort through me; I felt as if she were disappointed in me. Haunted by the change in Maria's eyes, breakfast did not seem as appealing to me anymore. I pushed my food away and walked down the hall to the family room.

"It's a beautiful day," I said from the doorway, interrupting their conversation. "I'm going to take a walk—I need some fresh air. I'll be back soon."

"Okay, sweetheart, please be careful," my mother called after me as I turned away.

"Thanks, Mom," I called back from the kitchen. "I'll see you guy's soon." zipping up my jacket, I walked out the back door.

I returned to the wooded area, determined to discover where the path led. Listening to the whispers of falling leaves and watching their many colors glowing like stained glass. The warm sunlight drizzling through the open spaces in the treetops, I felt at ease, unconcerned by the possibility of growling dogs or shadowy watchers. The cool fresh air, clean and pure brushed against my face, pushed by the breeze that tousled my hair. It cleared the confusion I had allowed to consume my mind in the past two weeks. Like a character in a fairytale, I skipped through the trees as a dryad in an enchanted forest, surrendering myself to the warm sun and all the splendours the earth had to offer.

The path opened into a clearing before continuing from the far side, and I saw it in the distance, winding toward the lighthouse. I looked around, making sure I was safe and alone, and then continued along the path.

Walking up to the old abandoned lighthouse, I mentally recapped the time spent here with Joey. I wandered around its base then went inside, pausing briefly to absorb each second as I climbed the stairs, placing my hand on the wall reliving that moment. When I finally reached the top of the stairs, thoughts of him had left me smiling.

Looking out over the vast, never-ending ocean, I wished that one day I would be the place he ran to. Captivated by the notion, I gazed through the glass window, as if I might see a reflection of him standing behind me. In fact, I saw his image, and it seemed to be coming closer. I smiled as if it was real rather than imagined; it seemed as if he were there — as if I could hear his heartbeat and his breath from behind as his image came closer. I closed my eyes to prolong the fantasy.

"Gabriella, what are you doing here?" he questioned. I jumped in awe as my throat dropped into my gut.

My eyes shot wide open. *He really is here!* Utter embarrassment made me feel as if I was suffocating and I choked trying to speak. I had lost all ability to function. My hand flew up to cover my mouth. Otherwise, my whole body froze and I stood there, catatonic. How did I not hear him walking up behind me? How had I not seen him when I came up? Was it possible I had hallucinated, either from stress or from the realistic intensity of my imagination?

Finally, I pulled myself together and turned around to look at him. I poked him hard with my index finger to make sure I am not gone crazy. No, he was real.

"What is wrong with you?" he guffawed, shaking his head.

"Oh my God, you scared me to death," I cried, feeling I would collapse with relief. Then I remembered how I'd gawked and sputtered at first, and I covered my face with my hands, wishing I could just disappear.

"I'm sorry. I can't believe you didn't notice me up here. You looked so focused staring out in your own world I didn't want to interrupt your train of thought when you first came up." He pressed his lips together, holding back his laughter.

I had less control and broke out into near-hysterical laughter that proved infectious—he started snickering and soon we were both laughing loudly.

"I thought I was alone, and I thought you were a hallucination or I'm just going crazy." The admission came out in gasps between my fits of laughter; I was having a hard time catching my breath.

"Sorry you're not crazy—I am."

Silence settled over me quickly. I looked at him, unnerved.

"Not literally," he hastened to assure me. "I mean I'm crazy to scare you like that." he sighed and stared at me with his deep-set eyes as he stepped closer. "I'm never able to say the right things around you, Gabriella."

"Um, I'm sorry about yesterday," I blurted to change the subject. "I didn't mean to sound ungrateful, it's just that I have a lot of things to adjust to." I turned to look at the ocean, trying to distance myself from him.

"How do you find it, living here?" he asked as he sat on the floor with his back against the inner wall.

I turned to look at him. "It's a big change for me. Everything is different." Comfortable again, I sat down across from him.

He lifted one eyebrow then narrowed his eyes. "You didn't answer my question."

"There are a lot of things I like—at least, I guess I do." I smiled at him, thinking, *you are one of them.* "Do you enjoy living here?" I redirected the spotlight to him.

"Yeah, I do. But I can't wait to be free to do what I want." He looked down at his fidgeting fingers. "My family expects a lot from me, which can be too much sometimes."

"Trust me, I understand," I said, feeling pretty much the same. "We have to make the best of what we are given. You can't change the path God puts in front of you." My hand came up to brush my hair away from my face.

"I would love to see the world from your eyes and feel what you feel," he murmured, his eyes meeting mine. "You seem free and passionate for life, whether it's good or bad."

"Speaking of," I said, realizing how much time had passed, "I have to head back home before my mother starts to freak out." Getting to my feet before I said something stupid, I added, "I have a long walk back."

"I'm going too." He rose. "Gabriella thanks for the talk." then he shrugged and grinned. "I parked my car on the road, if you want, I'll drive you home."

"That would be great my feet appreciate your offer."

He smiled at my cockiness.

We talked about school and the Halloween dance on Friday night during the drive to my house. I had him drop me off on the side road, hoping to keep my mother from seeing him. "Well, thanks" I said as I got out.

"Gabriella! Will you —" he shouted, as he rolled down his window and hesitated a moment, as if dumbstruck. "Uh, say hi to Allison for me..." he mumbled.

"Yeah, I'll do that." I waved and walked away, secretly wishing he had asked me to the dance. *Wishful thinking,* I told myself. *I am his new friend, his neighbor, and nothing more.* Still feeling embarrassed about how he had caught me at the lighthouse, I laughed to myself as I walked to the house.

"How was your walk?" Maria asked when I entered. She smiled at me with love, her mood contrasting with the disapproval I thought I had seen in her earlier.

"Hey, sweetheart, I was starting to worry." my mother said. "Did you enjoy yourself?"

"It was amazing I feel recharged." I said with a big smile.

We had some things sent down before the move that we had to unpack and arrange, being mindful that there still was a lot in storage from previous homes, as well — the last few places were not nearly as big as this one. There were six big bedrooms to fill in this house, and that was not counting the rooms downstairs. Though the house was stunning, it was too big for just us two, and that opinion was based on what Maria had shown me in our initial tour; I knew there had to be a lot more to this place than met the eye. All three of us were acting like children on a scavenger hunt, exploring every room deciding what should go where, once the movers brought the rest of our stuff.

I felt uneasy as we entered the cellar near the end of the day; it reminded me of my childhood home. The cellar in that home was where my mother taught me many spells, as my father watched. I settled on an old trunk to conjure memories of the past, while my mother and Maria wandered farther into the depths of the cellar, laughing and talking and occasionally exclaiming over something they'd found.

I remembered all my mother had taught me, of the three lineages of Bruxa, only we the Malicus are able to manipulate all four elements with our minds.

BRUXA

There are the Conjures, who dealt with spells and sprits, and the Lougaro shape-shifters. We all had originated on the Iberian Peninsula, which is nowadays in southern France, Argon, Andorra, Spain, and Portugal. Only we Malicus carry the purest form of Grigori bloodline; we were the most sacred lineage of the Bruxa society — a society with origins well before the advent of Christianity.

Through the ages, many groups had called themselves witches; people seem intrigued by all that is supernatural, which is good for them when put to good use. Unlike the dogma of those groups, a Bruxa does not know the whole truth until an elder decides you are strong enough in your will of obedience toward God then, only when you understand your gifts, are you able to read the Books of Truth and shadows. A true elder has not appeared for a few hundred years, it is said that it is an archangel. The head of each family, 'the council' has substituted in the elders place.

"Gabby, stop daydreaming and join us for dinner." My mother called, jarring me from my thoughts. I had not even noticed her and Maria going back up the stairs. Now there she was, shaking her head and smiling at me from the doorway at the top of the staircase. She looked around at the shadowy cellar. "There is a lot of work to do in this place, isn't there?" She sighed. "I know how you feel; my mind is also too preoccupied to remember anything right now."

She put her arm around my shoulders in a comforting hug as I reached the top of the stairs. "It's not that I've forgotten about our Sunday ritual," she explained. "I am sure, after this month, we'll be settled in and we'll get back to normal."

"Thanks, Mom." I smiled back at her.

"Oh — I forgot to tell you. Allison called."

Maria had prepared a satisfying meal. I ate too fast to appreciate it, eager to finish so I could call Allison. As soon as the dishes were cleared away Mom smiled and jerked her chin toward the phone, and I grinned and ran off to call my friend.

Twirling my hair anxiously while I waited for Allison to pick up, I wondered why Joey had mentioned her name earlier. Did she know something?

"Hi Gabby," she answered.

"Hi — Sorry I didn't call earlier it's been crazy all weekend."

"Don't worry; things have been the same with me." Her voice rose to a near squeal of delight. "Oh Gabby, Paul is amazing! I feel as if we have known each other for years!" She caught herself before she could act any more euphoric. "So tell me about what's been keeping you busy?"

"It's been an interesting one; my mother surprised me — she came yesterday. We've been doing a lot of catching up."

"Oh, that's who answered earlier." Allison said. "Anyways, are you coming to the dance next Friday?"

I felt a tiny surge of disappointment; I covered with, "I don't think I'll make it. I'm going to be busy, and I won't even be attending school this week."

"Oh, come on" she drawled. "What kind of excuse is that? Well, if you change your mind, you are welcome to come with Paul and me and..."She snickered.

"I did bump into Joey this weekend" I said. "He told me to say hi to you."

"Um-hum..."she mumbled as if knowing more. I knew she did not, but she definitely had her own suspicions.

"Allison, he's my neighbor and nothing more." I said in an exasperated tone, though I wished he were more. Determined to protect my pride, I'd never talk about my secret crush for Joey.

"Okay," she said as if she didn't believe me, "there has to be something terribly wrong with you, if you don't think he's hot."

"I do think he's attractive, that's it."

"Oh, please, Gabby! I don't believe you." Before I could protest, she changed the subject. "Anyways, if you want, I'll collect your schoolwork for this week and drop it off for you."

"Thanks, Allison, my mom took care of everything." I hesitated, hearing the clean-up continuing in the kitchen. "I have to let you go before my mother reminds me of the dishes." I sighed heavily.

"Okay, I'll keep in touch. Please, think—or beg your mom—about Friday I would love you to be there with me."

"I'll think about it, no promises." I smiled wistfully as I hung up the phone. I would love the chance to be Joey's date.

Chapter 5

TRICK OR TREAT

My mother's excited expression seemed tattooed on her face as she unlocked the front door of her soon-to-be shop. "Isn't it amazing!" she squealed as she flicked on the lights.

Maria and I exchanged an apprehensive glance, as we stood in a huge empty white space. Listening to my mother as she described in great depth the products she planned to offer, the blending counters, and the back room clinic. Her ideas were indisputably inventive; they would require a lot work, in less than two months.

BRUXA

"You're planning to have this place up and running in six weeks, Sonia?" Maria said skeptically, her eyebrows drawn together.

"Maria, did you forget my mother is Samantha the witch? With a twist of her wrist she'll put the preparations into fast-forward mode" I laughed, though I was only half teasing. My mother had always talked of doing this, creating personalized products for individuals, and what better way than to sell potions? If she wanted it, she would make it happen.

"Oh please," Mom protested, waving my exaggerated praise away. "I wish I was that talented." She smirked. "I will definitely have to cheat a bit to do it."

Closing up the shop, Maria and I exchanged a look of sadness, knowing our next stop was at the airport. Selfishly, I wished she didn't have to go back to Brazil, but I knew she had her own life she had to return to.

As we drove away from the airport, silence filled the car. Maria returning to Brazil definitely was the low point of the day. I hated saying goodbye to my godmother; I took comfort in knowing I would see her again for my eighteenth birthday coronation.

"Tomorrow is going to be a long day," Mom said, breaking the silence as we pulled into our driveway.

"We have a lot of stuff coming, I think we'd better call it a night."

A short time later after settling into bed, I heard a knock on my door. It opened letting in a crack of light as my mother poked her head around the door. "Is it okay if I come in?"

"Yes, of course you can." I sat up.

"I know the last couple of weeks have been rough," she said as she sat down on the edge of my bed. "I should have exposed you more to the real world sooner." she flashed a bittersweet smile. "Gabriella, I know you're not a little girl anymore. It's hard to believe you're almost a woman." She moaned. "I was just a little older then you when I married your father."

She paused and studied my face. "I see confusion hovering over you. Is it this boy, Joey? Or is there something you have to tell me?"

"Where to begin," I moaned. "All these different sensations are coming to me, things I have never felt. I keep seeing glimpses of the other side, and I have to admit, it scares me. An uneasy feeling comes over me. And Joey—it's strange; I can't read him at all, it's as if there's an unspoken connection to him."

Mom nodded knowingly. "Things are going to change for you this year. Sometimes our life path is a hard road to walk. Soon you will be eighteen and become one with your power. You're not just any Bruxa — you're of the Malicus lineage." I thought she was going to say more, but she just looked at me with sympathetic eyes, then leaned forward and kissed my forehead. "I love you. Now get some sleep."

****

Unprepared for all the things the movers brought in, I found the sight of all those crates, boxes, and pieces of furniture mentally exhausting. An ancient chest that two of the movers brought caught my attention. Curious, I examined the finely detailed angels carved into the chest's aged amber wood and the exotic ancient writing. I decided that Artistry this astonishing could only contain something truly wonderful. The only thing standing between the sealed mystery chest and me was the key.

I asked my mother for the key. She frowned and looked around, saying, "I'm not quite sure where I put it." In other words, "You are not getting it."

We spent hours unpacking as I searched for likely hiding places for that key, with no luck. Finally, tired and frustrated, I collapsed on the couch. My mother joined me and we both sighed.

****

Worn out by a week of unpacking and painting, I forgot all about the Halloween dance. Allison, of course, had to remind me. In fact, her persistence won the battle. Even if I tried to, there was no way of getting out it. I should have used my better judgment when Mom wanted to invite Allison over for dinner. Big mistake. They hit it off instantly, and Allison soon discovered I used my mother as an excuse not to go, when they teamed up and bulled me into going to the dance.

Now it was Friday afternoon, and the pile of rejected clothes on my bed was growing as I tried to decide what to wear. It looked as if an explosion had hit my room. It had been years since I dressed up in a costume. I was glad Allison, my fashion savoir, was coming over right after school to help me with my outfit, then spending the night.

I still could not believe what I had gotten myself into. Yes, secretly wishing Joey would show up with Paul—one thing was for certain, Joey was a big incentive for me. Anxiety overwhelmed me; it would be the first dance I have ever attended. I was concerned if everybody would laugh at me, or even worse. I pictured the scene from the movie *Carrie*, when she went crazy. I watched the minutes pass, waiting for Allison's arrival.

BRUXA

When the front doorbell rang, I tensed right up. Then, taking a deep breath, I ran downstairs and opened the door to admit Allison.

"Hey! I'm so excited…"Her voice trailed off and she frowned at me as she stepped inside. "Wow, you look sick; are you okay?"

I shook my head mutely.

Sudden realization dawned and she threw up a hand and said breezily, "Ah, your mother warned me this would happen. Relax, Gabby, you'll have a great time." She gripped my arms and gave me a friendly shake.

"I'm nervous," I groaned. "I've never been to a dance. What will happen if I fall on my face? Or, even worse, look like a flying chicken? "I felt ashamed, I loved dancing. The question was, could I dance?

"Don't worry, just copy what everybody else does," she said. Then she assured me, "If you want to leave early, we will — I promise."

I led her up the stairs to my bedroom.

"Did you find something to wear yet?" she asked, looking at the carnage on my bed as she tossed her overnight bag on a chair. When I shook my head, she exclaimed, "What are we waiting for? Show me what you've got and we'll figure something out."

I held up two handfuls of clothes. "These are a few things my mother gave me; I think your stuff might be better." That finally made me crack a smile — Allison is a wiz at this type of thing, and her excitement was infectious. I needed to feed off her energy.

"Well, let's see what we have to work with." Allison started digging through the mountain of clothes. "Here, Gabby, try this on with my skirt." She handed me the outfit and waited expectantly while I put it on.

"Oh my God!" she exclaimed when I whirled in front of her. "Gabby, I love it, you sexy gypsy!" she announced, her eyes bright with approval.

I stopped and studied myself in the mirror. "Thanks. It doesn't look too much?" I asked uncertainly. This whole costume thing perplexed me. Still looking at myself in the mirror at the long shirt draped to the floor, hugging my curves as the blouse slid off my shoulders. I remembered Disney's Hunchback of Notre-Dame I looked just like Esmeralda, but with topaz eyes. Liking what I saw, I finally said, "I think this is going to do." I still felt ridiculous; I assured myself that everything would be fine. I needed to relax enough to enjoy the evening.

Allison insisted that she drive, I think she figured if given the chance I would sneak away otherwise. My stomach churned with both enthusiasm and fear, and I struggled to keep my composure as me the gypsy and Allison the genie got out of her car.

"Oh Gabby, I love it!" Cindy squealed running over when she saw me get out of the car. She waved the rest of the pack over. "We've missed you this week."Cindy promptly threw her arms around me.

"It's good to see you, Gabby," Ashley hugged me.

"Hey, it's 'I Dream of Genie' and 'Esmeralda," Rayne quipped, and laughed.

Ashley and Rayne looked cute dressed as Bonnie and Clyde; Cindy, of course, was Marilyn Monroe, and Ana a cowgirl. My fear vanished when I saw everyone else dressed up. I put my nerves to rest and decided to enjoy the whole experience. Hearing the music ooze from the gym and seeing everyone energized and full of life made me glad that Allison and my mother had forced me to do this.

I felt disappointed when we approached a boy in an astronaut costume realizing it was Paul, standing by himself. "Hey girls, I bought your tickets already," he said, smiling and waving our tickets. His eyes slid to Allison and his whole face lit up; it was obvious that he adored her. After all, she made the perfect genie.

I could not stop my eyes from secretly searching for Joey as we entered the auditorium. I finally gave up and decided to enjoy myself. The loud music made it hard for conversation, so I opted to join my other friends on the dance floor, leaving Allison to absorb as much of Paul as possible. Losing myself in the moment, I did not care as my dancing fears vanished.

Definitely in need of some hydration, I left my friends on the dance floor and went to buy a bottle of water. I was so thirsty I gulped down the whole bottle without stopping. Gradually I became aware that somebody had been standing beside me, watching. I lowered the bottle and looked toward the bystander. My heart jumped into my throat, and quickly I put on my game face.

"Hey, nice costume, Care to read me my fortune?" Leaning against the pop machine, Joey held out his palm toward me.

"Sure, Zorro let me get my crystal ball from my pocket," I quipped. "Oh, I don't think you can afford me," I added, then laughed with him. I did not think it was possible for him to be any sexier. His dark costume hugged his body, highlighting every curve and groove. The black mask made his eyes and full lips seem even more alluring.

"Tell me this, gypsy," he said seriously, "there's a girl I wanted to ask to dance, or maybe hang out with me all night, but you see, I can't ask her. She's, um, difficult to understand at times, and I'm scared she'll say no." He stopped and looked me dead in the eye, waiting solemnly for my answer.

"If you like her you shouldn't hold back; you'll never know unless you go for it." I smiled hoping it had been me.

"All right. Thanks, gypsy," he said, then turned and walked away. I had little pity for his lack of confidence with this girl, I admit jealousy took over. I gritted my teeth, wanting to slap him upside the head.

I retreated to my friends, concealing my poor, defeated heart. How stupid could I be thinking he was talking about me?

Just when I thought my night could not get any worse, I heard the music change to a slower song. Discomfort took over, and the last thing I wanted is to watch couples swaying together on the floor. Trying desperately to escape my wounded pride, I made my way to the door.

My mood shifted immediately as a faint smell of sulphur pierced my nostrils. Something foreign triggered inside of me. My pulse quickened with the burn, but it stung with a fury. My teeth clenched with an overwhelming urge to strike something. Where had that smell come from? I desperately scanned the crowd of lambs, then, ashamed and mortified by this unknown rage, I bolted to the doors.

The burning in my veins cooled as I stepped outside. What had come over me? I rounded the corner and found a private spot where I could hide, cupping my face, praying to God for help and tried to calm myself by concentrating on my breathing. *I am the master of this,* I told myself firmly. *I own and control this burning.*

As I convinced myself to relax, the familiar unknown angelic voice whispered in the cool night air, "Its okay and I've got everything under control. Enjoy your night." His voice soothed me and eased the tension from my body. I leaned my back against the wall and tipped my head up, exhaled the unwanted feelings as it washed away. Now replaced with curiosity over the identity of my phantom visitor, I opened my eyes hoping to catch a glimpse of my silent protector.

"Gabriella! I wondered where you ran off to," Joey shouted, breaking me from my trance. He stopped in front of me and peered with concern. "Are you okay?"

"Don't mind me, I had a mild panic attack," I said, shaking my head and laughing at myself. I stepped out of the corner.

BRUXA

He gestured toward the door to the auditorium, as I walked along with him. "I took your advice and I tried to ask her, but I couldn't find her anywhere," he said, sounding disappointed.

Right now, the last thing I wanted to hear about was this girl. One thing for sure, I did not understand the male gender. Why in hell would he hunt me down to tell me he couldn't find some girl he liked? Jealous, I had no desire to help at all. "I'm sorry; you seem quite taken by her—don't worry, you'll bump into her again," I blurted, then bit my lip, and looked away, trying to hide my jealousy.

As we approached the glass door, he shouted, "Oh my God, there she is!"

I stared through the doors, thinking, *He has to be kidding if he thinks I am going to look at her.*

"Do you see her?" he asked excitedly.

This was ripping me apart inside. I ignored him and kept walking.

He grabbed me by my shoulder and turned me around to face him. "I found her—she's right in front of me." His eyes behind his Zorro mask were piercing.

I reflexively looked around, saw nobody else besides me, and pointed to myself. He nodded. I quickly looked down, feeling incredibly stupid.

"Of course it's you, Gabby," he said softly.

Relieved, shocked, embarrassed—a jumble of emotions ran through my head. I covered my face with my hands. How could I be so foolish; how could I let my inexperience with boys be so apparent? However, that did not matter anymore. I lowered my hands, revealing my face, and smiled as I gazed into his deep brown eyes. When I laughed, it felt like a release.

He hung his head, misinterpreting my response. "I feel stupid."

I quickly shook my head. "I would love to dance and hang out with you all night," I declared, sounding a bit desperate.

His head came up, and he smiled. Our eyes locked, and we both laughed. I felt giddy, still adjusting to the fact that he had wanted me this whole time. Everything wrong or bad that had happened minutes ago disappeared as he grabbed my hand. I bit my lip, trying to hide the smirk of a lovesick fool. What I wanted to do was scream, jump around, and tell the world that Joey Davale liked me!

When we walked back into the auditorium, heads turned and I saw awed expressions, as if we were Cinderella and Prince Charming making our entrance. The fast song that had been playing ended and a slow song came on. Joey pulled me into his arms, then chuckled and lifted my arms around his neck before dropping his to circle my waist. He pulled me in closer, and nothing else seemed to exist but the two of us. I felt his heart beating against my chest. A strong energy force ran through us as we looked into each other's eyes. I saw everything he felt. For the first time, I could read his thoughts—he was allowing me to peek inside his mind. There was something uniquely different about him, yet very familiar.

"I told you we had a lot in common," he whispered in my ear, sending a shiver down my spine. At that moment, the pieces fell together, and I knew he was of Bruxa blood.

The song ended, and we parted and walked off the dance floor together. "Did you know the whole time?" I asked as we made our way to an empty table.

"From the first moment I saw you, you bewitched me," he replied. "I can't read you, I sense your energy. I didn't have the courage to look at you or speak to you until you knocked me off my feet," he confessed, stroking his index finger lightly over my face.

"I thought I repulsed you."

"Are you kidding?" he exclaimed. "You are the most beautiful thing I've ever seen. And…you are the first girl to ever make me nervous," he admitted.

"Really? I'll never forget the first time I smiled at you—it killed me," I confessed, remembering my wounded pride.

"It scared me, how much I wanted you," he said, dropping his gaze to his fidgeting fingers. "I knew there was something different about you; it wasn't until my first encounter with you in the woods that I knew you weren't one of the lambs."

"So that explains the pesky dog situation." I smirked.

"Hey guys, it's about time!" Paul shouted as he and Allison approached. "Joey, if I had to hear about this for another week…"He shook his head, lips pressed together in mock disapproval; then he grinned as they sat down at the table with us.

Hours later, when we were getting into bed back at my house, Allison caught me off guard. "You know, I've seen you and Joey in my dreams," she said. "I know you both carry a great secret. You'll carry a burden unwillingly, and changes are heading your way."

My mouth hit the floor—my friend is clairvoyant! How had I not seen it?

"It's okay," she continued casually before pausing to yawn. "You don't have to tell me anything, I'm always here for you." Smiling, she slid into the spare bed and pulled up the covers.

BRUXA

I sat in my bed, gaping in disbelief, contemplating the strange, animalistic instinct that consumed me tonight. Never before had I experienced smells so strongly; nor had I felt this desire to attack or hurt anything. This thing growing inside of me was not a normal Bruxa trait.

Chapter 6

THE ROOM

My mother's knock on the door the next morning woke us. "Good morning, girls!" she called. "Breakfast is ready."

"Thanks, Mom," I called, and looked over at Allison. She looked as tired as I felt. Groaning, we rolled out of bed and dragged ourselves downstairs.

"How did it go last night?" my mother blurted the minute we entered the kitchen. Her eyes were wide, her expression eager.

I smiled. "It was good." I sat down at the table.

"We had a great time, Sonia," Allison said, then added with a smirk, "Your daughter has a secret admirer." I nearly choked on my orange juice.

"I knew it! He talked to you, didn't he?" my mother said, sounding like a schoolgirl.

"Okay, please—enough!" I said, and then changed the subject. "Allison, what are you doing tomorrow?"

"I have church at nine, and I'm meeting up with Paul later. Why? Do you guys want to double date?" Allison asked perkily.

I flashed her glare. She was excessively cheerful for first thing in the morning. "I didn't know you were religious," I said, determined to keep the subject off Joey and I. In truth, I did not want my mother to know about us until I knew it was serious—just in case something happened, or worse, to prevent my mother from planning my wedding. I did not even know for sure what was going on—I had never dated a boy. In fact, I never even had a crush before. For now, all that mattered was that I knew how he felt about me.

"I had a lot of family issues and personal problems in my life before," Allison answered. "God saved me and I found my salvation." She spoke proudly. It was clear that the blood of Christ protected her, which, I realized was why I was unable to read her wholly.

After Allison left, I decided to hang out with my mother, tagging along as she drove into the city and picked up a few things for her shop. As we drove past Joey's property, I stared out the window, unable to contain my smile. I started wondering about relationships. After a while I asked, "Mom, how did you know Dad was the one?"

She glanced my way and smiled. "I knew from the moment I saw him," she said, her voice tender. "It's funny — we should have hated each other; I guess God had other plans for us."

I hesitated, chewing the inside of my cheek before asking my next question. "Mom, I need to ask you something else. Does the smell of sulfur mean anything? Is it bad to feel a yearning to attack?" I finally threw it out there.

Her face went pale. She pulled over and stopped the car on the side of the road, momentarily looking at me with a blank stare. "Oh, great, I forgot my wallet on the dresser," she said, sounding flustered. She glanced at me again, her face still expressionless, she quickly turned the car around. "Sorry, hon, I didn't mean to cut you off. I completely forgot I have a meeting. I've got to take you back home." Finally, with clear reluctance, she sighed and said, "Gabby, I don't know. Why are you asking?"

I quickly tried to think of something to say to alleviate what looked like panic. "I got water from a machine yesterday and it smelled like sulphur. It enraged me; I was so thirsty, and I felt extremely aggravated that I had wasted my money." Listening to myself, I cringed, I came across as a moron. *I suck at lying.* I didn't need to be telepathic to read my mother's reaction.

"You're absolutely unbelievable," she said, laughing.

She pulled into the driveway and ran into the house. I got out and stood beside the car, knowing something else was up and not understanding the effect of what I said had on her. It obviously was not good, according to her reaction.

She came back out of the house. "Sweetheart, I want you to stay here and enjoy this amazing, warm autumn day," she told me. "I completely forgot about my meeting with the contractors. You'll probably want to pick up something to eat—I'll be late tonight." She gave me a quick kiss goodbye, hopped back into the car, and raced off. I stood there, wondering what she was really going to do.

Confused with the change growing inside of me and my mother's reaction scared me. With so much on her plate with her new shop, the last thing I wanted to do was add more stress. My mother has always catered to my life, and now she starting her own following her dream and opening her shop.

I got in my car and took off to the lighthouse, hoping Joey would be there, waiting for me to distract my thoughts.

When I pulled up in front of the lighthouse, I saw the bike he had been riding that first day we came here together. I got out of my car, eager to see him, needing to hear his calming, tender voice. My stomach fluttered as I approached the lighthouse. Then I started second-guessing myself, as my nerves possessed me. *No*, I told myself, *things are different between us now.*

He was leaned against the doorway with his hands tucked into his pockets, the sun illuminating him as if he were a Greek god. I hesitated when I saw the look of uncertainty on his face. Is he going to tell me that he did not mean what he said last night? Did he want to be friends after all? *How could I be so stupid?* My thoughts started to betray me while I approached him.

"What took you so long.?" he asked, then laughed, and threw me a helmet.

I sighed in relief as I caught the helmet. "How did you... Never mind; as long as you can't see my thoughts, we'll be fine." I smiled, shaking my head.

"What are you waiting for? Let's go." He placed his hand on my back and guided me toward the bike.

BRUXA

I could only bite my lip in disbelief at this new-found affection. I swung my leg over the saddle and held his waist firmly when he got on. This would be our last bike ride of the season, I knew because the weather was getting colder. This just made the rush of complete freedom even more special. It felt right. I didn't have to pretend to be "normal." We were all that existed; nothing else mattered.

The wind of our passage as it blew around my body fuelled my excitement, ended briefly when he slowed the bike down and turned down an alley downtown.

He pulled into the parking lot of the local bistro and parked the bike. He swung off the bike, and I watched him take off his helmet. Then he turned to me and smiled, taking my breath way. "I figured you must be hungry," he said.

Preoccupied, it took me a few seconds to register what he said. I took off my helmet and shook my hair out, then shook my head. "It's okay." I compressed my lips, feeling irresponsible. "I left my purse in my car," I admitted as I swung off the bike. The last thing I wanted was to look cheap.

"I wouldn't let you pay in any case... come on, let's get take-out." He grabbed my hand, and I felt his energy surging through my veins. His touch drove my heart to a frantic pace as his spirit danced in my mind.

We took our meal back to the lighthouse. As we pushed ourselves up the steep stairs, I definitely burned off any carbohydrate indulgence from the past week. Not that I cared. Then it dawned on me as I realized how thirsty the climb made me: "Oh great, we forgot to get something to drink."

"Don't worry," he said smugly, "it's all taken care of."

"I can't believe you!" I exclaimed as I topped the stairs and stopped to stare at what he had done. I grabbed him by his shirt and tugged him toward me, then released him and turned to look again at the blanket he'd spread on the floor of the lighthouse catwalk, complete with cushions and a wine bucket full of bottled water. "Is this our real first date?" I quipped, my voice crackled.

"I wanted to celebrate the first moment we ever spent together," he said, and then his tone lightened. "Let's eat—I'm starving." He brushed his hand across my back, and a tingle of exhilaration slid across my skin.

We ate, talked, and laughed, enjoying every second of our official first date. After the meal, we stared at each other in a tongue-tied moment of silence.

"I think we should walk this off and watch the sun set," he said suddenly, breaking his stare. He began to gather our stuff and cleaned up the mess we made while eating.

"I can use a walk," I replied, leaning forward to help tidy up our mess. "I wanted to thank you for preparing all this for me," I added, pausing to look at him.

His face broke into a smile. "Gabriella, you don't have to thank me. I'm glad you're here with me!" He scooped up the bags full of our picnic waste, and we made our way back down the stairs and put everything in the bike holster.

Offering me his hand, he led me down to the shoreline, making sure I did not trip while we clambered down the rock path, to a small cleared sand beach. We sat on a big piece of driftwood that laid half embedded in the sand and stared out at the ocean. The breeze that played with my hair felt cool against my face. I pulled up my legs and wrapped my arms around my knees in an attempt to stay warm. Then I looked sidelong at him, hoping my cheeks did not redden.

"Mr. Joey, it's your turn to tell me about yourself," I said.

He shrugged. "There isn't much to tell." He paused and thought a moment. "I was seven years old when my family emigrated here from Andorra, I have a ten-year-old brother who drives me crazy. My parents expect way too much from me, and I'm a Christmas baby — I'll be eighteen on December 25th." Again he paused, frowning in thought, and added, "I love studying history, especially that of our own kind." He looked at me. "So, Miss Gabby, are you going to tell me about *you*?"

I chuckled self-consciously. "It might bore you!" When he just waited, watching me, I continued. "Um, my father died when I was seven years old, since then we've moved around a lot — I have lived pretty much everywhere. I love feeling free and I love the splendor of nature." I smiled at that, and then the smile faded. "Ever since we moved here, I've been confused about my gifts and who I am. Right now, you're the only thing that makes sense in my life." Feeling my cheeks heat, I looked out at the ocean, suddenly wondering if I should throw myself out there. Maybe I was being a little too honest for my own good.

"I understand, I feel the same as you," he said, and my shoulders sagged in relief. "I'll be eighteen soon and I'm scared. I know we haven't known each other long, we're not like the lambs; things are different to us." He lifted my hand and kissed it. "I feel that you are a part of my life's purpose. I know

111

this is all new to you. I want you to know that, even though I'm used to being around girls, this is new to me as well." He leaned in and lowered his head toward mine.

I quickly ducked my head and our foreheads bumped. "I'm sorry," I whispered, struggling to pull away. "As much as it feels right, I can't right now." I was terrified! I had never kissed a boy, and I had no idea what to expect. I wanted to enjoy him for a while without making it complicated.

He left his head leaning against mine. "It's getting chilly," he said. "Do you mind if I warm you up?" He wrapped his arms around me.

We sat there, enjoying the peacefulness, aware of each other's emotions. He traced the lines on my palm with his fingers and held his hand next to mine to compare them. Occasionally we would gaze at one another, harmonious in our silence.

Finally, he released me with a groan. "We'd better get going before your mother gets home."

"Yeah, you're right," I pouted getting back onto my feet, not wanting to leave.

He walked me over to my car and stood behind me toying with my hair while I unlocked my car door. I looked at him over my shoulder, smiling. "I guess this is goodbye for now," I said, turning to face him.

"For now," he agreed. "I'll find a way to see you tomorrow." He kissed my forehead, then stepped back and smiled "Get going."

I hated driving away. I could have stayed in his arms for an eternity. Clearly, he had bewitched me, as well.

Twenty minutes after I got home, I heard a key in the front lock. I rushed downstairs to the foyer as my mother stepped inside. "Hey, Mom."

"Hey, beautiful, how was your day?" She smiled and set down her bags, then leaned forward to dig through one of them, saying, "Gabriella, I have something for you." I stepped closer, curious. "Oh, here it is." She straightened and held out a small box to me. "I hope you like it; I wanted to give you something special. I know this move and sudden exposure to the world has not been easy for you." She nodded toward the box I held. Her smile was unconvincing. "It's a protective charm for you to wear."

"Thanks, Mom." I opened the box and gasped. "Mom, this is unbelievable! I don't know what to say," I exclaimed as I stared at a carefully detailed silver angel, its hands cupped around a bright red ruby carved into a small vial. A pearly white animal fang served as a cap, and the angel's wings extended upward to form the loop for a long chain that reminded me of something medieval. "It's so beautiful! Where did you find it?" I held it up, staring at it in awe.

"It belonged to your father," she said. She looked at me with a small smile. "I had to get it cleaned. He wanted to wait until your eighteenth birthday to give it to you, but I could not resist. Look—" She caught the charm and turned it over in her palm. "—there is an inscription on the back." I peered at it. "I'm sorry, I have no idea how to read it," she admitted. "I think its ancient Hebrew."

She gently lifted the chain and dropped it over my head. "You have to promise me you will never take it off," she said solemnly. "The thought of you losing it—this is precious to our family." She stared into my eyes.

"I promise I will never take it off," I said solemnly, then giggled and wrapped my arms around her in a tight hug.

I stepped back and lifted the charm to examine it. This was the most exquisite piece of jewellery I had ever seen. The details of the angel were incredible, so lifelike, and the fang corking the top of the vial suited the piece perfectly. I dropped it to my chest and felt its mystical power as the charm settled close to my heart. I took a deep breath and exhaled. Everything felt clear to me again as if all my confusion, all my worries and stresses had faded away.

"Thank you, Mom, I love it." I said, my voice deep with appreciation.

My mother's smile seemed relieved—she was probably thrilled to see me in high spirits at last. She rested her hand on my cheek. "I love you more than you will ever know. There are many things we will soon need to discuss. Please do not leave me in the dark; come to me with your concerns. I am your mother, and there is nothing you can say or do will ever change that," she said sincerely.

Later we settled in the family room together, each curled up on opposite ends of the couch, sipping coffee. I opened up to her, revealing my bottled-up emotions, telling my mother everything about Joey. I got so caught up in describing my feelings toward Joey that I skipped mentioning the watcher in the shadows of the woods, the insistent draw of the singer Alvero, and the foul smell I had noticed.

I had never realized how easy it was to talk to her. We laughed and talked about love and boys all night. For the first time I saw her as a woman, not just a mother. I realized how similar we are.

The next morning I sat up in bed and stretched my arms wide feeling refreshed, alert, and ready to take on the new day. It had been a while since I had actually felt so energized upon waking. Grabbing my clothes, I practically bounced into the bathroom eager to attend church with my mother. I stood in front of the mirror for a few seconds, taking a good look at my reflection. I saw something different about my eyes. They seemed much more alluring. My mother's call broke me out of my self-examination.

Feeling ashamed at my recent absence made it awkward walking into the church. I looked up at the murals and felt as if God's eyes were upon me as we walked down the aisle between the pews. I felt curious eyes on us, though neither of us paid them any attention as we sat down. Halfway through Mass, curiosity got the better of me and I looked over at them, now that their heads turned away.

I saw the families of the rat pack. Joey turned around and secretly smiled at me, as if he felt my eyes on him. Glancing first at my mother to make sure she was absorbed in the service, I shot him a smile back, and then he turned back around. I could not wait for the service to be over.

I sat back and observed them and their families as they took their sacraments. Joey's mother was sophisticated with her beautiful, rich, dark hair cut into a classic blunt. She was an average size, with features similar to my mother's. His father was tall and brooding, a handsome older gentlemen with light brown hair and a pale complexion. The younger brother was a younger version of Joey, though he took more after his father, while Joey had his mother's features. Joey carried his father's strong, tall physique, though. They were one of the better-looking families.

After seeing his family, I wanted to flee before an awkward situation could arise. My mother, bless her pure, naïve soul, found the good in everything bad. I jumped to my feet as soon as the service ended; she narrowed her eyes in a disapproving glare. I looked at her, knowing that if I did not sit back down, there would be hell to pay.

"If you walk out now," she hissed between her teeth, "those Bruxa families will think you're corrupted or, even worse; they'll think you're weak." She paused and gave me a crooked smile. "I don't want to stay here either." I looked at her in disbelief. Never had I seen this cunning side of my mother.

As each family passed, they looked our way and nodded. My stomach fluttered when Joey and his family passed. They smiled, though his mother's smile was accompanied by probing eyes. Finally the last family passed — Paul's family, and by far the friendliest. His mother had a youthful glow and his father was dark and handsome, reminding me of an older version of Paul. His sister, Angela, had the same brown hair and blue eyes as her mother.

His mother stopped and approached my mother. "Sonia, is that you?" she asked, her eyes focused on Mom.

My mother hesitated, then exclaimed, "I can't believe it—Ana! You look amazing." She rose and they hugged. Paul and I looked at one another, baffled.

"Sonia, your mother didn't lie—she's gorgeous," Ana said, looking at me. Then she looked back at my mother and her expression filled with remorse. "And I'm sorry to hear about your husband. This is my son Paul, and my daughter Angela, and my husband Tony," Ana said proudly. Mom and I smiled and nodded at each as she introduced them. They were pleasant and sincere souls.

"It's nice to meet you all. This is my daughter Gabriella." My mother was just as proud. She and Ana walked away together out of the church, smiling and laughing like old best friends. Paul and I exchanged glances again. Obviously, our mothers had relations of some sort. I went to the car to wait for her.

"Oh Gabriella," she said when she finally opened the driver's side door, "Ana is an old friend from Portugal! Our mothers were best friends. I haven't seen her since I was fourteen years old." She slid behind the wheel and sighed. "As for what I said in church, we were only one of many different and mixed lineages there.

I know I have not exposed you to our kind before or educated you on our history — especially that of our family. We are the last of our kind — your grandfather is the last noble left. That is why they all stared and nodded inside. If you had gotten up and left, that would have looked really bad." she blurted.

My mother dropped me off at home and took off to the city to take care of some business. I paused at the front door to turn and wave goodbye as she pulled away. As I closed the door behind me, I realized how little I knew of our kind including my Family. I decided to snoop around and find the key to that unique chest I had seen the movers carry in. I was certain that it held something that would put to rest my curiosity.

Maria had told me to use my instincts. Closing my eyes, I focused on my thoughts as I walked around. Feeling my way with my hands, I followed a magical thread as it pulled me. It led me to the study, a room I normally neglected. I continued probing, and sensed a strong force tugging at me. I opened my eyes, knowing there was something here. When I looked around, I saw nothing but book shelves.

I moved along the shelves, noticing a small, cleverly concealed door. I opened it, put my hand inside, and felt around. I found a lever and pressed it. When the bottom shelf slid aside, I crawled through the opening. Able to straighten up once inside, I could see a narrow winding staircase illuminated by natural light from above. The air was stale and heavy with the smell of old books and dust. With no hesitation, I darted up those stairs.

I entered a room where time seemed to have stood still, as if somebody dropped me in the medieval times. A thick layer of dust covered everything, and cobwebs papered the walls, highlighted by the sunlight filtering in through a four tiny circular windows, one on each corner acting as skylights. A sundial stood in the center of the room. A desk and shelves filled with books, and an astonishing number of foreign historical objects lay here and there. Freaked out by the webs and sneezing from the dust, I turned and went back down the stairs to get the cleaning supplies I needed before pursuing my personal treasure hunt.

I made a quick stop at my bedroom and changed into sweats and an old shirt. I ran back downstairs to grab a broom and duster from the cleaning pantry. Before I could gather more, I heard a knocking at the front door. Annoyed to be distracted from my excavation, I headed toward the door, yelling, "Wait! I'm coming." In the foyer, I glimpsed myself in the mirror—I looked like a dirty bum. Shrugging impatiently, planning to get rid of the visitor quickly anyway, I opened the door.

My mouth dropped open. There Joey stood on the veranda. He looked me up and down, grinning. "Nice outfit."

Groaning inwardly, I stammered, "Hey! I wasn't expecting anybody; I was going to clean."

"It's the day of rest," he replied. "So why don't you get your shoes and jacket on and come relax with me?"

"I would love to go out with you, but look at me. I have a lot to do." Just thinking about all the cleaning I had to face made me exhausted.

"You can give up half an hour of your time today to drink coffee."

I sighed, tempted. No, I had too much to do. "If you want you can come in and have a coffee with me," I compromised. "I do really need a coffee right about now."

He grinned. "Actually, I grabbed some before I came here." He leaned over and picked up a cardboard tray containing two paper cups. His persistence won me over; I opened the door wider. "By the way, I love this new look," he teased as he stepped past me.

I closed the door quickly. "It's getting cold; I can feel winter coming," I muttered, accepting one of the coffee cups and wrapping my hands around it to warm up.

"I know, no more taking the bike out! How did you like Mass today?" he asked with a trace of sarcasm as we walked toward the family room.

"It was odd, feeling all those inquisitive eyes on us." I shrugged. "Nevertheless, it was nice."

"My mother thinks you're beautiful," he told me as we settled on the couch. "She also said you have a strong gift and that you and your mother are the last of the dynasty."

Again, I shrugged, this time in annoyance. "People always tell me that. I have no idea what they're talking about."

"I noticed your mother talking to Paul's mother Ana," he said as he wrapped his arms around me.

"I guess they're old family friends."

"She's an amazing woman." He cradled me tighter. "Our family carries the strongest Lougaro gift; our Alpha skips a generation. My father's uncle is the head of our clan."

"My father isn't a Bruxa or any kind of witch. My mother's family disowned her when she married my father." Feeling ashamed of being a half-breed, I looked down.

"You have nothing to be ashamed of. To me, you're perfect. My parents recognized your mother—she is of the royal house of Malicious, the strongest of all Bruxa bloodlines. I guess you're my little lost princess," he teased.

Sitting in the comfort of his arms, I wondered why my mother had never told me any of this. Am I my mother's shame? Is that why I never had the chance to build relationships with any other Bruxa? By now, I should be mastering my gifts. The only thing I could master was reading the thoughts of the lambs and my protective shield. My mother moved things with her mind, healed people with a touch, and conjured spells with air. I never understood why people kept telling me I am so strong.

"I better get back to cleaning, before my mother gets back," I mumbled.

"Oh, okay. Do you want me to help you?" he asked, sounding anxious.

"Actually, I have a lot of things to catch up on. I will see you tomorrow in school." I wasn't trying to blowing him off, I just wanted to be by myself right then. The whole talk about families bothered me.

"Is everything okay?" He paused for a few seconds and looked at me with concerned eyes. "Have you changed your mind about things?"

"Oh—of course not. I just didn't expect…I have a lot to do today," I stammered.

"Well, if you need help, I can help. I know you mother won't be back until dark." He sounded desperate.

"What—you have some kind of K-9 radar?" I teased and chuckled. I relented, with the admonishment, "Only if you promise not to talk about the Bruxa or family matters. One more thing: you have to swear an oath that you will never tell anyone about what I'm about to show you." I held my hand out, for him to shake on our oath.

"I promise, no talk of families, and I swear by oath to lose my tongue if I should ever tell a living soul," he said solemnly, grabbing my hand. I felt the burn of his oath as our hands met.

He agreed to hide his car, in case my mother came home earlier. I put a quick end to his excitement. Smiling, I led him to the cleaning pantry and started passing him the cleaning supplies. In the back of my mind, I feared my mother's disapproval for inviting him into the house while she was gone. I reminded myself that it was completely innocent; we were just cleaning the secret room.

I led him down the hall into the study. "Well, this is it," I said, turning to him. "I want you to stand facing the hallway while I open it." I giggled as I turned him around to face the door.

The Room

He let his eyes rove around that side of the room while he waited. "Oh, I love your home," he said. "I've always wanted to see inside. The person who lived here before gave an uneasy feel to the property."

"What do you mean the person before—how long ago was this?" I asked as I reached to pull the lever.

"I don't know, a few years ago. Nobody ever saw him—or maybe her. I have to be honest: this house used to freak me out. Ever since you've come it's felt welcoming."

"Okay, you can turn around," I said gleefully, clapping with excitement.

He looked around for the source of my excitement, frowning with confusion until I pointed to the floor opening. "Oh wow! A secret entrance," he exclaimed bending down to look in. Like a kid, he rubbed his hands together, grinning. "I'm eager to explore."

I raised an eyebrow. "Are you ready?"

We crawled through and pulled the cleaning supplies in after us.

His face lit up as we stood in front of the narrow spiral staircase. "Wow, I can't believe this, this is crazy."

I grabbed his hand and directed him up the stairs. Stopping on the second last step, I turned, biting my lip in anticipation to cover his eyes before we entered the secret room. "Okay, one step, and then we are going to make a left, and *voila*!" I pulled my hand from his eyes. He stood there speechless, looking around. Uncertain of his reaction, I asked, "So…what do you think?"

"Wow, this is insane! We'd better start cleaning before the dust or spiders consume us." His expression was still unreadable.

I was unsure if inviting him up had been the right decision, but he did not once mention anything about our families. We goofed around, which made cleaning amusing. Exhausted we dropped to the floor.

"Are you hungry?" I asked. "God knows I am."

"You finish up, and I'll run out and get something for us," he suggested. "What do you want?"

"Honestly, whatever—I'm not picky, Wait, I'll walk you out," I said, pushing to my feet.

I walked him to the door. "I'll be back soon," he said, smiling, and walking backward down the lot, waving. He tripped over his own feet as he turned around. "It's all good," he called as he jumped back to his feet.

I couldn't resist laughing as I watched him walk away. Closing the door, I released a sigh as I leaned against it, realizing how much I loved being with him. I returned to the secret room and looked around with an open mind. I wanted to discover something that I could claim. As I traced my finger over the books, I could hear them whispering my name. However, one screamed out to me, and I lifted it. As I opened it, a raw energy poured out, sending shivers through me; I snapped it shut and put it aside for later.

My eye went to a jewellery box sitting on the desk. I opened it, and saw an old skeleton key with my name carved into it. I froze, and the box slipped through my hand. I was relieved the beautiful box did not crumble to dust when it hit the floor.

How was it possible that my name was on a key here? Had it been placed here for me to find? I grabbed the key, ran back downstairs, and closed up the concealed entrance. Then I went outside and sat on the front veranda, taking in the cool breeze and playing with the key and my thoughts. *No*, I thought logically. *It is impossible that the key purposely been placed there for me to find. But then again Gabriella had been a popular name in the past; it must be a coincidence.*

My eye caught a glimpse of Joey's graceful strut as he got out of his car and approached. I became more aware of how much of him I required — mind, body, and soul. As our eyes locked, I realized he was my protective shelter, clearly the light in my dark confusion. I knew it was time to let go of absurdity and focus on what was real in my life.

Chapter 7

BEFORE THE STORM

Weeks passed and I never found the use for that key, but my attention had been consumed with school and Joey. I began to feel like a normally functioning teenager with a regular routine. Joey waited on the side of the road for me every morning before school. At lunchtime, all of us hung around the same table. I had become an official part of the rat pack; we had formed our own coven. I had to admit, I loved being around the twins, David and Scott. They definitely were the pack's entertainers. I would laugh instantly when David made his crazy facial expressions. They were my big teddy bears, treating me as a sister, always having my back in any tiny disagreements. This is the way of our kind: we protect one another.

Sitting in my last class of the day, I wondered if I would be able to find time to revisit that secret room. I had been too busy, my time consumed with Joey, school, and helping my mother. Especially Joey. I was immersed in his world and daydreamed of him constantly, wanting as much of him as I could get. It never felt like enough.

I still had not found the courage to kiss him. With Christmas around the corner and knowing that he would be leaving for Europe to spend the holidays in Andorra, I felt the pressure was on. The thought that I would not see him for three weeks or on his birthday killed me. I wanted to plan something amazing for him before he left. I only had a couple of weeks to pull everything together. My friends and the rat pack had pulled together some ideas.

My mother was hardly ever home now; she was getting things ready for her grand opening on Friday night. The house always felt empty with her gone. I had two more days until the real stress would be unleashed. My mother pulled me out of school for Thursday and Friday to be her personal slave.

Leaving my last class and walking down the crowded hall as all the students eagerly burst from the classrooms at once, I realized how much I loved being at school. For the first time in my life, I felt I belonged, that I mattered. Especially being around the rat pack — my own kind, bounded by our loyalty and our secret way of life.

At my locker I gathered all my assignments and packed them in my bag, grumbling. I wouldn't see Joey for a few days. School had become our safe ground; we both were terrified to meet one another's families.

I sensed him come up behind me before he rested his head on my shoulder. "So, four whole days — I don't know if I can handle it," he groaned softly against my neck, then rolled away to lean against the locker beside mine. He pouted, with his chocolate brown eyes that melted into my soul.

"Please don't remind me," I said. "I'm trading my happiness for enslavement." Rolling my eyes, I shut and locked my locker door. I grabbed his hand with a smile as we made our way out of the school.

I jumped back into his car while my car warmed up. It was freezing outside. He rubbed my arms in a sad attempt to warm me up. Then he moved his hand from my arm to lift my chin up and gaze deeply into my eyes. "Gabriella, I love how your face can be so animated." He gently brushed his lips over my forehead. "I love the way you look at life."

His lips moved to my right cheek. "I love how you make me laugh." He kissed the opposite cheek.

I sensed where this was going, and panic flooded in as he leaned in towards my mouth. I had never kissed a boy and had no idea what to do. My heart beat rapidly to a point I thought it would explode out of my chest. I felt the tension of breath, our desire undeniable. He softly ran his fingertips across my lips and leaned in closer. There is no more time for timidity.

"I love everything about you," he whispered as his soft lips pressed against mine. An electrifying jolt ran through me as he kissed me. He lifted his head away and looked at me, seeking my approval. I placed my hands on his face and closed my eyes as I leaned in to kiss his bottom lip. He kissed the top of my lip gently then pulled back, leaving me wanting more.

"I couldn't resist. You are my life, the air I breathe. You are embedding deep in my soul. I loved you from the moment I first saw you," he whispered, twirling my hair in his fingers. "I've met a lot of girls, I can't explain but when I first saw you... I sound tacky, but I could see my life in you."

"From the moment I saw you my life began, and now I know beside you is where I want to be; you have captivated me, Mr. Davale," I confessed, and his eyes danced. I looked away, declaring, "It scares me, how much I feel for you."

His eyes strayed over my shoulder. "You'd better go before your car runs out of gas," he said abruptly.

"I guess you're right." I bit my lip. "Well, I can't go four days without you; if you have the chance to sneak away, will you meet me?" I asked desperately.

"Of course—text me when and where and I'll be there." He smiled. "Oh Gabriella, I do love you." He reached out and grabbed my hand. "I know you feel the same, even though you can't say it to me." He grinned.

I leaned forward and pulled him in toward me and kissed his lips again, then looked him straight in the eye. "It's amazing, how easy it is to fall for you." Then I turned to go to my car. "I'll see you tomorrow," I yelled out.

I held my composure all the way home, parking my car in the driveway and looking around before releasing my excitement in screams of joy. Pulling myself together again, I entered the house and locked the door to make sure I remained alone, then jumped and screamed with exhilaration as I ran around, professing my sentiments as at the top of my voice like an idiot. I traced my lips with my fingertips, pretending his warm, supple lips were on mine. More than ever, I wanted to give him a gift with a lot of meaning.

Knowing I had time, I decided to explore the secret room, certain I would find something unique there that would only belong to him. I grabbed one of the oil lanterns from the fireplace mantel and crept up to the secret lair, lighting the lantern before making my way up the stairs. I knew I had maybe an hour before it got dark.

I had forgotten how medieval the room looked. Old emotions emerged as I stepped into it; everything looked the same as I had left it, back on the day we had cleaned. Seeing the jewelry box I had dropped still lying on the desk, I placed the lantern down beside it and knelt to pick up a couple of things I missed. I put everything back into the box, closed it, and placed it on the desk, then forgot about it as I started to snoop around.

There were too many interesting things to look at. Most of the book covers were embossed with the same coin-shaped seal, with ancient writing running around its perimeter and another circle within bearing the image of two mounted knights, each holding a shield and spear. I opened a few of them but all of them written in an unfamiliar language.

As I put the last one back, I noticed a thin wooden box tucked between two books nearby. Intrigued, I pulled it out and opened it to reveal a square of dark purple satin folded over something. Lifting the fabric aside, I gasped at the sight of an exquisite silver dagger, its brilliant sheen almost blinding me as it caught the lamplight. The handle was made of either ivory or some bone-pale wood, and the hilt was inlaid with a bright red gem carved with the Star of David. I ran my fingertips over the imprint, knowing this was valuable. I was disappointed when I did not sense anything enchanting from the touch. I closed the case and putting it back.

Opening a cupboard, I failed to notice before, as I discovered an oval jewelry box small enough to fit into the palms of my hands. It was exquisite. With twelve blue topaz stones embedded around its edge and one rock in the center, it had a shape like an eye that also had the Star of David carved in it. Beside the jewelry box rested a tiny chest. I lifted the lantern for a good look around—what else had I missed before? The secrets in this room remained a mystery; they gave me an uncomfortable feeling as darkness fell. I grabbed the jewelry box and the chest and made my way back downstairs.

In the kitchen, I set everything on the table and prepared codfish for dinner. While waiting for it to bake, I opened the tiny chest and saw an amber prism; when I held it up to the light, I saw the Star of David in its golden depths. I set it down and moved to the jewelry box, sifting through its contents. Seeing a pair of tarnished rings that matched the same pattern that was on the tiny chest, I lifted it out and looked at it before slipping it onto my finger. It was much too big for me, the workmanship beyond exquisite, with a ruby in the center of a cross. Holding it up to the light, I knew this would be the perfect gift for Joey.

The next morning, knowing I would be enslaved to my mother . Helping her setup the store for the next two days, I dreaded opening my eyes. I jumped out of bed and saluted her as she came into my room. "Yes, ma'am!" I said with Southern twang.

She grabbed my pillow and threw it at me, laughing at my sarcasm. "You're a brat, I love you." She giggled, then sobered. "We will be leaving in an hour, so get everything you'll need — it will be a long day." She exited my room.

I packed up everything including the rings, hoping I could find time to take them to the jeweler for cleaning and restoration.

The drive did not feel long, with my mother talking about the things that we needed to do. My duties were putting together little gifts for the open house.

She had invited all our neighbors and the local shop owners with well-to-do names.

Then she said, "Gabriella, I know you and Joey have been spending a lot of time together. I think it's about time you introduced us officially." She smiled.

"Mom, do you want to meet him tonight?" I was desperate to see him again and this struck me as a good opportunity. Raising my eyebrow, I waited for her response.

She smirked sheepishly. "I know how much you care about him and I also know these next few days are going to kill you, not seeing him. I realize you are not my little girl anymore. So I already talked to Allison and asked her to bring Paul and Joey after school to help out."

I smiled, and then asked, "Mom is it all right if I run out to a jeweler this afternoon?"

"Of course, with those extra hands tonight I might not even need you until late tomorrow," she agreed as we pulled in behind her shop.

My mouth dropped open as my mother unlocked and opened the door. I could not believe how the shop had transformed. It became a heavenly oasis of magic and rustic yet contemporary style. She had placed a consultation bar right at the front of the shop for everyone walking by to see. I was astonished at my mother's vision and her drive to set it all in motion.

"What do you think?" she asked anxiously, cupping a hand around her chin while waiting for my approval.

"Mom, I can't...I can't believe you did this!" I paused, playing with her nerves. "This is incredible. I love it! It is the coolest shop I have ever seen. It is inviting and enchanting. I'm proud of you, Mom." I hugged her.

A few hours later, exhausted from setting up the products on the display shelves, I looked around to see that we were halfway done. "Mom, is it okay if I run out now?" I asked with puppy dog eyes, eager to run away.

"Go ahead, sweetheart. There is a jewelry shop at the end of the block. If you don't mind, picking up something for us to eat, there's a place right beside it." She was distracted, her eyes straying around the shop as she handed me some money.

I could not walk fast enough. I was relieved when I stepped from the wintry cold into the restaurant's warm air that laden with delicious aromas. I placed an order and ran over to the jewelers.

"Hello, how may I help you today?" a mature woman with fire-red hair greeted me. I looked up from my inspection of one of the display cases.

Regardless of how loud her hair and makeup were, she carried herself well, and I could tell she had years of knowledge.

"As a matter of fact, I need to restore these rings, please." I smiled and placed it on the counter.

She picked it up to inspect it, her eyes wide with disbelief. "Were did you get this?"

I saw her thoughts; the rings were very old — indeed, medieval — and worth a fortune. I knew if I told her I'd found them, she would call the police. "Actually, they're a family heirloom. I want to restore them for my mother, as a surprise." I smiled, killing any suspicion.

"Is your mother opening that new shop down the block, called Craft?" Her voice had softened and her smile now reached her eyes.

"Yes, Sonia is my mother," I answered.

She nodded. "Your mother brought in another fascinating piece, an angel pendant wrapped around a vial." I pulled out from under my shirt. "Yes, that's it; unbelievable." She shook her head slowly in appreciation. "I believe that is an ancient Hebrew inscription is on the back." I read her curiosity: she wondered if we were Jewish.

When she asked if my father had been Jewish — apparently my mother had mentioned last time that she is a widow — I couldn't say much but that, I had no idea so I was curious to know myself. I already knew she couldn't read the Hebrew text. "You wouldn't happen to know anyone who could translate the inscription, would you?" I asked.

Her eyes lit up. "As a matter of fact, my cousin studies ancient Hebrew. Wait, I'll give you his card." She ruffled through her counter drawer. "Oh yes, here it is." She smiled and handed it to me.

"Thank you. So, do you think it's possible to restore these rings for me?" I asked again.

"Oh — of course. They won't be done until tomorrow afternoon."

I nodded. "Thank you again for everything, I'll see you tomorrow." I waved as I made my way out.

I appreciated our warm food as I walked back to the shop with it; the warm air radiating through the bag dulled the bite of the icy air hitting my face. Too preoccupied with thoughts about who may have owned the valuables in the secret room, I had a hard time sensing any imprints; I knew there was a great secret hidden amongst everything.

Later, after ending my call with Allison, I started to tense up — I was introducing my mother to Joey! It felt extremely odd that she seemed okay with me having a relationship with a boy. My mother spoke flawless English but she had that old fashion Portuguese mentality: no boys allowed in our home unless they were family, and no sleeping over at anyone's house. I took a deep breath, thinking only if she knew how often Joey came over. I had twenty minutes to prepare myself before Allison arrived with Paul and Joey.

When I heard faint voices at the front of the shop, I took a deep breath to relieve my anxiety and left the back room. My palms felt sweaty and my throat seemed to constrict as I arrived in time to see Paul and Allison greeting my mother at the shop entrance, with Joey waiting behind them.

I walked up to Joey. "Joey, this is my mother Sonia. And Mom, this is Joey," I said, too fast. I watched closely, looking for her approval as they shook hands.

"Well, it's nice to meet you, and I appreciate you helping us out." I sensed my mother prob-ing him inside and out—she was a master mind reader and could read almost anyone or anything other than the Lampir and me. The inability to read the minds of immediate family members is common.

"It's nice to meet you as well, I'm excited to help you guys," he replied with a huge smile. However, his smile did not reach his eyes. Bothered by this, I wondered what my mother saw. I don't think he realized how strong she was.

"Well, let's get cracking," my mother, announced, clapping her hands together. She delegated Allison and me to make up the gift bags while Joey and Paul helped her with the products and displays.

I laughed and joked around with Allison as we packed the gifts and tied them with ribbon. My eyes kept drifting to Joey and Paul as they arranged display cabinets, placed furniture, and hauled boxes as my mother cleaned around them. What had my mother seen that bothered him? Was it her disapproval? Anxious to find out what had happened, I couldn't wait for this night to end.

"Thank you so much for your help," Mom finally said. "I think it's safe to call it a night. You guys go, I am going to stay here a little longer. Joey, it was nice meeting you. Do you mind if Gabby catches a ride with you?" She smiled. "I think you both need some time to catch up." She practically pushed us out the door. That boggled my mind—if she didn't like him, she would not be sending me home with him.

Paul and Joey ran out to warm up their cars while Allison and I finished our last two gifts. I saw unease in my mother's face as I said goodbye. Hugging her, I whispered, "Are you going to be late? Should I wait up for you?"

"I'll probably be another hour or two." Her smile comforted me a bit.

Allison led the way to the parking lot up the street. Out of nowhere, I felt the burn run through me again, a lot more powerful this time than previously. I looked around frantically as my head started to spin. Then I fell to my knees, my vision blurring as Allison shrieked for help. All I saw was a brief glimpse of Joey running to my aid before things started going dark.

When I came to again, the fury inside me had subsided. Joey wrapped his arms around me, his presence revitalizing me. He lifted me up and carried me over to his car. I heard worry and the panic in my friend's voices while they quickly ran over.

"Gabby, are you okay? Should I go get your mother?" Allison asked urgently.

"No." I shook my head, I didn't want to stress my mother out a day before her grand opening, I'll talk to her after her opening night.

"Gabriella, are you okay?" Joey echoed, stroking my face.

"Yeah," I finally managed to mumble. "I'm sorry, I think I pushed myself too much today. I think I just need my bed." I grimaced at the distress I saw on their faces.

"I think you should stay with her until her mom gets home," Allison said to Joey. "Make sure you

143

call me after and let me know how she's doing," she ordered as she left with Paul.

His heartbeat against my cheek soothed my pain. I felt his finger caressing my face and lifted my head to look up at him with uncertainly. Joey's face full of concern as he pushed my hair away from my face and gently kissed my forehead. "Let's get you home," he whispered. "Gabby, do you want me to stop anywhere?" he asked as we pulled out of the parking lot. "A drugstore, maybe?"

"No, I don't know what's wrong with me." I frowned, thinking. "It's as if something wants to tear out of me, and you are the one thing that calms my pain," I confessed, holding his hand close to my face.

He looked at me, not saying anything. He held my hand tight as he drove, periodically looking at me with an apprehensive expression. "Gabriella, there is something we need to talk about," he finally said. "I might be able to help you." He started rubbing my hand, as if he were nervous.

Sensing he was choosing his words carefully, I looked at him, suddenly concerned.

"Well, you know that we have our gifts," he continued after a moment. "Mine is shape-shifting. My lineage is Lougaro, I developed it when I hit puberty. I remember feeling similar to what you've described, until I learned to control it. Everyone is different—maybe because of your dad, you are a late bloomer. Or maybe somewhere in your mother's lineage there is cougar blood." He paused and looked at me with a face full of empathy. "In the next couple of weeks, I'm going to teach you how to control yourself, and how to own it so it doesn't own you."

As ridiculous as he sounded, I knew what he said was true. Still, I knew it was impossible for me to be a shape-shifter. "Nice try, it's not in my lineage," I said. I giggled knowing he had been that annoying Rottweiler. "You do make a cute dog." Even so, I wanted to learn how to control whatever was lying within me.

As we pulled into my driveway, I knew there would be no way he was going to leave my side until my mother returned. "Wait, let me help you," he demanded as I opened the car door.

"I am perfectly fine now," I protested, continuing to get out of the car. "I appreciate that you want to help me, but I can manage."

He persisted, holding my arm as I walked to the front door as if I were some helpless child who needed monitoring. He waited downstairs as I washed up and changed. Now I found myself questioning the truth as I looked at my reflection in the mirror.

"Wow, you're fast. I thought you would be a while," he blurted when I came back downstairs and caught him snooping around. "Is this your father?" He gestured at a picture on the fireplace mantel, the last one taken of our family.

"Yeah, that's him." I stood beside him, looking at the photo.

"You definitely have his eyes," he noted, still focused on the image. "If you don't mind me asking, what happened to him?"

"He died while away on a business trip in Europe." I sighed and shrugged, tucking my hands into my sleeves. The details of his death were unclear to me: this is the excuse I use to tell everyone.

"Is that your only family picture? I noticed you don't have other pictures displayed," he commented as we walked over to the couch.

I sat down next to him and rested my head on his shoulder; he wrapped his arm around me. "My mother has an old book of her family pictures," I replied. "My father's family all died when he was young, so he really didn't have a family. If you don't mind, I'd rather talk about something else." I did not want to be rude; I had enough on my plate, and the last thing I wanted to do is reopen old wounds.

"Sorry, I should have known better. One thing's for certain, I'm grateful that they created you." He leaned forward and kissed my forehead.

I snuggled closer against his chest, enjoying the warmth of his embrace and remembering how pleasant our first kiss had been. At that moment, I wanted nothing more than to kiss him. I feared my mother's wrath—unfortunately, this is her home, and she is a Portuguese Bruxa! After today, remembering her and Joey's silent reactions as they shook hands. I wanted to test the boundaries.

"I wondered, what exactly did you think of my mom?" I asked, tilting my head up to look at him.

He chuckled, shaking his head as if he had been waiting for me to ask. "How did I know you'd ask that? I have never met anyone who could actually get into my Mind—it freaked me out a bit. I have never had people read my mind or channel into my thoughts. She was right in there; with just that brief touch, she knew all there is to know about me, and she made herself known. I have to honestly say, it threw me off." I could hear his disbelief in his voice and see the awe in his eyes that she possessed that much power.

"What did she see and what did she say?" I asked, consumed by curiosity.

"Well, she wanted to know my intentions with you, of course, and she questioned my faith more. She told me to always be honest in my heart, whether I live or die. Then she said to be careful of my heart." He wrinkled his nose as to shake off what my mother had said. I saw the ghost of a smile, and I wondered if it truly bothered him. "I had a talk with my mother last night about you, and she insisted that you have to come over for dinner next weekend and meet the family."

"Wow." I hesitated, sitting straight up and pulling my hair back. The thought of us being serious made me nervous. "Wow, this is it — what did you tell her about me?" I tried to hide my anxiety. He was the first boy I'd ever cared for and I could not shake a strange feeling of doubt.

"Well, I didn't say much. She saw it all over me when I walked in yesterday. She was excited that I had chosen you. She started talking about our lineage and something about the ravens." He shrugged and ran his fingers absently through my hair.

I stared into his eyes, saw the love, and leaned over to kiss him.

He held me away. "Trust me, there is nothing I want more, but your mother is coming home and I know she is going to freak out that we're here alone — I'm hoping, under the circumstances, she'll understand." His face showed his torment. "She'll be here soon, especially if she knows what happened to you. I'm going to wait outside until she gets here." It was clear that my mother had put fear into him.

"Wait, I'm going to join you," I announced, jumping off the couch to follow him.

Bundled up nice and warm, we walked around the yard, holding hands in the moonlight. I caught sight of an owl. Covering his mouth to silence him, I pulled Joey casually toward the wooded area, pointing out the owl. When we were a few feet away from it, the owl turned its head and stared at us. Then it opened its wings and glided off into the moonlight. Frustrated by its departure, I leaned against an oak tree and watched it soaring away.

"Isn't the moonlight breathtaking?" I murmured, staring tranquilly upward.

Without warning, his hands pressed against the tree on either side of me and he leaned in, looking at me. I saw his adoration flowing from his eyes. His index finger traced around my lips, and he moved in closer and whispered, "You are my raven."

I felt the steam from his words fondle my lips. I hungered for the warmth of his lips against mine. Staring into his eyes, I slid my hands through his hair, then down to his face. "You are—"

Before I could finish he grabbed me and kissed me passionately. My blood rushed through my veins at an exhilarating pace. I ran my hands back through his hair. We both felt our natural instincts forcing us together as we kissed. I felt so light;

it was as if we levitated a few inches above the ground.

He suddenly pulled away and we slowly dropped back to the ground. "Your mom is coming down the street."

Dusting ourselves off, we walked toward the house, hiding our guilty pleasure. We sat on the porch steps until her car pulled into the drive. The glare of her headlights stung my eyes. Worse, I felt the glare of her eyes through the windshield, and I closed my eyes and focused desperately on projecting my thoughts to her, reassuring her and explaining why he was with me.

I felt Joey's body tense as she got out of her car as he prepared himself for a tongue-lashing. "Don't worry, she knows—Allison already called her," I whispered, and felt him relax.

"Thank you, Joey, for watching out for my daughter," Mom said as she approached us. "I relieve you of your duty."

Still not sure of her true feelings, he jumped to his feet. "All right, good night and good luck tomorrow. I'll see you both at the opening…And Mrs. Fragoso, I mean no disrespect to you, Gabriella wasn't doing too well before," he blurted.

"I know, Allison left me a message. I'm sure she'll be fine now." Mom smirked and waved good night to him.

I followed her into the house, turning in the doorway to wave good night to him.

"Good night, Joey," Mom said firmly, nudging me aside to stand in the doorway, watching him drive off.

I drew a deep breath and waited with trepidation for her to close the door and reveal how she truly felt.

Chapter 8

TRUTH

Anger consumed her face as she slammed the door behind me. My mother eyes scanned my face, and for a terrifying moment of silence, I wished I knew her thoughts. Then her eyes started to tear up and her gaze dropped to the floor. I was bewildered. Clearly, something else bothered her.

She pressed her lips together, and exhaled, "I told you to tell me everything! What happened to you tonight? This wasn't the first time, was it?" Her tone, though still harsh, was a smidge kinder, her eyes showed a fear.

"Yes, Mom, it has happened a lot since we moved here. I did not want to stress you out, with you trying to get settled in your new shop. The last thing I wanted to do was distract you. Trust me, I've been dying to tell you; I'm petrified — I don't understand what's wrong with me." I threw my arms up releasing the tension and fear that resided within me.

I began crying, hoping for the same assurance she had given me when I was a child. Confessing did provide relief, almost a sense of freedom. At last, I might get the answers I needed.

"We need to talk." Her voice turned hard, her body stiff. The look in her eyes was all too familiar — the same look she had when my father died.

"What is it, Mom? What's going on?" I cried, grabbing her shoulders and turning her to look at me.

"Oh Gabriella, what have I done?" she moaned. "I should have known, but you never craved...I still should have known better, you have his eyes and you're so different." She babbled hysterically and avoided eye contact. Releasing a sob, she looked up to seek help from heaven.

Concerned, I urged her to sit down. "Mom, what are you talking about? You are freaking me out! Just tell me what the hell is going on," I wailed.

She sat there for a few minutes in silence, struggling to regain her self-control. Whatever she was babbling about had conjured a deep fear in her. Her reaction terrified me. What did this all have to do with my father's eyes, with me? Did this involve the change occurring inside me? Did I inherit some strange human curse from my dad, something to be concerned about?

"Mom, tell me what's going on…please!" I begged, desperate for her to tell me the truth.

"Oh, sweetheart, I love you so much. You need to promise me that you'll tell me everything that is going on in your life," she insisted as her calm demeanor returned. She lifted her hands to my face; they trembled, revealing her continued stress. "There are many things I need to tell you. You know that your eyes are the doorway to your soul, don't you? Well, everything is going to change for you, and I have no idea how to help you." She looked down and moved her hands to cradle her head.

"I don't understand—what is wrong with me? Please get to the point," I demanded.

She looked up at me, her eyes wet with tears. "You know how much your father and I loved each other," she said in a voice strangled with agony. "You were a gift from God—we never thought it possible to conceive a child. You see, nobody except Maria knew what your father truly was." She lowered her eyes as the moment intensified. "Your father was a Lampir," she whispered in shame.

Shock hit me like a tidal wave. Her words seemed to linger in the air between us as I struggled to resister them, even though I knew exactly what she said. Silence and regret filled the living room. Then I collapsed slowly to the floor and my mind went blank. I sat there, emotionless, trying to grasp a proper train of thought. I had always known something was off. Lampir! How we hated them. My father was a bloodsucker, a vampire— nothing like what the legends portrayed.

"You showed no sign for us to worry about. My bloodline was strong in you. I noticed something different in your eyes the moment I arrived here, but I blew it off. Your father was good, looking for God's redemption and grace. You have to believe that you are more human than…the other." Regret made her choke out her words. "I knew one day I'd have to tell you the truth," she moaned.

I sat still, processing facts and finally understanding the change that I had been experiencing these last couple of months. That is what has been crawling within me; that would explain those dreams. I squeezed the bridge of my nose, wanting to release the pressure. Then I felt her arms wrap around me.

"What are you saying—I'm half witch and half vampire? I am cursed to feed off the wicked and kill? I can't be! There's no way!" I screeched in anger. I felt betrayed. My whole existence had been a lie. I pushed her away and ran to my room.

Never had I been this angry before. I paced back and forth in my room, trying to comprehend the truth. In all honesty, I knew something was growing inside me. I started breathing fast, nearly hyperventilating. The life I knew would never be the same. I was unprepared for this truth.

I ran to the mirror and stared at my reflection, then broke down and cried, vowing to myself I wouldn't let it control me. I most defiantly won't allow it to turn me into a dark creature of the shadows. I examined my reflection, searching for the person who stood in front of me.

There was a soft knock on my door, and then my mother entered. Standing behind me, she whispered, "Gabriella, we will manage this. Your father was not evil; he never killed for pleasure, only for duty. There is much you need to learn and understand. I didn't know for sure what to expect, that is why I always tried to protect you. You're coming of age and need to learn how to survive. The world you are about to enter can be dark and hard." She paused. "You mustn't breathe a word to anyone about who or what you are. The Bruxa hate the Lampirs. There are those who will try to destroy you, and those who follow the dark path will try to convert you into something we all fear. I know that you and Joey have formed strong feelings. Unless his heart, mind, spirit, and soul belong to God, he will never love the other part of you."

I heard the pain in her voice and knew she was hurting as much as me, if not more. I stood motionless before the mirror. I squeezed my eyes shut, as she closed the door behind her. Breaking out of the shock, I regained whatever was left of me. I was forced to face the ugly truth that I carry the blood of my enemy.

****

Hesitant, I walked down the hall to her bedroom door and slowly opened it. Pain and regret clouded the room. I gasped for breath, I pushed myself inside her room. Hunched on the edge of her bed, she was weeping. I hated that the truth caused this much anguish. I stood in front of her, wanting to reassure her that I knew her love for me.

"I'm sorry to have reacted so cruelly to you," I said when she lifted her head. "It's…hard to digest."

I sighed and knelt in front of her, hanging my head in shame.

She reached out and placed her hand gently on my head. "There is the chance you will never turn and live as a Bruxa," she said, a thread of hope in her voice. "We need to prepare for the chance that you do."

She rose and walked across the room to the beautiful chest with the angel carvings the movers brought that I had admired so much and had been obsessing to unlock it. Waving me over, she pulled the key out from around her neck. "This was to be your dower; I truly hoped I wouldn't be opening it before your eighteenth birthday. Your father left a letter for you to read in case this happened." We knelt down together in front of the chest.

She blew on the lock, and it lit up as her breath touched it. She inserted and turned the key, and the lid flew open. A tiny gust of wind rolled out, sounding like angels whispering a hymn. A faint glow seeped from the chest as if signaling approval. It had been magical, as if it waiting solely for me. "These things belonged to your father and now belong to you," she whispered with a smile. I knew there had been a reason why I was drawn to that chest — it is a part of who I am.

BRUXA

She pushed the lid open wide, revealing what lay within. I saw many ancient scrolls, stunning pieces of jewelry, crowns, goblets, spear tips, and a dagger. She reached in, grabbed a sealed letter, and placed it in my hand. "Start with this first. It will help you understand your father." She sighed. I knew how much she needed him now. "Gabriella, please try to understand that your father loved you so much, he sacrificed himself to protect you. Only Maria and another know of you. The visitor in the shadows that you spoke of has been watching you; he might be the other one.

"The letter is only intended for you to read; the paper will be blank, so you'll need a drop of your blood to release the secret message he left you. The words will disappear once you've read it, and the paper will disintegrate, it's forged from Bruxa and Lampir magic." Her voice sounded sad, and she knelt there as if broken.

I stood back up. "I'm going back to my room. I need to process everything and allow my mind to absorb all this." I hugged her tight and kissed her good night, that bit of normalcy setting both our minds at rest.

I returned to my room, turned on the lamp on my night table, and fluffed the pillows behind my back. Closing my eyes, I stroked the envelope that held my father's note, savoring the moment; my fingers lingered for his impression. His heart and soul stained these few pages. Relaxing back into the pillows, I reconnected with my spirit, preparing mentally. Then I tore open the envelope and pulled out the note to read his words.

A chill ran through me as I unfolded his note, as if his presence were standing next to me. I looked around, smiling, to let him know I am aware of his spirit. Then, taking a deep breath, I pricked my finger.

The tiny drop of blood hit the blank paper and magically, the script slowly lit up like a firebrand on the page. The glow faded, leaving clear, crisp handwriting. It evoked a childhood memory: I was little and running around, distracting my father from his studies until he gave in and chased me around the room until he caught me and threw me, giggling, over his shoulder. He would bring me back to his desk and, his eyes filled with love, to try to explain the art of writing.

Without a doubt, I knew how much he loved me. I would always be his little princess. I let that push back my prejudice for Lampirs, and read, striving for understanding.

BRUXA

To my beloved daughter Gabriella,

If you are reading this, my worst fear has been realized, and I am unable to protect you. There are many things you will need to know; and I have planned for this, if you have not already discovered my hidden study. There you will find all the information you will need to learn about our history and legends. Under no circumstance must you show anybody this room. There are sacred things hidden there.

Now, about me.

Yes, I am a Lampir, a vampire, immortal, or whatever names you might prefer. I know your views have been misguided by books or movies and especially by the Bruxa. Yes, there are those of us who are soulless and selfish. They are the fallen Brethren, or children of the fallen. Most of us were not designed to be that way. The Brethren were crusaders for God, handpicked by one of the three sons of the Grigori (the watchers). Many of us, over the centuries, became angry and resentful, hating the lambs we had sworn to protect. It was the lambs and the Bruxa who betrayed us.

Forgive me, child. This is the hardest thing to try to explain briefly to you, for the change may come rapidly and you need to know who to trust and how to control your hunger and the strength you will develop. Things will be unique for you because of you mother's blood, I can only tell you what I know of mine.

I had been sent by the Brethren to destroy your mother before she came of age, for she was the last of the Malicus bloodline. Her power, passed down to her progeny, was an imposing threat. They feared her powers and her strength.

Watching her as prey, I could not help but be enchanted by her beauty, her trusting soul, and her love for life. She knew I had been watching her and refused to believe I would destroy her – she was right. She bewitched me the first moment I looked into her eyes.

We married secretly and hid our love, running away to Canada shortly after she found out she was pregnant. You were unexpected, but definitely our greatest blessing. I never questioned my blessing, for you are the first ever to be born from the Brethren Lampir. I never thought it possible.

In fear of anyone knowing the truth, we hid in the Canadian Rocky Mountains. I convinced the elders that your mother was no longer a threat. I agreed to watch over her and strike her down if she made one threatening move.

Here we were, soon to be parents, with many fears. Your mother's pregnancy seemed to be normal just as any human pregnancy. Neither of us knew what you would be like when you came out. Yes, we feared you would have fangs, or have skin so porcelain-pale it would burn in the sunlight. I admit I thought the worst, picturing you as a savage beast we would need to tame.

Maria is an old friend, the only human to understand me. She was a Lampir one of the originals in her past life, put to death by the Inquisition. She already knew of your coming and showed up a day before you were born to help us deliver you and show us how to care for you. Your mother had no experience and was disowned by her family. I knew nothing about fathering. With Maria's help, it somehow all became natural.

I will never forget how your mother screamed as she was going through labor; I thought for sure you were killing her. Maria kept reassuring me that all women act this way while giving birth. She finally kicked me out of the room because my worry was stressing your mother more than the labor.

I went through my own hell outside the room, pacing back and forth and wanting to break through the door when I heard your cry and nothing from your mother anymore. I finally threw it open and saw Maria standing beside your mother wearing a huge smile. It is forever branded in my mind, the smile, and the peace radiating from your mother's face when she looked at me and told me it was a girl.

Maria took you out of your mother's arms and brought you over. From the first moment I held you, I felt the ultimate power of love. I sobbed, feeling all my *convictions of what I was, and grateful that God had shown you mercy – you were perfectly normal.*

Not until a Lampir consumes the blood of a lamb do they become immortal. Please, whatever you do, never take a life – no matter how much you may crave for their blood or even if they deserve to die. You may carry the blood and have our powers, or you also might remain mortal.

You must own and control the power and never tell anyone. Know your strength and how to control your powers as you have been blessed with from both your mother and me. Unfortunately, the real holy war has not begun. Be ready to protect yourself. You must learn how to master your gifts.

Your senses will all change. First, you will experience different smells. Evil carries the foulest smell, that of sulfur. These are the ones who have no souls; they live to kill the lambs, mentally and physically. They disguise themselves in lambs or as beautiful creatures that play on the sympathy of others – never trust them. Trust your senses; only a Lampir smells those foul beasts.

Your hearing will become acute; you will hear and be able to channel in sounds from miles away. This will come to you when you block out everything else and focus on just hearing.

When encountering another of our kind, you will feel your heart race; we call this signal "the burn." It is hard to know if you will be able to detect them or not. Usually we can detect our own kind, for we are not human; we have become children of the Grigori. Those who walk in the path of the Brethren are harder to detect. Those Lampir who are fallen are everything man and Bruxa fear. Their evil is easy to detect.

Contrary to popular belief, we do not hunt the lambs unless it is required out of duty or self-defence. Those who have darkened souls need to prey on humans to quench the thirst in their evil hearts. These Lampir, better known as the fallen, are the ones who walk in darkness. They are the lost Brethren who have turned against our cause. Some have returned and converted back to the Brethren; many do not.

Sunlight will only destroy the fallen, ones whose souls have been blackened. Cursed are those who have turned their backs on God. They may never see the light of day and must roam the darkness. For those of us who still belong to the Brethren, the sun will reflect the truth of our age and stings the skin – for daytime is when truth is free and the lambs play. Night is always full of mystery, lies, and deceit.

If you ever hunger or crave for the taste of warm blood, please refrain from feeding on the lambs. I suggest you try wild animals. As long as your heart beats, you will never need blood to survive, nor will you have to hide in the shadows, for you are still living.

The fall of the Templar's was the fall of us. Uneducated lambs who believed the lies of the corrupt church officials and money-hungry kings and Bruxa nobles who polluted their minds executed them. Not easily destroyed, half the Brethren turned their backs on the lambs and became hateful toward their weakness. Without their protection, many innocent lambs were tortured and slaughtered at the hands of their own kind. The ignorant and hateful who were guided by true evil masquerading as orders in God's name.

There are only a few of us left who follow the true code of the Brethren. We act as the council, handpicked by the Watchers. We have the power to maintain order among the Lampirs and make sure things stay in balance. We are the law-enforcers.

The devil disguises itself by offering false peace and hope for humanity and twists the works of God to mislead the lambs into a world of hidden lies, murder and rape, serial killers, wars made to enslave the helpless, and genocide. All these have occurred after our fall. The lambs were unaware of what they unleashed by destroying the Brethren.

Yes, there are lambs who do find true faith in God, and they become servants of truth and are free from personal bondage. Always trust those who follow the true light of God. These people see the world for what it really is: a hidden war.

The Bruxa still fight the hidden battle, maintaining a balance with the real world and the spirit world and helping guide the lambs. They are similar to the lambs; some are weak and want too much. You must be careful whom out of the Bruxa you trust. They still are human, maybe a little different, they are flesh and blood, the same as the lambs. Of course, be aware of New Age witches — they do not understand all the complexity and most of them are easily seduced by the dark and don't even know it.

All the Brethren carry the Seal of the Templar on their inner right wrists. Remember, when in despair, follow the Star of David. It will guide you away from danger, and you can call upon the angels for protection. Be careful on the full moon, the day the angels rest. I have a special necklace with an angel charm and a vial that will allow you to ask for their protection.

Every day, you have to practice and channel your powers and your strength, for you are going to need to be prepared for the worst. Make sure you take time for meditation and prayer. True faith is the hardest gift to master; none of us are perfect beginners.

There is a lifetime of explaining and knowledge I want to help you understand. Unfortunately, this is the best I could do for now, having no idea what will become of you and how you will develop.

With all the my love,
Your Father Mathias

After taking some time to process the information, I felt relieved, a lot better, in fact. Everything seemed much clearer. Sighing in relief, I absorbed all the information. I watched in amazement as the note curled up and burst into a heatless flame. The note had disintegrated and vanished. I laid back feeling my exhausted emotions as my head hit the pillows and I instantly fell asleep.

Chapter 9

NEW DAY

I opened my eyes to a new day, a new life full of uncertainty. Stretching out my limbs, I let go of all the built-up stress, then glanced casually at my alarm clock—and promptly jumped out of bed. It was noon! Panic took over, and I wondered if my mother had also slept in or if she had gone to the shop without me. I scurried down the hall, yelling out for her, and flung open her bedroom door. She was not there. I ran down the stairs, calling out again for her. Again no answer. She must have left. I made my way to the kitchen to ease the rumble in my stomach, and saw a note she had placed on the counter.

BRUXA

Gabriella,

I figure you needed your rest; I know last night was overwhelming. You can choose if you want to join me later. If you choose not to I understand, and I still love you, no matter your decision. Your breakfast is in the oven.

Love, Mom

I ate, then rinsed off my plate. The running water flowed through my fingers, making me aware that a part of me had also been "washed away." Still uncertain of who I was and what my destiny held, I stood there in contemplation until the water numbed my hands. At least I knew what had been growing inside of me. I guess my life, already being nothing like normal, made it easier to comprehend everything. I shut off the taps and gazed absently out the window with only one enormously big concern: Joey and me. I may have been aware of the truth, but I was still in denial in some cases as I struggled to accept what I might become.

I finally belonged to a group of friends and had a boyfriend. The last thing I wanted to do was give it all up for something I was cursed with. Knowing this, was I being selfish? Joey is my world, and I couldn't walk away.

I glanced over at the tree where we had shared our twilight kiss while getting into my car and smiled sadly. I knew this was going to change everything.

I knew there would be no way to tell him without knowing how he truly felt about the Lampirs. Doing what I do best, I blocked out my worry and left it behind as I drove off.

I made a quick stop at the jeweler's before meeting up with my mother. The jeweler was as talkative as she had been the day before, too distracted and unable to focus, that her thoughts and conversation seemed muffled. I thanked her and paid, then left. As I pulled up to the back of my mother's shop, my concerns of yesterday choked up in my throat and my stomach clenched. I took a deep breath to ease my nerves and got out of my car.

Before I even touched the door, my mother was standing there. She swept me into her arms and held me tight. "Thank you. I love you so much, sweetheart. We will get through this somehow—it will work out in the end." She gave me a warm smile.

The afternoon flew by, with no time to talk or even look at each other. She wanted to avoid me as much as I wanted to avoid her. I focused on helping set things up and getting to know her staff. All day my mental energy focused on Joey, knowing that if I could see his smile, my stress would somehow evaporate.

Finally, I found time for myself and sat in the back room to pull the rings from my bag and examine them. I admired their gothic elegance, which I found enchanting. Placing one on my index finger, I turned my hand back and forth, examining the delicacy of the work. A force of confidence swept over me, as if the ring possessed a special power — I admit I enjoyed the thrill, though it also made me uncomfortable. I took the ring off and threw it back into the box, which I tucked back into my bag as I heard my mother approaching.

"We have an hour until the guests arrive," she said as she sat down beside me. She awkwardly giggled. "I'm actually nervous. I wanted to thank you for all your help; I couldn't have done it without you."

I dropped my eyes and sighed, apprehensive. "Mom, do you think things between Joey and me will fall apart because of what I am?"

"Well, I think if he really does love you, it will hard at the beginning to accept the truth. It may be a problem. It is hard to say. When I read him, I saw his own great confusion with his family's expectations; he has not had a chance to find himself. This is a journey you must both make yourselves."

Her words were encouraging, but not quite the answer I wanted to hear. "His family wants me to come over next week for dinner," I told her. "Or should I put an end to us before it gets too complicated? I don't want to give up Joey," I groaned. "I think I'm falling in love with him. He is my shelter, the one thing that tames my burning."

"I think you should live your days as if they were your last. Do not give up hope—you may never change into your father's kind, or perhaps you will have some of his powers. I don't know—God is the only one to know your fate." She smiled and stood.

Watching her walk back out, I realized that I did have to live day by day and hope for the best.

The night proved to be a great success for her. Everyone showed up, the guests were overwhelmed by the magic they felt as they entered, and they all loved her products and the concept. She was booked with appointments from the New Year until late February. I was proud of her accomplishment; she achieved what she wanted, and solely on her own.

As for me, I desperately tried to maintain my composure while inside I was falling apart. My mother sensed my stress and once things died down, she sent me home, telling me her employees would help with the rest of the night and with cleaning up.

Disillusionment consumed me as I pulled into the driveway and did not see Joey there waiting for me. It had been crazy busy at the open house, and I didn't get much of a chance to talk to Joey, everything was so chaotic. Even the introduction to his

BRUXA

parents had been brief. I just did not have time to examine what was going on, period.

I felt the emptiness that lingered in the cold breeze as I closed the car door. I walked to the spot where we had our moment last night. Reaching out and touching the tree, I imagined him standing there. It generated mixed emotions in my mind. Laughing to myself, I pressed my back against the tree, looking up toward the stars and thinking of him.

The cold breeze slid heavily against my face, the chill focusing my thoughts and opening my mind. I attempted to concentrate on my hearing, blocking out my other senses. I heard something moving in the night, as smoothly as a razor slicing through the air. My heart hammered with fear, yet also intrigued. Hearing the familiar breathing, I closed my eyes as the burning warmed my inner core. I knew the visitor from the shadows was here, standing somewhere nearby.

"I know you are there and I know what you are—reveal yourself," I demanded, still fighting fear. Unsure of its intentions, I still welcomed it.

I opened my eyes wide and looked around as I stepped away from the tree. I found the courage to challenge it again. "Show yourself," I yelled louder, then gasped for air as fear hugged me. My heart pounded violently, as if going to burst out of my ribcage. Tired of being toyed with, I wanted to know why it lurked in the shadows, silently watching me.

I froze as a cold presence wrapped around me, breaking my courage. I could feel it standing behind me, its cold eyes boring into my back. Too terrified to turn and look it in the face, I stood motionless. As the presence took a hold of me, fire burned through my veins.

"You're not so brave now, little one." His angelic voice held a hint of arrogance as it whispered in my ear—as he stood right behind me, inhaling my essence. "You are interesting to watch; your heart beats like that of a Bruxa but your scent is like one of us." His words echoed through my body, rendering me helpless.

"I admit I would love to destroy your innocence, but I am compelled to help you, youngling." His words pressed against my neck. I instinctively found his voice and presence alluring, appealing to my soul in a way I never thought possible.

"I need to know why you are watching me," I said, finding my courage again. "What do you want with me?" I had had enough of his toying. He had invaded a secret place inside of me.

His voice softened. "I guess I feel sorry for you and your father." He stepped back from me.

"My father!" All my fear vanished. I turned and in that, second he was gone. I sighed in disappointment, standing lost in his words.

Walking back to the house, I felt my fears confirmed — I truly am a half-breed, a full mix of Bruxa and Lampir. No longer could I deny the truth. I had to acknowledge and take pride in what I might become. The shadow watcher's presence captivated an inner part of me, a potency that flowed through me. I felt a hunger deep in my soul, as if it starved for more. I felt his eyes watching from a distance as I walked toward the house. My blood burned with a fiery heat that dispelled the cold in the air.

I had forgotten about my life — until I saw Joey's car drive in, the car's headlights momentarily blinding me. Their glare reminded me of my life, and I resented myself for being weak. I felt ashamed for my thoughts and my desire to accept what I can be, as if I had surrendered. Now, consumed with guilt, I struggled to find the courage I needed to look at him as Joey got out of his car and leaned against the driver's door.

"Hey, beautiful," he shouted, waving me over. When I sauntered up to him, he said, "Hey, I wanted to make sure you were all right; you seemed so stressed and distracted tonight." His gaze slid to the trees behind me for a moment. "Plus I sense something bad in the woods — actually; I've sensed it a few times this year." His ominous tone crawled up my spine.

"I haven't noticed anything," I lied. "Thanks for checking up on me. Sorry, Joey, I am exhausted and I hear my bed calling me. Is it okay if we talk tomorrow?" I kept my eyes on the snow I was kicking with my foot, hoping he did not notice my obvious dismissal.

"That might be a problem." He grabbed me and pulled me close. "You're not getting off that easy, not without kissing me good night."

He pressed his lips against mine and I responded, kissing him back, all guilt forgotten. Then I pulled back, laughing nervously. He tipped his head forward and as our foreheads touched, I felt connected to myself again. "Nice try, Mr. Davale," I teased. "I have to admit I enjoyed that. Tomorrow is another day." I stepped away.

"You're all mine tomorrow, Miss Fragoso," he warned, grinning, before he got back into his car.

I turned at the front door to wave goodbye. Joey will always be in my heart and always be my shelter. His car disappeared. I shook my mind free of feelings of desire and probed for the shadowy stranger I had encountered in the woods. Though I hadn't seen or touched him, the power of his voice plagued me. I sensed nothing. After a moment, I unlocked the door and stepped into the house. My bed was calling me; that had been no lie.

Thoughts filled my mind as I lay there in bed, desperately trying to fall asleep. I felt torn by two worlds, and the mental and physical stress exhausted me. I at last dozed, and in that area between dreaming and wakefulness, I ran wild and crazy through the night, my blood burning, as the watcher in the shadows followed me. Just as I thought I saw his face, I heard Joey calling my name in the distance, and as I turned to look, I found myself back in my room again.

When sunlight warmed my eyelids, I woke abruptly and looked around, finding it strange that my curtains were wide open—I hadn't opened them. I rose and walked over to the window, feeling the chilly breeze blowing through the bottom, as if it were cracked open, not closed properly. Uneasiness surged through me. Was I dreaming last night? Or had I in fact been running around wildly? Alternatively, even worse, did somebody break in last night while I was sleeping? Closing the window tight and relocking it, I gave it a tug just to make sure, and then headed downstairs.

The house felt empty, which also made me feel uneasy. Gripping the banister, I closed my eyes and probed for anything unwanted that might be lurking around our home. I was unable to detect anything. I knew something had been in my room, and I wanted to know what, or who. I was bothered that my personal space might have been invaded while I slept.

I stood in the shower, letting the water pour over me as if it might wash away who I was. I wanted to forget all that I would become, wanted to pretend someone would save me from myself. I was too preoccupied with the night visitor and my dream and the voice that enthralled me so — curious to look upon the owner's face. As I rinsed off the soap slathered on my body, I wished I could do the same to my thoughts.

Today I did not intend to call Joey; I had a great deal on my mind to absorb from the last two days. I needed time to search deep into my soul without worrying about relationships. Right now, I knew, I was my own worst enemy. I was lying to myself, still unprepared for the truth, wanting only to be normal. How I envied the lambs and there simplicity.

Going through and cleaning up the pile of junk that had built up on my dresser in the past week, I noticed the card the jeweler had given me with her cousin's number. I held it up. Isaac Bernstein. Tapping the card in my palm, I wondered if I should call him. Yes, I decided, I would like to know what the inscription said. With my mind made up, I eagerly dialed the number, hoping he would not think of me as a bother.

I let it ring a few times then, just as I was about to hang up, a man's soft, calm voice answered. We talked briefly; as soon as I mentioned his cousin's jewelry shop, he cut short further conversation and said he wanted to meet with me as soon as possible. We set up a meeting for the following Wednesday at 7:00 p.m. at his antique shop, located in downtown Boston.

Hanging up the phone, I paused to think a moment. I would be one step closer to discovering the missing pieces of my father's secrets. I was still haunted by what had slipped through my window while I slept. I checked my window again, making sure it was sealed shut, and then went through the whole house, checking every window, and making sure to lock all against any intruders.

The doorbell rang, and I answered it. I should have known it would be Joey on my doorstep. Though normally excited to see him, I felt indifferent toward him as I opened the door. "Hey," I sheepishly muttered, hoping he did not detect my hidden emotions.

"Hey. Remember, today I have you all to myself."
He leaned in with an eyebrow raised and devilishly
grinned

"Sorry. It's been a crazy few days. Come in. Give
me a few minutes and I'll be right back." I motioned
him inside, and then bolted up the stairs, squelching
my concern until I was alone, changing. Then I gave
myself a pep talk and pushed back my fear before I
went back downstairs.

"Hey, beautiful," he drawled as he tried to read
my expression, "I should have called, something
came up. I figured we'd go for lunch and a movie,
because tonight the guys want to take me out, if you
don't mind?"

"Of course I don't mind, I need a night off in any
case." My smile reassured him. I was finding it hard
to conceal my fear and concern from him, so a boy's
night out came as a relief.

"Wow, that was easy," he chuckled, sounding
surprised. "The boys made it sound like it would be
a lot worse. You're not upset, my going with them?"

"Why? They are a part of your life, too. There
will be times I'll need to do the same, so go and have
fun tonight." I flashed him another smile as I pulled
on my boots.

"You are amazing." He kissed my cheek, then
lifted me up and squeezed me in a bear hug.

BRUXA

We drove to a restaurant and, while waiting for our food, we discussed our movie options. Resting my head on my palms, elbows on the tabletop, I watched him roll up the sleeves of his well-fitted cashmere sweater. The thought of losing him began to ache within. What would happen when he found out the truth?

We agreed to see a new horror flick. I laughed at his movie choice: it was about a vampire who had to choose whether to live or die. *A typical immortal choice,* I thought. Since it meshed with recent revelations about my personal situation, I didn't argue with him. *It might actually work in my favor; I can hear firsthand his thoughts, all in innocence, concerning the secret within me.*

We found seats and I snuggled into his shoulder. Now would be a good time to start probing his views. "What is your opinion about the Lampir?" I whispered, watching his face. "Or should I say vampires?"

He grimaced. "Honestly, from what I know of them, they disgust me." His voice grew venomous. "They prey on weak, lost souls; they're selfish and cold. ...But there is something about them that is fascinating," he admitted. "Why? What do you think?"

A cold hand clenched my stomach. "I think there is good and evil in everything, especially us Bruxa,"

I replied, slowly pulling away from him and placing the tub of popcorn on my lap, so he would not be suspicious. "I mean, Christians hate us, based on the misconception that all witches are bad. I think it's the same for vampires — there are no absolutes."

I was concerned about our relationship and what I would have to endure later on. Sitting back and staring at the movie on the screen, I thought about his comments. The movie's protagonist was a French nobleman who had to choose whether to die or live on as a vampire. He struggled to stay human, but evil kept pulling him in deeper, until he chose to be a vampire because of his wife's murder and he wanted to avenge her death. I hid tears at times. I could relate to parts of the story.

"What did you think about it?" I asked Joey after the movie.

He shrugged. "It was all right. I hate how people try to romanticize them, though. They are creatures with no souls or hearts. However, they *are* interesting." He looked at me. "Did you enjoy it?"

"Yeah, I did. My heart went out to him, and the decisions he had to make — an eternity of pain and regret just to avenge his wife's death." I lowered my head and sighed, on the surface looking sympathetic but really hiding my shame. Would Joey's opinion be different if he knew the truth? I looked at him in this different, uncertain light. I saw his passion for me and knew how much he cared for me. He is all I wanted and more; concealing the truth from him would rip me apart inside. I hated deceiving the one person who meant the world to me.

The cold breeze numbed both my skin and my thoughts as we walked back to his car. Still shivering while we sat inside the car, I waited as it warmed up. He tugged off my gloves and wrapped his big hands around my cold fingers, smiling as he rubbed them together.

"I am grateful to be blessed with you," I said, pulling one hand free to rest it on his cheek. I leaned in to kiss him.

"I wish I wasn't going tonight," he confessed. "I'd rather be with you. You are a drug I cannot get enough of — the more I have of you, the more I want. I don't know how I'll manage, leaving you for three weeks." He looked away and absently twirled the keys hanging from the ignition.

"Don't worry, you'll have fun tonight, and two and a half weeks will go by fast," I lied. He was my balance, never letting me tip into my other half. With him no longer around to shelter me, would I transform into what I feared and become the thing he hated most?

He drove me home, and I turned around at my door to wave goodbye to him as he pulled away. *Only one more week left with him before he goes to Europe,* I thought. I still had to plan something special for his birthday. I went inside and called Allison to see if she wanted to join me tonight and help me plan something for Joey's birthday. However, she was busy "with an English essay due on Monday," she groaned, I decided to visit my mother at the store.

Chapter 10

FIRSTTASTE

The nights were getting darker a lot earlier now, and I had to turn my headlights on as I drove into the city to my mother's shop. The road had been quiet and empty until I got to the outskirts of Boston, where the streets slowly filled. Finding parking on a Saturday evening was hellish, even though it was still early. The closest parking lot I could find had to be at least four blocks away from my destination. Preparing myself mentally for the cold that awaited me outside my car, I got out and hit the lock switch, reminding myself that I would be out of the cold soon. I had expected a warm welcome from my mother when I walked into her shop.

BRUXA

Even Samantha her employee ran to give me a warm hug. My mother peeked around the corner with folded arms, Samantha reluctantly released.

"Gabriella," she said calmly, "may I talk to you in the back?" I knew from experience that was her angry tone. I didn't expect this reaction from my mother. Clueless about what might have caused her displeasure, I took a deep breath and followed her toward the back room.

"Yes, Mom?" I asked hesitantly as I peeked through the door.

"Close the door behind you," she ordered. Then, when I had complied: "What the hell were you thinking, coming here by yourself, and not calling? You know there is a full moon—how could you be this irresponsible? I'm disappointed with you." Her words sliced through me like razors as she flung her black hair off her shoulders and stood glaring at me with her arms crossed.

"I'm sorry! I thought it would have been nice to surprise you. We haven't talked much since… "I paused, holding back my tears of frustration. "Apparently I made a bad decision by coming," I said coldly.

I snapped, feeling my hurt resurface. "You're always trying to protect me. You won't save me— you are hurting me more by shutting me out. I am a half-breed of the worst kind and here I thought I was descended from a family of noble Bruxa blood. All my life you sheltered me from the worst, and now I've discovered my whole life has been a lie — you weren't protecting me from others, but from myself! You have no right to tell me about danger, with what I have growing in me." My voice dropped just shy of a whisper.

"When were you going to tell me — when it was too late and I had blood on my hands? You should have prepared me to deal with what I am and how to protect myself. You should have taught me how to use my own power for the greater good, instead of lying and denying what I am and what I am capable of doing!"

The look on her face nearly killed me. She stood there, frozen in her own shame. I had never disrespected my mother to such a degree before. She had to realize that by holding me back, she welcomed danger. If I had been taught how to protect myself, how to own and control my powers, this would never have been an issue.

"I guess there's nothing else to say. Enjoy the rest of your night." I turned and opened the door, then looked over my shoulder, preparing to say more. I choked on the words and could only whirl and walk away, holding back my tears long enough to wave and smile good night to Samantha, not giving her a reason for suspicion. I exited the shop consumed with emotions of resentment and hurt.

I roamed the streets, feeling lost and empty. The brisk winter air didn't even faze me anymore, fuelled by my anger. I gave into instinct and as it started to kick in, a foul smell of sulfur tickled my nostrils. The burning within coursed through my veins and my blood flared up as if ignited by a wild fire. I followed the smell to an alley about a block away from my car and peered into the darkness, spying three figures hidden in the dark shadows. I heard their repulsive thoughts as they tormented a poor girl, like cats toying with their prey. The burn took control, and I walked into the alley with no fear of consequences, led on by the smell and the anticipation of what awaited me. I felt my canine teeth extending into tiny daggers.

My burn intensified and I inhaled deeply, welcoming the Lampir in me, prepared mentally to destroy them. I stopped a few feet away and flung back my long dark hair. The trio stood staring at me, not knowing what to think of this situation. Two of them were skinny and tall, while the third one— their leader, I sensed—the fat, bald, foul excuse of a man. The girl was around fifteen years old. Reading her mind, I learned one of her tormentors is a distant cousin.

"Is there a problem here? I would hate to think you've been tormenting this poor girl," I snarled, slowly circling around them. Some small part of me felt shock about what had come over me; I would never have done this before. Looking at the fright-ened, helpless girl as they released their hold on her. As she stumbled to the cold ground, it fired up an uncontrollable burn inside of me.

"Go home, Cara, your mother is worried," I ordered, and she sobbed in relief and leapt to her feet and ran off.

"Who the hell do you think you are?" the fat old one growled, raking me up and down with his eyes, sizing me up. "I have to say, it will be a pleasure to have you instead."

"Carlos, didn't your mother ever tell you God's always watching, even in the shadows?" I sneered as he approached. I grabbed him by the chin and held him up high enough that his feet dangled an inch above the ground. Carlos's eyes widened in fear, and the other two bolted in terror.

I wanted to rip him apart—I struggled with myself not to. Hearing his regret playing in his mind, I released my grip and watched him col-lapse to the cold cement. Now he only looked weak. "Remember: God always watches," I warned him. "If you ever touch another girl inappropriately, I will rip your head off." I loomed over him. "This is your chance to start a new life. I suggest you find God. Now go, before I change my mind."

I watched him scramble to his feet and run away, amazed at how natural this felt. I heard the wind whip strongly behind me, and I instantly froze when I heard hands clapping in a dark corner. I turned and saw nothing, but very aware of my visitor.

"Well, well you *are* daddy's girl. Nice perform-ance; I felt for that disgusting, fat lamb—or should I say, filthy pig." Arrogance saturated his words that seemed to press against me.

"Why do you watch like a mouse but tease me like a fox?" I challenged him. "Why can't you face me? Are you too cowardly to let me see you?"

"I have looked you straight in the eye, and it was too much for you to bear." His voice seemed softer, and I heard a shuffle as he stepped back.

"I don't know what you're talking about, at this point nothing is too much to bear," I said. "I need help to will and control this; I know you're always watching me and you haven't attempted to kill me. Will you teach me? I am ready to look upon you," I pleaded, and then held my breath as I stood waiting for a response. I heard nothing, and I knew he was gone. I felt lost, as I stood there alone in the dark alley.

Confusion lingered with me as I left the alley and headed back to my car. The city streets had bloomed with nightlife. Crowds of people flowed by me like blurred watercolors. The noise faded to mumbles and my feet felt heavy, my mind lost in a whirlwind. I turned the corner and crossed the street to the parking lot. People continued to pour around me. I was unable to make out any of the faces; they all looked like lost sheep. Before getting into my car, I took a good look at my surroundings, seeing everything through a different set of eyes.

The clock on my dashboard read 7:35 p.m. — I could not believe it. It felt as if hours had passed. On the drive home, my thoughts populated with more questions. Without a doubt, I was my father's daughter. My fears had come to life when I had to restrain myself from ripping Carlos apart. I readily admitted that I enjoyed being fearless and free. How could I conceal this new aspect of myself from Joey?

I parked my car taking a deep breath as I got out, exhaling as I stood there staring at the full moon, lost to the world until I heard soft footsteps behind me while making my way to the front door. I stopped dead realizing I was not alone.

"You're right, I am always watching," he whispered.

BRUXA

I turned to face him, his head downcast, and his face hidden in shadow. "Will you teach me and tell me about my father?" I asked again, glad he had returned to me. I bit my lip, wondering if I had pushed my luck by asking about my father.

"Yes, I will help you." He voice softened, no longer sounding sinister. "Your father was an old friend in my past." He stepped out of the shadows and into the moonlight.

My body seized up in anticipation of the long-awaited introduction. My heart skipped a beat as he slowly lifted his head into the moonlight, the light from overhead making him seem angelic and highlighting his perfectly sculpted face. I gasped, and then struggled for breath, remembering his face.

"Oh my God, it's you." My voice cracked. I stared in disbelief, while my heart pounded out of control. Alvero, how could I have forgotten that night I first saw him? How he picked away at his guitar captivating the crowd at Jazz. It all began to make sense the unbearable feeling that had taken over me the moment our eyes met.

"Yes. My name is Alvero," he said formally, holding out his hand.

"You already know my name—Gabriella." I reached out to shake his hand. As our hands met, instant energy surged along my spine straight to my soul. I blinked, stunned—and he was gone.

"You'll have to become quick and fast with your defenses," he said, disappearing and reappearing from a dark corner. "This will be your training." His voice fell to a whisper. "Close your eyes and let the burn flow through you. Feel it as if you're dancing to its music."

I found it hard to concentrate while still in a state of awe. Those full lips and turquoise eyes made it impossible for me to fully concentrate on anything but him. In an effort to get him out of my thoughts, I closed my eyes and just let go, feeling the burn crawling from my head to my toes. I felt my body swaying with the wind, gliding back and forth.

"That's it, let it go, Gabby. Release your human concerns and let yourself be free of judgment," his voice sang as he glided by me.

I felt myself again free and careless of worldly restraints, with no worries harnessing me. I floated like driftwood on water. The sound of moving cars faded into the distance. The sounds I heard were so minute: mice scurrying across the frosty ground, the rustle of a bird's feathers. I was entirely submerged in my newly discovered world.

"Your mother is coming," he said in a normal voice that broke my concentration. When I opened my eyes, he had vanished into the night.

BRUXA

I did not want to confront my mother again. I ran into the house and hid in my room. I opened the journal I'd found in the secret room, hoping it would be a good distraction. Hearing the front door unlock, I listened in silence, waiting for her next move. I held my breath as she marched up the stairs, counting on my fingers the seconds until she barged in my room.

She opened the door. "We need to talk," she said firmly. She came in and sat on the edge of my bed. "You're right," she sighed. "I can't pretend you don't need to learn how to will your powers and understand your lineage. Forgive me for all the secrets." She looked away. "I've enjoyed living normally too long."

After a moment, she turned to me. "I grew up under heavy expectations, constantly training and studying—my parent's trophy. Much like you, I was so free spirited. I yearned to be free of my birthright. I never wanted my family to control you as they did me, which is why you have been kept in the dark. That's why I refused to take you back to Europe after your father's death."

"Joey talked about your family," I said. "I felt so stupid, not knowing the extent of my lineage. Basically, I'm the ultimate weapon—and I have much to learn in little time." I hesitated. "I am scared for my salvation. I do not want these powers to consume me, and I don't want to live forever in the shadows. I know the Lampir is strong in me." I looked away, fighting tears as I spoke, knowing what just happened tonight.

My mother curled up beside me and cradled me as if I were a child again. She explained how the Bruxa female birthrate had dropped to nearly nothing, with only one in five female children born. All three lineages had slowed, especially the Malicus line. To make it worse, Lampirs in the past killed females before they were able to produce offspring.

She told me her father, the last of the royal line, had married a Conjure. The most common lineage, my grandmother had royal blood from previous generations. They married to produce a female. "No one is able to read your mind or your future, that in itself will protect you," she told me. "And since you walk in the light of God, nothing can harm you. You must not lose your faith or your fear of God's judgment; God created all and may destroy all." She lifted my head up and smiled at me. "Good night, angel. We will start training tomorrow."

She left me feeling reassured. Seeing things in a clearer light, I resumed reading the journal until fatigue blurred my vision and I sank into deep sleep.

Chapter 11

MAGIC

Sitting in church, feeling my stomach twitch with mixed emotions, I tuned in and out, as the priest gave Mass. I was anxious to get home and start my training with my mother. Noting Joey's absence and seeing the rest of the rat pack here at mass dampened my spirits and unsettled me. I brushed off the unsettling feeling, telling myself he had slept in. I smiled as I left the church; it must have been some crazy night for him.

At a young age, I had mastered the ability to channel in and out of the minds of the lambs. I had also been taught basic conjuring and healing spells. Now I needed to learn to will and control my invisible force of light, the ability to move objects with my mind. My mother was able to move objects around with her mind; her power came from a natural energy of light and thought.

"Start by focusing on this object as if there is an invisible thread holding it up," she instructed me, placing a cup of water on the floor. "Then pull the string with your mind." She sat on the floor with her hands resting on her legs, and demonstrated. As she stared at the cup, it rose above her head, and then gracefully sank back down, with no water even rippling inside.

Seeing her toss her beautiful black mane over her slender shoulders was so magical in itself. I wished that one day I would be as beautiful and graceful as she was. When she maneuvered with her magic, her beauty was indescribable. Now I understood why she had captivated my father.

"Wow, you make it look so effortless," I said. "Okay, I guess it's my turn." I mimicked her position on the floor, then blocked out all thought and focused. I felt the force and willed it with my fingers. The cup wobbled, but didn't rise. I tried for a good half-hour with no progress at all. Determined to master it, I was not going to give up.

"Listen to your inner self and try to relax. You're thinking too hard." Her voice softened my tension and she rested her hand on my shoulder, urging me to relax.

Sitting with my legs crossed, focusing on inhaling and exhaling, I went into a meditative state. I focused my energy, allowing it to become one with me. Just as I did with the burning, I let my light force flow through me as I raised my palms, directing the object with calm and steady movements of my fingers. Still focusing mentally on the glass of water, I opened my eyes to see it suspended in mid-air, three feet off the ground!

"Good job. Now try moving it side to side," Mom whispered in a calm voice, trying not to break my concentration.

I deepened my focus as the energy surged through my fingertips. I guided the cup to the right with the invisible thread I imagined. I gestured the opposite way with my finger, and the cup followed — then dropped to the floor, a victim of my excitement. I had never realized I had the power to do that with my hands.

"I did it! I can't believe I did that! It's amazing!" I shouted gleefully, jumping up to dance around. I stopped and looked at her, still grinning proudly. "Thanks, Mom. Are you going to show me more?"

"One thing at a time," she told me. "You must practice this every day. You did well but you need a lot more work." She smiled. "Our Fragoso bloodline is known for our mind powers—that is what made us powerful. Your grandfather is the ultimate mastermind. His blood line is one hundred percent pure Malicus."

"I know this is off topic, but why do the Bruxa hate Lampirs? I mean, how did this hatred start?" I asked, taking advantage of her openness.

"Where to start? They turned their backs on the lambs as the Inquisition started. They killed many of the Malicus and the Lougaro who guarded them. It has been hundreds of years since the war. That day I saw your father, I knew he was there to kill me. Knowing he would not because he was my raven, I showed him love and the compassion he had lost. It was we who betrayed them." She hung her head in shame.

There were so many questions that I wanted to ask, now that I could accept what I am. However, she had already sacrificed an hour of her time to teach me my new lesson, and I didn't want to harass her. Besides, I needed answers. I also needed time to digest the overload of information I had received recently.

The afternoon dragged on as I finished the rest of my assignments. I was troubled by the fact that Joey had not bothered to call me yet. Realizing how much it troubled me—first his absence from church and now not calling — I called his cell phone. When I got no response, I tried his home phone.

"Hello, Mrs. Davale, may I please speak with Joey?" I said when his mom answered, feeling nervous to be talking to his mother.

His mother's voice warmed when she learned it was me. She told me how delighted she is that I would be joining them for dinner the night before he leaves. She said he had slept in; and he had things to do today. "I'm sure he will call you when he gets back."

I thanked her, relieved our conversation was short, and hung up the phone. A chill ran through me as I sensed that something was wrong.

Curled up on the window seat in my bay window, I tried to do some reading. The words blurred no matter how I tried to focus; my mind was elsewhere. My eyes drifted out the window. What looked gloomy and grey now had brightened up with white flakes of snow twirling down, reawakening Father Christmas. I hated the cold, but I had to admit there was something magical in a snowfall. Watching as it covered the earth in a white, cottony layer, I longed to touch it. I tossed the book aside and bundled up nice and warm.

I slid my feet into my boots and tossed on my parka, then pulled on my gloves. My head filled with childhood memories of playing with the descending white snowflakes, catching them on my tongue. I ran outside then stopped, captivated by the untouched frosting of snow that blanketed the earth in calmness. I watched the snowflakes falling one by one, sparkling in the light like diamonds as they descended. Feeling a sense of peace, I let go of myself, heightening my senses and closing my eyes to let the burn take over.

I glided through the falling snow into the wooded area, stopping there to give in to my light force. Lifting my hands, I controlled the pattern of the falling snow like a conductor directing an orchestra. Testing my senses, I listened as the earth hummed. Hearing a faint whispering, I locked in on it and focused in deeper to hear the words.

"I can't believe he did that, your foul thing of choice," Alvero muttered, sounding disgusted.

"What are you talking about?" I blurted, instantly breaking our connection.

His words plagued my mind. Consumed with curiosity, I tried and failed to regain our connection. Angry about giving in to my human curiosity, had he been talking about Joey? Would this explain why I felt an unsettling concern? My feet felt heavy now as I ran back to the house to call Joey and settle my mind before it went into overdrive.

I burst through the back door. As I was about to grab my phone, I heard the front doorbell ring twice. Tracking snow through the house, I ran to the front door, knowing it had to be him. My heart raced as I opened the door. Relieved and overjoyed, I wrapped my arms around him and held on tight.

"I was just going to call you. This is better," I said, pulling back to smile. I noticed his embrace was stiff and he stood quiet. I frowned in concern. "Are you okay, Joey? Something is definitely wrong with you." I stood back to study his face. He looked emotionless and empty.

"You're right, something is not right with me. It is cold and I have been standing here for at least five minutes, waiting for you to answer the door. Were you outside this whole time?" he grumbled with an avoiding glare.

I felt him trembling inside his soul. Though confused by his behavior, I pulled him inside, out of the cold. He went over and sat on the couch. "Wait here, I'll be back—I'm going to make something for us to drink." I flashed a warm smile, still unsure of his attitude.

My mind disconnected from him as I waited for the cocoa and the secret ingredients to simmer and merge. I wanted to give him time to calm down; his behavior planted more seeds of doubt in my head.

BRUXA

What would his reaction be if he knew the truth? That second of coldness is all I ever wanted to bear.

I looked at his face as I carried in our drinks, noticing it had become harder, his light duller. I set our cups down on the coffee table in front of him.

"I don't deserve you; I shouldn't have snapped. It's selfish for me to think that we could ever be like the lambs," he said, his voice full of remorse. He grabbed me by the arm as I was about to sit across from him.

"Trust me, I should be the one saying that to you," I said, thinking, *If he knew the truth of who I am…*

"Gabriella, you have made me weak and unfocused. I have used girls in the past and hurt many of them, but you are my kind. If possible, I would give everything up for you. What I did yesterday is what I am; you're distracting me from my duties." His voice was distorted, as were his words. He released his hold on my arm.

"What are you talking about? What happened last night?" I asked my voice high with concern. He avoided eye contact, and it felt as if my chest were caving in. I wrapped my arms around myself. This was killing me! Why couldn't he get to the point? I sank onto the edge of the couch, watching him.

"Last night, the guys and I met up with another clan of Bruxa, who attend a college we've all applied to. They invited us to a frat party. The night had been great until they wanted me to stay after Paul and the twins left. Being stupid, I stayed and everything seemed normal. Then they wanted to take me out for a hunt. They dragged me along to show me how it is done. They found some random Lampir and picked a fight with her. Obviously, they knew my powers and used me to track her down. They toyed with her. She was unprepared for what happened."

He shook his head, and his eyes fell to the floor. "The way they did it felt wrong. It was as if they did it out of sport not duty. They called me weak as I walked away from them. I froze and choked when I heard the way she screamed. Unsure of what really happened, I ran back to see. Out of nowhere, another Lampir came and pushed me to the ground. It happened so fast, the only thing I remember him saying is, 'Your friends will pay for this, and I will snack on them one by one.' His words tattooed in my mind." His voice, consumed by remorse, cracked with pain. He covered his face with his hands and cried.

For the first time, I looked at him with resentment and hate, judging him. Nevertheless, another part of me was glad that he had not taken part in the torture. *He led them to her,* a part of me thought. *What if that had been me instead?* Part of me hated him and another part felt pity for him because I knew that is what he is designed for—killing Lampir.

"I don't know what to say," I began. "Why didn't you stop them? I believe there is goodness in all of us. It's all in how you use your gifts." I bit my tongue to contain my rage. "How would you feel if that were me, and the situation was reversed?"

"I admit I would love to destroy an immortal," he said. "I hate those leeches. I have been taught to attack if they are stepping out of line. I would kill if that had been you. I'm designed to kill them, but what the Bruxa did was wrong." He looked at me. "Out of all people, you should hate them the most. It's funny; I don't think you know how deep our hatred is toward them."

His words, strong and passionate, etched a wound in my heart. Not knowing what to say or how to react, I sat in silence, watching him sipping his drink. *I am falling for someone who utterly hates a part of me. If he did have a conscience for the Lampir, could there be hope for us?* Even if I were not a half-breed, I would never have it in me to judge or hate something so much without a personal reason.

"We are not ones to judge the other children of the Grigori," I murmured. "Yes, we may be different, there is as much evil in us as there is in them,—your friends are proof of that. It is only God you should concern yourself with and his judgment—for you should have stopped them. I don't want to sound harsh…but it's the truth." I felt torn within. I knew he felt guilty as hell. I pasted a reassuring smile on my face and placed my hand on his flushed cheek, showing him compassion.

"You leave Sunday night, and won't be back until the fourth—wow, three weeks," I said in a lighter tone, changing the subject. "It's going to be difficult; I'm scared you'll come back different." I looked away, fearing that he would change for the worse, after already seeing a change in his temperament.

"Why would you say that? I will be with family. Nothing will change; I will just be stronger and more aware, especially after my coronation. My family has many expectations, and if they knew about you I'd be the envy of them all," he boasted. He set down his cup, smiling, and rose to walk to the door.

Still bothered by his view of me as his prize, not to mention what had happened to that girl, I said, "Sorry, I don't carry my title; it's my mother's birthright, not mine. Don't think you'll have me at your side to gloat over." I disguised it as joking, but I was serious as I walked him to the door.

As I reached over to pass him his jacket, he grabbed my hand. "Why do you take such offence?

You should know how much you mean to me," he said, turning me to face him.

"Not to sound ill-tempered, but why do you always mention my status? I don't even interact with them myself. Sorry, my noble family knows nothing about my life. I will not be locked up in a tower for observation." I stopped and covered my mouth, unsure where that had come from. He was looking at me with uncertainty in his eyes. "It's been a rough week," I apologized. "I know you do care, and I'm sorry if I offended you." I bit my lip.

"Sometimes I wish I could hate you," he said with a devious smirk as he leaned in to kiss me goodbye.

I chuckled, shaking my head at him. *If he only knew...*

I wanted to make something special for my mother and block out what had happened with Joey. Looking into the freezer, I decided it was a toss-up between steak and seafood. It had been a long time since I had had steak. I ended up grabbing both. While defrosting the steak and seafood, I sautéed the onion. Once it turned golden, I threw the garlic in for the last few seconds before taking it off the burner and pouring a cup of wine into the mixture. The aroma reawakened my culinary passion. I reached for the meat and some herbs and spices.

Magic

My head started spinning in repugnance as I stabbed the fork into the raw meat, releasing some blood. Without hesitation, I threw it into the pan and placed it back on the burner. The sight and smell of cold blood made me want to heave.

Despite my nausea, my efforts were a success. My mother delighted in the fact that I had made an amazing dinner. Even I was proud of my culinary skills in the kitchen. Later we nestled up on opposite ends of the couch sipping our lattés. We started joking around and talking as we used to do before the move.

She sobered when I showed her the ring I wanted to give Joey for his birthday. She explained how inappropriate it would be to give to him, and said we would go out this week and get him something else.

We reminisced how we used to. I told her how Joey had acted, realizing how much it ate at me. Putting my cup down, I rested my head on her lap.

"You know, Gabby, I love you so much. You know I'm always here for you," she said as she stroked my hair.

"Why did things have to change?" I moaned as I sat back up to look at her. "Don't get me wrong—I love having friends and having Joey around."

"Why do you think I have sheltered you and kept you away from the Bruxa?" she replied. "I have wanted you to be stronger in your faith, not in the way of the Bruxa. I have never hid what I am from you because it is a strong part of you. I lost my noble privileges when I denied my father's pick of husbands and ran away with your father. You have never met him or seen him; I don't doubt he would love you." She smiled at me.

"Can you tell me how we came to be?" I asked, hoping she would not reject my question.

Her voice took on a storyteller lilt and I settled back to listen. "We are all children of the Grigori. They were the angels God sent to watch over humankind. It came to be that they desired the daughters of Eve and took them as wives. Many of the male children exploited their power and were easily influenced by evil. They challenged God by being immortal and God destroyed them with his mighty fists in the great flood. The obedient daughters of the Grigori were sent to live on an island, away from the lambs, never to live among them until the New Covenant.

"Throughout the centuries, our people flourished. They soon forgot their obedience to God. Our ancestors accomplished things you couldn't have imagined; we were becoming full of pride and vanity. With great power comes great evil. God destroyed the island, leaving six women and their children, who served God fully with all their hearts so they were spared. They came to the Iberian regions, where they made a new convent with God. That is why only the female may carry on the blood-line, for her obedience to God." She sighed sadly and looked away. "Times have changed a lot, there is less use for us. Most lambs welcome demons freely and no longer fear God."

Later, looking out my window at the moon's reflection bouncing over the dark ocean, I thought of Alvero and wondered about my soon-to-be teacher. It is going to be a challenge to stay focused when my teacher is the most gorgeous creature I had ever seen. His voice alone stirred something deep inside of me.

Chapter 12

FADO

Dense fog consumed the daylight and I felt lost within its grasp. The farther I walked, the thicker the fog got, making it harder to see anything. My blood burned wildly as I savored my fear of this unknown domain, slowly forgetting myself and the world I belonged to.

I stumbled over a large black rock and fell into tall, damp grass that buried me as if I had fallen into another place and time. I pushed myself up on my elbows and shook the otherworldliness from my mind. A cold, uneasy, burning sensation replaced it. Fear kicked in as a black cloud approached, hissing profanity. Looking around in panic, I realized I didn't have the faintest idea where I was. My heart raced with terror.

To my right, about fifteen feet away, I noticed a cobbled path. I quickly picked myself up and ran toward the path. The uncomfortable chill pressed harder against me, becoming frightful as I tried moving faster. Continually looking over my shoulder, I looked for the dangerous threat that felt as if it were approaching rapidly from behind me.

In the distance, I saw a cross on top of the steeple of a small wooden chapel. I pushed myself to run faster, but my feet were not moving. Frustrated, I jumped into the air and glided toward it, so scared I didn't think twice about the fact that I was *gliding*. I just wished for the protection of that chapel. The clouds opened above it and a ray of sunlight descended to illuminate the humble chapel, as if it were welcoming me into its protection.

I sighed in relief as I reached safety, releasing the terror that had consumed me. Peace consumed my fear, as I looked around. The mountainous terrain was magical in its splendor. Snow dusted the mountain peaks, and a soft mist nestled in the valleys between them. Beyond that, it was as if darkness had devoured the world.

I walked around the chapel, seeking the entrance. I ran my finger against the aged wood as I went, and

I released a silent giggle, relieved to be in the light. When I reached the front of the chapel, I stood looking at the finely detailed inscription carved deep into the wood above the doorway, flanked by four faceless angels, arms outstretched as if they were inviting me in. Taking a deep breath, I pressed my palms against the heavy oak doors. A gust of wind blew out from within, as they swung open, rushing by me as if released.

I felt a pure simplicity upon entering this new domain. The walls were bare and modest, unlike the rich trappings of a traditional church. A rainbow of colors seeped through the stained glass and lit up the chapel with dancing shards of reflected light. The room was empty except for one monk swathed in brown cloth, his back facing me. He stood still in front of the altar, a wooden cross-hung above it.

Peace came upon me as I strolled in; I knelt and made the sign of the cross as I got to the pews. I was aware of the monk as I knelt down to pray; he did not budge or flinch. I closed my eyes and began to pray, and in that second, I felt an energy surge within me.

I whirled as a hand gripped my shoulder, my eyes flying open. The monk was nowhere in sight. It was as if he had never been there. I got up to look around, desperate to find him. When I didn't see him inside, I dashed back outside. Dark clouds had swallowed the sun. As I turned to go back inside, something abruptly whisked me up into the air.

It felt as if my heart had stopped. I sat bolt upright in my bed, awaking from my nightmare. My hair stuck against my neck and back with the rapidly chilling sweat of fear. Seeing the steam of my breath in the air and noticing how chilled I felt, I sensed a presence in my room.

The burning sensation in my blood warmed me as a silhouette emerged from the darkness and made its way toward the light. My survival instincts kicked in and I flung myself off the bed, to stand on its far side in defensive mode.

"Relax youngling. You are so predictable," Alvero said in a mocking voice. Stepping into the soft light filtering in through my window, he leaned forward. His eyes glowed a mint blue- green.

"What—what are you doing in my room? How dare you come uninvited? Who the hell do you think you are?" I hissed hoping not to wake my mom. I relaxed a little, and folded my arms across my chest. I felt exposed, standing before him in nothing but a slinky tank top and pink boxer shorts.

He chuckled. "Yes...you are most interesting to watch, especially when you dream. It is about time you figured it out. You're still such a foolish human

Bruxa," he murmured as he came closer. His luminous cat eyes changed to sparkling green diamonds.

At a loss for words, I stood as he circled around examining me. Chills shivered down my spine. My heart raced with exhilaration and fury. For a quick moment, time seemed to stop.

"Uh… are you done, or do you enjoy making me uncomfortable?" I muttered angrily, breaking out of my trance. I grabbed my blanket to cover myself. I was angry that he had such a power over me, to make me blush feverishly.

"I'm not that fond of the human in you, but watching you I did glimpse something that did appeal to me." He paused and scanned me again. "Why are you covering up? I liked those little pink shorts." He teased me with a sly smirk, stepping close enough to twirl a strand of my hair. My knees quivered as I felt my hair sliding through his fingers. "I guess you made me curious to learn how you mortals live."

I ignored his beauty as my anger boiled over; right now, I wanted only to rip him apart for driving me crazy. In that second, he vanished into the night.

With a huff, I walked over and relocked my window, then returned to my bed. I never wanted to see him again. I hated how he came uninvited, violating my mind and my space as if I were some toy to play with. If I had never known my father, I would have despised the Lampir as well, after seeing firsthand how selfish they could be.

I tossed and turned through the rest of the night, my mind not allowing my encounter with Alvero to evaporate. My dream did not even disquiet me as much as he did. As much as I wanted to hate him, I could not stop thinking about him and those cool green eyes.

I must have hit the snooze button five times before getting out of bed the next morning. Then, realizing I had half an hour to get ready, I flung aside the bedcovers and leapt out of bed to dash around like a lunatic. After throwing myself together, I jumped into my car, anxious to see Joey. I hoped he would have the power to remove the bitterness that still lingered from last night's episodes.

I quickly parked when I saw him getting out of his vehicle and waving at me. I was in such a hurry to run over to meet him that I tripped over my own feet on a patch of black ice and landed right on my butt. Watching, Joey flinched. I wanted to cry. Instead, I burst into hysterical laughter at his expression. The more I looked at him, the harder I laughed. He started to chuckle as he helped me up.

"You're a disaster today," he said, still laughing as he shook his head.

"You have no idea about my morning." I struggled to speak, still savoring my embarrassment. I guess this happens when you welcome anger.

I regretted my commitment to hanging out with my girlfriends at lunch and hated the fact I wouldn't see him until the end of the school day. He was not thrilled; I think he secretly knew I was preparing for his birthday party. As we walked into school, I stared at him wondering how I was going to survive not seeing him for three whole weeks.

My morning classes felt long, and my mind still dwelt on last night's visitor, Alvero. It was evident how much he despised the Bruxa, and completely apparent that he considered me a chore. For whatever reason, he felt compelled to help me—probably in honor of my father. I knew he must be over a hundred years old, maybe older, but he acted like a college brat and he looked it as well. I did wonder how old he was. He seemed a complete opposite to my father, a distinguished young man, noble and sophisticated.

"Gabby, hello…is anyone there?" Cindy called, waving her hand in front of my face. Ana stood behind her, smiling and shaking her head.

"Oh, sorry—I got lost in a zone." I gave my head a shake.

"Let's go, we have a lot to talk about." Cindy chuckled as she grabbed my arm.

BRUXA

Though we ended up sitting at opposite ends of the cafeteria, Joey and I made frequent eye contact. I could not help admiring his well-constructed face and strong chest, and shook my head in utter disbelief that he belonged to me and no one else.

"Gabby, please try to focus," Allison said. "Paul and all of us agree we're going to take Joey to Jazz Friday night for his birthday." She crossed her arms as if to say there is no point in arguing. Unfortunately, I was outnumbered.

I choked on my food. "Isn't there anywhere else, something different?" I asked in desperation. I could not go back there! What if Alvero was there—he'd give me away! Talk about an uncomfortable situation. Not at all how I had planned to spend one of our last night's together.

"Well, not really it is the only cool place that is all-ages. Besides, both our friends agreed on that place. Why? Is there any particular reason you don't want to be there?" Allison smirked as if she knew something.

"No, I just thought it would be nice to try something new and different," I answered, burying my worry; by now I should have known that my life was a constant disaster.

****

Fado

The next day started much better, I slept like a baby and woke energized and seeing things a lot clearer than I had the day before. What was the big deal about going to Jazz? Even if Alvero were there, it would not change anything. He blended in fine; they would never know he was a Lampir. Still, the possibility of discovery loomed over me.

The week had passed relatively fast, and now here I was, locking down my locker for the Christmas holiday. I hesitated, knowing that Joey and I would be apart until the holiday ended. I was ecstatic to be away from school, I was not thrilled about that three-week separation.

"So I'm going to pick you up at 7:00 — be ready," he yelled out his window after dropping me off at my house.

"You do realize this is the third time you've reminded me," I called back, chuckling, before stepping through my front door.

I had about an hour before he came back to get me. After I got ready, I took a moment to admire the gift I planned to give him tomorrow night: a coin medallion on a sliver chain, with a lighthouse on the front. On the back, I engraved *my air, my light, my life — you are the beacon* in Latin all Bruxa's mother tongue. The phase reflected my true feelings. He is my life — or at least the life I would prefer.

BRUXA

My heart jumped when I heard the door, and I dashed to greet him like an army bride greeting a husband on leave. Smoothing out my soft teal silk blouse dress that hung loose but faltered all my curves, I opened the door on my picture-perfect Joey, standing out in the cold as his leather jacket hugged his strong fame. He did not say much until I pulled him inside.

"Wow, you look amazing," he said, looking me up and down. Then he grinned. "I think I'd rather stay here alone with you instead."

"That would be nice, to have you all to myself— but we have people waiting for us," I teased back, zipping up my jacket and flinging my mane of straight dark hair as if I were performing in a music video.

I paused as I was locking the front door and took a deep breath as I thought of the possibility of bumping into Alvero. I exhaled, willing my concern to leave me with the expelled breath. Our drive there removed any anxiety I may have harbored, as a laughing Joey reminded me of my wipeout. Then his tone grew serious, telling me about his family in Europe, and how excited he is about his eighteenth birthday coronation. He intended to spend the weekend before in preparation, so he could bring himself, clean and pure, to the elders for their judgments.

He spoke with such passion as he described all the rituals he would be doing for his preparation. His charisma sparked a pride in me. It amazed me how his face lit up with pride in the honor of being a Bruxa. He loved the idea of being a soldier and bringing the wicked to justice. Our drive had become a Bruxa seminar.

A few minutes after 8:00, we pulled into the Jazz parking lot. I could not contain my laughter as I thought back to our first encounter as we walked hand in hand toward the entrance. "Do you remember that night we first talked?" I giggled. "You told me you liked my hair color." My giggle turned into a laugh. He grabbed me and pulled me closer to wrap his arm around me, biting his lips in attempt to restrain his own laughter.

There was already a line-up at the front door. Mentally thanking Cindy for being a step ahead and booking birthday reservations, I smiled at the ox-like bouncer at the door. "We have a reservation for the Davale party."

"Okay, go right in." He lifted the rope from the pole and motioned us inside.

The place was already filling up. We pushed through the crowd, me taking advantage of Joey's height and letting him spot our friends and lead the way. Of course, typical of my unfortunate luck, we were sitting right up front.

Cindy jumped up right away when she saw us. Before we even had a chance to sit down, she was at my side. "Oh my God, I'm so excited!" she gushed as she grabbed my arm and pulled me slightly away from Joey. "Isn't this amazing? Did you know that singer from last time—Alvero—is performing three sets tonight? That is why it's so crazy in here tonight. Oh Gabby, I cannot wait! He's so sexy," she squealed.

I smiled, trying hard to hide my feelings. *If only they knew,* I thought. As soon as I heard his name, I knew this would be a night from hell.

As everyone ate, I zoned deep into myself, preparing mentally for the night. Now that I understood my burning, I didn't think it would be bad. I found it a lot easier to control my reactions. Turning a negative into a positive as the host introduced Alvero for his first set; I realized this could help me learn to contain the Lampir within.

Similar to a domino effect, silence rippled back through the crowd until the entire room went to a quiet mumble, everyone waiting for the first notes of his mystical music. He sat quietly on his stool, cradling his guitar, until every eye focused on him. Then he strummed the strings of his guitar like a

Spanish gypsy. The passion in his music enslaved the crowd; his words flowed right into their souls. No matter how I despised him, I could not help falling in love with his music. He sang with conviction and passion, and I realized there had to be much more to him then his egotistical attitude.

"This is called a *Fado*," he said as introduction to his next piece. "My mother sang it to me when I was child, and for the first time, I want to share it with all of you." He stared right at me, knowing I would understand what he was saying, since Fado is a Portuguese style of music.

I recognized the song within the first few seconds and a painful memory of my father ripped through my heart. This was a song he sang to comfort me, something I used to hum to myself as a child. Alvero's words tainted my thoughts and I found it harder to control my mind. Each word he sang slashed at me as if somehow he knew how his words would affect me. I refused to get up and walk away. Instead I sat there, hiding in Joey's arms, glaring at Alvero. Everyone except me clapped as his first set ended. Relieved he was finished, I was determined to enjoy the rest of my night; I would not let him destroy it.

"Hey beautiful, if you squeeze me any tighter, my arms will fall apart," Joey amused, patting the top on my hand, making me relax.

I loosened my grip. "I'm sorry. It's that song—my father sang it to me as a child," I muttered.

"If you feel uncomfortable, we can leave," he whispered. His adoring face melted my anger away.

I shook my head and soon got involved in joking around with the others, forgetting about Alvero's tainted presence. Just as my night seemed to be improving, I felt Alvero's presence and saw him approaching our table. He radiated arrogance as he stood in front of our table. "Well, you must be the birthday boy," he said to Joey. "I wanted to come over and wish you a happy birthday." With no shame, Alvero held his hand out and shook first Joey's hand, then the hands of everyone at the table, looking at each with sincerity. They have no idea what he is.

"You're a very lucky birthday boy," he said to Joey, his eyes on me. "She's one of a kind. Well, I hope you enjoy the rest of your night." He said to everyone then, raising one eyebrow, he inclined his head to Joey and glanced at me.

Listening to my friends' praise of Alvero, especially when Joey spoke his name with such admiration, I cringed. Alvero mocked all of them, and they were clueless. Feeling nauseated, I excused myself from the table, unwilling to hear anymore from the wannabe Alvero groupies.

I stalked toward the exit, hoping some fresh air would calm my nerves. Fury clouded my mind, though. I did not pay attention to which door I walked out of, only flung the door open, and stepped outside. Realizing I had exited through a fire escape into the alley just as the door slammed shut behind me, I clenched my teeth, angry with myself. Then, recollecting the skills my mother had me practicing, I closed my eyes and concentrated all of my thoughts on making the door reopen.

"You're so predictable and stubborn."

My eyes flew open in surprise as I recognized Alvero's voice. I turned to face him. "Why do you constantly insult me with your arrogance, and how dare you mock my friends' kindness? Do you envy those with a soul, or do you just hate everything? You know what I pity about you? Living for eternity and filling your emptiness with hate," I hissed at him.

He darted forward and pinned me against the wall, his body centimeters from mine. Paralyzed with terror, I feared he wanted to rip me apart.

"You know nothing about me," he growled. "Who are you to judge, when you're the one deceiving them all? What will your precious Joey do when he discovers what you really are?" He glared at me and curled his lips back, revealing his fangs.

I stood speechless, hanging my head in shame. He spoke the truth. My body trembled with the burn, preparing itself for a fight.

His head swooped down toward my neck. As the tip of his nose glided over my jugular vein, I whimpered, "What are you waiting for? I can't believe I trusted you."

Alvero held himself still for a few seconds, perhaps while he fought his own inner battle. He pulled his face away from my neck, his eyes dark with pain. I cupped my hands around his face, blinking back tears. Uncertainty flared again as his hands came up to grab my wrists.

"What mind tricks are you playing with me?" he hissed as he threw my hands down. He abruptly looked away, and then vanished, catching the door after him before I became locked outside again.

"What took you so long, are you sure you're okay?" Joey questioned as he stood up to meet as I walked back to the table.

"Yah, don't worry I'll be fine." I bit my lip as he grabbed onto my hands.

"You know what, I'm not feeling this place, I don't mind leaving if you want to go." He smiled and leaning in to kiss my forehead. Hours later, I was grateful the night was over. I curled up in my pajamas on the window seat, looking out my bay window while the *Fado* Alvero sang played through my mind. One verse kept repeating in my mind like a skipping CD: "My love is deep, deeper than blood and water; I stand defenseless as you gaze upon my hidden sorrow, an angel who gives me the will to live—my life is yours, all I am is in you." Those words etched forever in my heart.

The next morning I woke to see my mother's gentle smile as she sat on the edge of my bed, watching me awaken. "I'm amazed how you have become a woman," she said softly. "I'm trusting in you to make the right decisions." She sat back. "I have to fly out tonight. There's something I have to take care of back home." She frowned with a deep sigh. "I hate leaving you especially now with everything you're going through, I will be gone for a week and a bit. I have spoken with Allison's mother and she agreed to check in on you. Samantha will be managing the shop in my absence," she said with a twinge of remorse, but I saw urgency in her eyes.

"Where are you going, is there a problem?" I asked, concern pushing me right out of bed.

"I have to go back to Portugal and take care of something of urgency. I wish I could take you, but your safety will be a great risk. I will be back soon. I love you." Her eyes glistened with unshed tears. She smiled and kissed me goodbye, then rose to leave.

"Mom, please talk to me," I yelled, stopping her in the doorway. "I need to know what's so urgent." I knew it had to do with her family—and me.

"It's your grandfather. I must claim my honor back and resume my responsibility for the sake of our kind. I will be back as soon as possible. I'm sorry for the short notice, it is imperative that I leave now."

Seeing and hearing the tension in my mother, I grabbed her and held her tight in my arms with a deep affection.

We did not talk much about her reasons for leaving as I drove her to the airport. She did not fail to give me a list of things to do and not to do. Well, she knew Joey was not going to be a problem, since he was leaving late Saturday morning. I was both scared and excited to be on my own for a week, even though my mother was hardly ever home, now that she had her shop to care for. "I figure you'll be fine," she told me with a wry smile. "After all, you have killer instincts."

Chapter 13

THE MEETING

My stomach turned inside out. Not even Joey's reassuring pep talk in the car had helped. Now I concentrated my efforts on each step as I approached his house and not on my unraveling nerve. His family did not scare me so much as the questions and judgments they might have.

With only an arm's reach from the door, it flew open and his mother burst out to greet us. I stood paralyzed with uncertainty as she wrapped her arms around me. "I'm glad you finally came over," she squealed. "We've all been dying to sit down and get to know you."

BRUXA

Behind her, the rest of the Davale clan stood waiting their turn. I felt almost betrayed by their overbearing welcome as they took their turns, giving a warm European welcome complete with kisses and hugs. This wasn't the response I expected at all. Their universal curiosity, as they all hovered around me as if I were a spectacle, threw me off balance.

"Come on, guys, let the poor girl take off her shoes," Joey quipped, shooing them off. "You've got all night with her."

"I don't mind, it's nice to meet you all," I managed.

"Gabby, do you want something to drink?" his mother asked as she headed back into the kitchen, the rest following her out of the room.

"Sorry," Joey whispered. "They're just excited that you're here, so don't mind them. Let me show you around." He took my hand and led me away for a house tour.

"I don't mind at all," I said, my stress and discomfort vanquished, now that we were alone again. "I just didn't expect them to be so friendly."

Joey's family had a grand home in a modern, open concept style. I particularly liked the atrium on the main floor, paved with polished marble with a pentagram design in the center. They spared no cost on the design and artistry. He led me to the basement, without a doubt a boy's domain. With three boys in the household, I wasn't surprised to walk into a sports bar/movie theater.

The grand tour finally ended when he said with a wink, "And at last we have reached my room." He gently pushed the door open.

"Wow!" I blurted, my eyes widening. "I didn't expect your room to look this way, especially after the boys' room in the basement. I have to say, I'm a bit jealous."

It looked more like an executive's bachelor pad. A French door opened onto the backyard. His bathroom even had a jet tub. Everything was neatly organized, even his king-size bed was perfectly crisp. By comparison, my room seemed messy.

"Wow, this is not at all what I expected," I said again as I wandered around the room. I stopped to examine his book collection, which had overflowed the shelves to flood the floor with tidy stacks. Then I moved on to peer out the glass door. "This must be a beautiful view during the day." I turned toward him, as excited as a child, and he came up and wrapped his arms around me.

"You know, all I want for my birthday is to hold you in my arms all night," he whispered against my hair as he held me.

"Hey Joey," his little brother announced loudly from the doorway, "Mom sent me to come get you." We bounced away from each other, smirking.

The dining room was set up as a banquet, with magnificently arranged fresh flower centerpieces. Mrs. Davale had put a lot of effort into this dinner.

"Gabriella, what plans do you and your mother Sonia have for the holiday?" Mr. Davale asked when we were all seated at the dining table. He glanced up at me with a smile, returning his attention to a piece of meat he had been cutting.

"Actually, my mother had a personal matter she had to attend to. Unfortunately my holiday won't be as exciting as yours." I kept the smile on my face as I put a bite of food in my mouth.

"Oh, that is too bad," he said, sounding regretful for asking.

Dinner was amazing. We laughed and joked, and his parents talked about Joey's childhood and the first time he discovered his gift. They treated me as if I were a long-lost relative and it was nice to feel a sense of belonging. It all seemed surreal how welcoming they were. A part of me did not feel right about the whole situation, as if it was too good to be true. Not only is my boyfriend conveniently my neighbor, he happened to a member of the Bruxa and his family is terrific.

His mother brought out a cake as we all sang "Happy Birthday" to Joey. She placed it on the table in front of him, and I noticed that one of the candles started tipping precariously, as if it were about to fall off the cake. Sure enough, as he blew out the candles, it did fall. Igniting the paper tablecloth, which caught on fire right away. Seeing what I wanted to happen in my mind, I twirled my finger and the water jug sitting at Joey's elbow rose as if on an invisible thread and tipped water on the fledgling fire.

They all froze, then simultaneously turned their heads to look at me. My confident smile was unconvincing, and I wished I could run and hide. Instead, I bit my lip and looked around, desperately seeking their approval, like a child caught dipping into the cookie jar.

"You are of noble blood," Mr. Davale declared, and bowed his head toward me. The others followed suit.

"Oh no, no — trust me, that's not necessary. I should bow to you, for being astonishing hosts and welcoming me over to enjoy this wonderful meal." I inclined my head to them, feeling my face heat up. I could not believe I said that. Distress grew toward panic in my mind, I wanted only to escape.

"That's okay, Gabby. Joey mentioned you don't like to talk about your family," his mother said kindly, placing her hand on my shoulder. Her touch sent an uneasy surge up my spine.

Other than my magic show, I had to confess that the night went better than I thought it would. I envied Joey for his large family—don't get me wrong, my mother is the best, but only two can be lonely. We hung around with his parents for a while after the meal, sipping on espresso. They hugged me tight as we said goodbye.

"This is crazy," Joey muttered as he was dropping me off. He looked away. "I can't imagine not seeing you for three weeks—I can't handle being away from you for a day! Gabriella, you're my life."

"I know, it's crazy. Do you remember your birthday wish?" I whispered shyly, eyes downcast, embarrassed by what I was about to say.

"Yeah…"His eyes widened.

"I wish you would hold me in your arms all night as well." I felt my cheeks flame with a blush at my tacky confession.

"Just so you know, my intentions are honorable and I wouldn't dare try anything—besides, I know your mother would kill me in my sleep if I did," he joked. I could see his sincerity as he cupped my face in his hand and tipped it up to look at him. "Give me an hour. I'll go back home — I don't want my family to be suspicious of you." His face glowed with enthusiasm.

I ran inside. I could not believe what had come over me. I felt alive and energized as I prepared a scented bubble bath. My heart drummed as heavily as the water pouring into the claw-foot tub. Giggling, I sat on the rim, waiting for it to fill up, tracing ripples in the water with my toes.

At last, I slipped into the bubbles, absorbing calmness from the hot water. I lay there, sinking deep within myself, dissolving the fear of being alone with Joey and fighting our teenage desires. I trusted him not to overstep any boundaries, but I did not know what to expect. Nervously I swept my fingers back and forth through the water.

After tossing on my yoga pants and tank top, I freshened up my hair so I didn't look like a complete bum. My heart pounded hard when I heard him knock on the door. I jumped up and realized I had to maintain some composure. I went downstairs, gracefully opening the door, and looked at him with a sultry gaze. I grinned when the porch lights highlighted his astonishing features.

"I can't believe we're doing this," he whispered as he stepped inside. "I feel guilty, what if your mother knew?"

"Relax, she left me a text,—she just landed in Portugal. You do not have to whisper. Beside it's not like we're having sex," I teased with a serious firm-reassuring look.

We fell silent, both feeling timid and awkward. I grabbed his hand and led him up the stairs to my room. My heart raced uncontrollably. This is the first time I had ever had a boy in my room.

"Listen, Gabriella, there's only you in my life, and that makes it right, and I would never take or expect you to…um, I think you know what I'm saying: there is nothing for you to worry about." He leaned his chest against my back as I opened my door.

"You are the one thing that feels right in my life." I turned to face him and ran my hands along his face. Then I turned around and stepped aside. "Well, this is my room."

He suddenly whisked me into his arms and carried me to my bed. Our smiles turned into an intense moment of silence as our eyes locked. Placing me on my bed, he bent over and kissed me urgently; I returned the kiss with equal passion. His soft lips tasted of milk and honey, and his warm mouth sent tingles throughout my body. Our passion grew, while our bodies slightly began to hover above my bed.

He slowly eased off before things got out of control as we fell back onto the bed. We inwardly laughed at what happened. We didn't speak a word; instead we engaged in one another's thoughts as we lay beside each other, our two hearts beating in sync. I knew we found in each other our own magic. He traced his index finger all over my arms and back, sending my mind into oblivion.

"You mean the world to me and I have a little something to give you before you go." I reached over him and grabbed the gift box, sitting up as I handed it to him.

"Gabriella, you didn't," he protested as he opened it. He sat silent for a moment, then pulled the chain out and examined the medallion in the light from my lamp. "I love it," he announced, and leaned over and kissed me.

"I'm glad you like it." I bit my lower lip in excitement at his reaction, then nestled against his chest, wanting to burrow as close to his heart as possible. I lay there, feeling the warmth of his body and listening to his blood pumping through his veins as he played with my hair. I wondered what life had in store for me. Could Joey be my one true love? If so, why did I doubt so much? Eventually I fell asleep in his arms.

"Gabriella, wake up. I have to leave now," he groaned, tapping my arm with his hand.

I did not want to answer, knowing doing so would end to our time together. "No, I want to stay this way forever," I whimpered as I rolled over to face him. We stared at each other in silence, taking a mental picture, knowing we would not see each other for three weeks.

He leaned in and kissed me gently, then smiled with love. "I will text and message you whenever I can. Oh, already I miss you." He kissed me again.

As he slid off my bed, I looked down in disappointment, feeling as if my heart were crumbling. I admired the muscular curves of his torso as he buttoned his shirt, wishing to hold him again. Three weeks was not long, but in my heart, it seemed like eternity. I jumped off the bed and held him tight, begging him with my eyes not to go, even though I knew he had to. Part of me was scared that this might be our last moment.

"Um...I really do..."I struggled to say it, he pressed his index finger against my lips.

"I know. I love you, too. Three weeks is nothing—we have a whole lifetime to share." He smiled and grabbed my hands and led the way down the stairs. "I will call you as soon as I'm settled in," he said, his adoring eyes telling me how much he cared. He gave me a final kiss goodbye.

The Meeting

Watching him walk away in the first pale light of dawn, I felt something unsettling about him leaving, like the closing of a book and opening a new one. I prayed he would not change, or worse, that I would not. He had been the one thing stopping the Lampir in me from emerging. Watching him drive off was like seeing my life disappear.

I felt lonely and lost, not knowing how I would fill up my days with no one around. I found it hard to remember what life had been like before Joey came around. I had never been alone before, my mother had always been looking over my shoulder.

Allison planned to come over to spend the night. She was bringing a bag full of goodies, including a couple of movies for us to watch. I pulled out the junk food and started prepping the entertainment room for us. I heard the phone ring, and I bolted to answer it, disappointed when it turned out to be a telemarketer. I knew his flight was only six hours and I would be hearing from him soon.

When I heard my phone beeping, I pulled it out to see a message from Joey, letting me know that he wouldn't be able to call me for a few days and that he'd arrived safely — and that he missed me. I was bothered that I would not hear his voice for a few days, but was glad he'd texted me at least.

BRUXA

"Hey girl, are you ready?" Allison exclaimed, giggling as she came through the door a short time later. "I brought over *Dracula* and I have another surprise."

"Oh, great," I replied hoping my expression was not obvious.

"Oh come on, it's a love story, it's not gory. Besides, Joey mentioned you loved that other vampire movie." She smirked as she threw down her bag. "This was what the guy at the video store recommended. I haven't seen any of them."

"Go ahead and pick whatever one you want to watch first," I told her while setting up for the movie. Of course, she passed me Bram Stoker's *Dracula*.

The whole time I watched the movie, I could not stop thinking of the monster growing inside of me. Could I ever take a life when the time came? Remembering what had happened in the alley that night put a new fear in my mind, about how easily my instincts took over.

I looked at Allison, who had no idea, what I was. For that matter, that the boy she loved is a witch. I felt consumed with guilt every time she made me laugh, knowing we all were betraying her. A select few knew the truth of what we were and the things we do. I hoped Allison could be one of the few someday.

Days passed, and my emptiness grew. I took comfort in my mother checking in on me by phone and talking to me every day. Holding the pillow that held his scent close, I fantasized about Joey, wanting to hear his voice again. A few days had passed since I had heard or had a text from him. It drove me crazy; why hadn't he called me or sent an email or a text?

Remembering the meeting I had with Isaac Bernstein at 7:00, I returned to the secret room. I had forgotten how medieval the room looked. I rummaged through everything, looking for things that had Hebrew text, and placed everything in a duffle bag. I started second-guessing myself, wondering if should show it all to him or not, and ended up putting a lot of it back. There was something unique about that dagger. For some strange reason I felt almost protective of it. I put it back.

I drove through a snowy haze, searching for Isaac Bernstein's shop location. When I found it, I realized this neighborhood is probably not in the nicest part of Boston. A sense of dread filled my mind as a slight scent of sulfur floated in the air. Finally, I found his building, and pulled into its parking lot, I regretted our meeting when I realized it was a pawnshop. Pushing away my prejudice, I walked inside.

"Isaac?" I called out looking around the tiny shop as I waited for someone to appear. The objects displayed exuded a feeling of despair. The dim light added to my discomfort. I felt like I had walked into some 1970s-biker movie.

"Yes, I'll be there in a sec," he yelled out from the back.

I waited, debating whether I should stay or leave and find someone else to translate the ancient Hebrew writings. Too late—at that moment, he stepped out from the back. To my surprise, he was a handsome well put together young man. He was about twenty-four years old, with an unruly mop of hair and striking hazel eyes.

"Yes, may I help you?" he asked while approaching me.

"Um, we talked a week or so back. I'm Gabby," I replied, thrusting my hand out to shake his.

"Oh, yes, sorry—I was expecting you a little later. Nice to meet you. I've been looking forward to this." He smiled with excitement as he shook my hand.

My mother had me practicing my channeling and tuning in and out others' thoughts, and now I put that to work, analyzing his intentions, as I looked deep into his thoughts. An honest soul who really loved history, he wanted to get his Masters. Even though he was built like a brick house, he lacked inner confidence and gave into pressure easily. The way he carried himself, his strong physique definitely would not give his inner weakness away. *His soul is pure and his heart walks with the light.* Overall, I liked his persona.

"I appreciate your time, I need you to keep everything I show you confidential," I told him. "These are extremely rare heirlooms I found with my father's things." I placed everything I had brought on the counter.

"Wow...these are incredible artifacts," he exclaimed, inspecting the charms and jewelry. "I can't believe you don't know what these are." His face became animated, as if he had won the lottery. "These things are incredible pieces of history. They belonged to the Knights Templar."

"Do you mean the first crusaders?" I asked, confused then shocked. I remembered my studies last year on the early Christians. "Can you translate the back of this?" I asked, pulling out my necklace.

He took it from me and inserted a jeweler's loupe. "Amazing, how finely detailed this writing is," he murmured. "It's almost a fingerprint."

"You're able to read it?" I leaned forward to peer curiously at the charm.

"It's hard to make out the words, they are so small, and some symbols confuse me. It says something about a holder of God's light destroying the darkness made by angels' hands." His eyebrows squeezed together as he concentrated. He looked up at me. "You must have a remarkable family history. If you ever need help with these, please feel free to call," he offered eagerly, clearly delighted to being handling the items, not daring to cheat me for fear that I had a powerful family. He looked at me with more respect, as if he were intrigued by the dark secrets of my family and by extension, me.

"Thank you for your time," I said, putting the items back into the bag. "What do I owe you for your services?"

"There's no charge. This honestly is my pleasure, Gabby. Do you mind if I take a picture of a few of these symbols so I can examine and interpret them better? Call me in a few weeks and I'll be able to translate everything better. If there are more things you need translated, please feel free to call me," he said, scribbling another number on the back of his card. "This is a number where you can reach me anytime."

"Thanks, Mr. Bernstein. Be careful—I'll be taking you up on your offer soon enough." I shook his hand again before leaving.

"Oh by the way call me Isaac next time, I am only a few years older than you," he shouted as he waved bye.

Once outside, I had to clean the snow off my car. A strong burning pain shot up my spine. My eyes widened, and I looked around in panic. I couldn't see or hear anything, which made me even more apprehensive. Tentatively I scanned quickly around before getting into my vehicle, and then locked my doors, feeling paranoid.

The weather had become progressively worse. I drove cautiously out of the city on roads buried under a thick layer of snow, visibility impaired by the continuing snowfall. The unsettling feeling still lingered. As I merged onto the empty highway, my car rocked violently. The burning returned, so wide-spread it threatened to consume me, making it hard to breathe.

I heard a heavy thump on the car roof and the car slid a bit. I concentrated on regaining control and I peered up to see a little dent in the car roof. Driving ten under the speed limit, I did not dare go faster. I wanted to flee, to get home to safety. My vision blurred and blood rushed to my head — a warning?

A moment later, I heard another thud and the car bounced, as if something heavy had pounced onto the roof. Trembling with fear, I turned the radio off to hear hissing and what sounded like two people on top of the car, wrestling. Something thumped on the roof so hard it caused my car to shake, making it harder to control the wheel. My blood boiled furiously with liquid fire.

The voices hissing faintly at one another became louder. Paranoia swallowed my mind, and I lost focus sliding on the black ice. My car went out of control, sliding back and forth across the lanes. I tried desperately to regain control. My hands were tight on the steering wheel, and the car slid right off the road. A thousand thoughts flew through my mind and it seemed that time slowed enough for my life to pass before my eyes. My car rolled off the shoulder into a field, and the airbag exploded open. My head bounced against it and ricocheted against the door window as it shattered.

Trickles of warm blood ran down my face as I pulled my body out of the wreckage. I felt disoriented and numb. I was unsure if I was going to live or die. My blood violently pulsed to my heart suggesting that I would live, at least for now.

Two figures kept flashing into my field of vision, and I heard hissing and cursing but one thing I keep hearing was the name Silvia. My vision was so fogged; I was unable to tell what was taking place. My heart raced out of control. Jaw clenched, I dug my fingers into the snow and tried pulling myself to safety.

A terrifying screech pierced me to the core. My blood trickled down my face, finally dripping into my mouth. Tasting it for the first time sent my body into frenzy. I began to convulse, and that is the last thing I remembered before my mind faded into whiteness.

I lay there, not knowing what had happened. I felt trapped in a body as if it were an empty shell. I could not move, talk, or open my eyes. Had I died? Or was this one hell of a nightmare?

The faint whispering of someone's voice suggested otherwise. I couldn't make out anything it said, but I sensed concern in its tone. It settled me into a peaceful state where I reconnected with my spirit and my body. Maybe I was hearing an angelic voice in the distance calling my name repeatedly.

Chapter 14

ALIVE

I reawakened within myself, unable to open my eyes or mouth. I breathed deeply through my nostrils and drew in the scent of angelica, basil, lemon balm, and elder bark. I heard something that sounded like water simmering at a low boil, and identified its steam as the source of the calming aroma. A strong hand slid under my head and lifted it to slip a thick pillow behind me. Then it urged me upward to a higher position.

I was astounded by how heightened my senses were in such a catatonic state. An angelic humming echoed through my body. The cold hand slipped under my neck again and tilted my head back. I felt a warm potion trickling into my mouth. As it slid down my throat, I felt it merging with my inner organs.

Feeling peaceful again, I zoned out.

When I came around again, I blinked at the soft glare of candlelight. Everything looked blurred. My heart jolted when I heard a guitar being strummed in some familiar ballad. Little by little, I eased myself up to a sitting position, my sore muscles protesting the movement.

"Um...thank—thank you," I mumbled.

"Shh—relax. You don't need to talk," a familiar voice whispered. I heard him approach, his hands urged me to lie back down.

Recognizing the voice, I cringed a little inside. "Alvero". I had forgotten how charming his voice sounded when he wasn't being arrogant. It revealed his compassion. His arrogance had to be a front that he put on to hide his inner pain, I suspected. Why would he go out of his way to help me, when he could have dumped me off at home and left me to fend for myself?

"How long have I been out?" I groaned, squinting, in a defeated attempt to see his face.

"Well, it's been over twenty-four hours, it's Thursday night." He had picked up his guitar again; I heard the strings whisper, then echo as he set it down.

"Oh my God, my mother!" I gasped. I threw the blankets off, and then realized I was not in my clothes. I felt a linen dress shirt hanging from my shoulders to my hips, and men's boxer briefs. I was grateful to be alive but traumatized by the fact Alvero had stripped me down and dressed me.

"Don't worry, she's not coming back until Tuesday night. I have been replying to her texts so she won't worry. She thinks you have been sick. And your car's in the shop, getting fixed." He sounded farther away. I heard some clattering, and I smelled something delicious—I assumed he had prepared something for me to eat. He smirked. "I'm surprised your car wasn't a write-off. You, on the other hand, were a different story. Sorry, I hope you like this—it's been a long time since I ate real food," he said, coming over to guide me to a chair at a table. "Wow, I must say your body heals as fast as ours—you looked like Quasimodo last night, your face all swollen, black, and blue. Now, twenty-four hours later, you don't have one scratch; it's as if nothing happened." He sounded amazed. I felt his eyes upon me.

I smiled with sincere appreciation, but was beyond overwhelmed. "I think at this point I'd eat anything. Thank you for everything." He set a plate down in front of me and I devoured every morsel, not even noticing what I ate. I gulped down a glass of juice while he watched. I couldn't see his expression; I imagined he compared me to a pig. I wiped my mouth with my sleeve, not caring about my manners.

"Sorry I had to bring you here, you had a tracker after you. Actually, they were after your boyfriend — unfortunately, you carry his scent. I had to wash the blood and his scent off you. I also changed you into fresh clothes." He chuckled when my face heated, seeing the red flush of my embarrassment. I lowered my head so my long hair would cover my face.

"What do you mean, I have a tracker after me?" I asked, breathless with fear.

"Well, they're not after *you*, as I said, you reeked of his scent. The one his friends tormented was a female and the one who tried to attack you was her maker, mate — whatever. He is no longer a threat; I brought you here just to be safe." He sounded as if it was no big deal. His hand came into my line of sight and grabbed my empty plate.

The meal seemed to have helped and I felt myself regaining strength. I tried to get up but my legs were still a little weak. Nevertheless, I forced myself to move around, feeling my way because my vision still a bit foggy. It was like looking through tinted glass. My legs buckled and I wobbled, setting myself back down on the couch.

I relaxed, listening to him play his guitar until I dozed off again. I woke a few hours later, feeling even more renewed, with only minor twinges of pain and some tender spots from bruising. My sight had returned, though my eyes were still sensitive to the light. Alvero stood staring out his glass balcony doors at the city lights, their distant glow highlighting his mystic aura. I looked around in disbelief at how airy and expansive his loft was. Still too dark to see his entire set-up, I noticed a lot of tribal art and historical pieces, many depicting angels. They gave the décor a slightly medieval flavor. I had pictured him living in an abandoned warehouse full of rust and stale air. This was nothing like what I had imagined.

"Wow…I'm impressed," I said, wandering around. "Your place is beautiful. There is a lot of emotion in these pieces."

I caught him off guard. He turned, startled, and mentally dropped whatever had been holding his attention. He looked at me with empathy, and a smile slipped out that even reached his piercing turquoise eyes. I returned his smile.

One particular statue of an angel caught my attention. So lifelike! I looked closer, its expression seemed neither happy nor sad. "It's strange," I observed, straightening. "You don't look the type to have so many tasteful things with obvious sentimental value."

He shrugged. "Of course, being a couple hundred years old, I have accumulated a lot of wealth, as your father did. The only difference being, I never shared my life with another. Like him, I have properties everywhere." He joined me and guided me to the balcony doors, and we looked out over the city lights bouncing across the bay.

"Stunning," I murmured, then turned back to survey his loft. I could see city lights anytime; I might have only this opportunity to view Alvero's home, with its clues to his true personality. "Are those from a hunt?" I asked, pointing to several animal skin area rugs on the floor.

"Actually, they are." He laughed and folded his arms over his chest.

"How old are you, exactly, and how old were you when you died?" I asked, dropping back down on the couch, hoping I wasn't overstepping my boundaries. I stared at him, already seeing him in a different light.

"It was so long ago. I no longer remember my exact age," he said. "I died hundreds of years ago, when I was twenty years old. I was soon to be married, until…"His voice trailed off, and he looked away for a moment. "Your father was my master. He was a good soul, all the way up to his death."

"I'm sorry for being rude to you in the past," I said, moving the conversation away from what was obliviously an uncomfortable topic.

"No, I deserved all you said, you were right. I do detest a lot of lambs, but not all are bad," he confessed, effectively concealing his expression by getting me another blanket.

I sank comfortably back onto his couch and watched him pick up the guitar again. He settled it against him as if it were a part of him. With each stroke of his fingers, the music captivated me. He strummed the strings as if his fingers naturally wove within the cords. He began to sing, and I closed my eyes and listened to his magical voice.

This change and his personality confounded me. I wondered how long before his hatred kicked in again. I wondered if this softer side he was showing me was an attempt to earn my sympathy. I could tell that my father had meant a great deal to him and wondered about their relationship. I knew my father's imprint was strong on him.

Wanting to know everything about him, I had many questions to ask but little energy left. I struggled to stay awake. The angelic melody that poured from him enervated me, relaxing every muscle, dissolving all my stress. Soon it rendered me asleep.

I flung my arm over my face, shielding my sensitive eyes from the morning sun that poured into his loft through the balcony doors. Squinting around, I quickly realized he was nowhere to be seen. I spied a note propped on my cleanly pressed clothes waiting beside my purse on the coffee table. I regained full vision, so after I dressed I took the opportunity to look around. The place looked as if ripped out of contemporary home magazine. Noticing a winding staircase in one corner, I followed it up with my eyes to a box-shaped room protruding from an outer wall, up near the rafters. It even had a window overlooking the main living area. For all I knew, he was up there watching me.

I giggled to myself, and walked over to the glass doors to open his note, strangely eager to read his message. I leaned my back against the door, unfolding the piece of paper I began to read it:

Hey Gabby, your car will be ready tomorrow, late afternoon, there are many shops within walking distance if you want to go shopping or pick up food. My keys are in the nook by the door. I suggest you find some comfortable clothes for tonight — your training starts at sunset, so be ready.

Alvero

P.S. If the door attendant asks, you are staying with Mr. Vero.

I lifted my eyes and looked across the bay. It brought memories of the lighthouse. I was instantly dumbfounded that I had forgotten about Joey. His face popped into my mind. I berated myself. How could I have forgotten about him, even for a minute? I went to my purse and pulled out my phone to see if I had any missed calls, but there was nothing. Bothered by his lack of regard for me, my mind betrayed my heart with doubt.

I found the washroom, a shockingly white room devoid of all personality and color that made it colder and less welcoming than the rest of the place. I stepped up to the sink and looked at my reflection in the mirror as I made use of the towel and the bar of soap over the tub to wash my face. There were no signs of injury, but I saw a different look to my face.

I found his house keys and left his loft, hoping to clear my mind. In the hallway, I paused to take a second look, memorizing the loft number and floor before entering the elevator. My head started throbbing. I was determined to be positive and behave like a normal human being.

Exiting from the elevator onto the main floor, I realized this place was no joke. To the right a security desk stood beneath high arches and walls adorned with modern art and sculptures. To the left, leather armchairs made the lobby inviting. Looking at the security guard behind the desk as I passed, I smiled and he nodded as if to say hi. He didn't seem concerned with me leaving.

The door attendant was more curious. "Hey there, you must be...?" he greeted me in a thick Boston accent.

I turned to him. "Hi, I'm Gabby." I held my hand out.

"I'm Sammy; you're staying with Mr. V." He shook my hand with one eyebrow raised. He looked like a middle-aged man with heartfelt eyes. At first glance, he looked like an Irish pit bull, but I glimpsed the big teddy bear hiding inside.

"How do you know that?" I asked in surprise.

"Oh, I was here the night Mr. Vero brought you in." He mused. "I don't know what you've done to him, it's nice to see a smile on his face."

"Oh no...No, it's not like that. He's practically a big brother, trust me." I chuckled. Nevertheless, I knew he had his own opinion. "You wouldn't happen to know a good place to eat around here, would you?"

Taking his suggestion, I followed his directions carefully, and then wandered around, taking in all the landmarks within walking distance. I never realized how much history lay in the streets of Boston. Amazed at all the love and labor that went into building this city, I could see why the people of Boston took pride in their city.

I was cold and tired after an afternoon of walking around and picking up a few things I needed. Feeling more at ease, I waved to Sammy as I returned to Alvero's building.

Alvero was still nowhere to be seen. Exhausted I dropped back onto his soft leather couch and kicked my feet up. I closed my eyes to daydream and develop a peaceful serenity, preparing my mind for that night's training.

I must have dozed off. When I woke, my eye wandered up toward the rafters. I saw Alvero, his chiseled torso exposed in the overhead cubicle window, stretching as he welcomed the dusk like a Calvin Klein model. He quickly looked down twisting his body in my direction. I instantly slammed my eyes shut and pretended to be still napping.

"How are you feeling today?" he asked as he leapt down the stairs. "Well, you *look* a lot better." He grinned sarcastically, knowing I had been watching him.

Pretending I had just awakened, I stretched and yawned, trying to hide the guilty pleasure. I was not used to seeing gorgeous men walking around with their chests exposed, he definitely brought a new meaning to the phrase "forbidden fruit."

"I feel amazing," I said as I stood up. "I appreciate your saving me, and taking me in for these few days. Is there any way to repay you?"

"Do you think I would let something destroy my best entertainment?" he said in his usual arrogant tone.

I bit my tongue on a snippy response, grateful to still be alive, hurt at being misled into believing he had a compassionate heart. I was only a form of entertainment, like a circus monkey. "You know, I'm sorry if your circus monkey is showing gratitude, a simple 'you're welcome' would have been fine," I muttered, crossing my arms.

Within a second, he stood right in front of me. My blood surged through my heart in a surge of surprise. "You're welcome," he hissed into my face. Then he stepped back. "Shall we begin? Close your eyes and look deep into yourself. Free your instinct and find your inner force as you block yourself."

Closing my eyes, I channeled deep inside me, letting the fire in my veins come out. Hearing a soft sound, nothing more than a razor cutting through the air, I blocked to the right then quickly to the left. This continued for at least an hour before he pinned me down.

"Get up! Push me away," he shouted.

The adrenaline merged my two blood types together, producing a little of my magic power. I blew him off and watched in amazement as he flew back, arms wind milling, totally out of control. I raised my hand to stop him before he flew out the glass doors.

He regained his balance once he landed back on his feet. I knew how he felt; I had no idea I would process such power.

"Why are you wasting my time—are you a Bruxa or one of us?" he grumbled like a jealous child, stomping up to me.

"Actually, I am both," I said in an icy tone. "And I'm sorry if that's a problem, you should know this…" I bit my lip frustrated. "I don't understand you. You hate me, you enjoy watching me, and at times pretend to be nice to me. I understand you feel responsible for me because of my father, but why?" I glared at him, awaiting his answer.

"Do you want to know the truth?" He shook his head and sneered, "You could not even grasp the whole truth." Then he relented, or simply wanted to vent.

"I feel sorry for the Lampir in you, who is locked away like a shameful part of you as your Bruxa part radiates from your exterior. Yes, I hate the fact that you are human still. The lambs think we are all monsters of the devil. Yes, just as the Bruxa do, we have good and bad, we have done more for those stupid lambs than any Bruxa has, and we are the ones who pay for the mistakes of the Bruxa. You ask me why I hate the Bruxa. You have no idea! I could not believe that your father, of all Lampirs, fell in love with your mother. He was one the greatest of his time. I loved your father! That's why I promised when the time was right I would watch out for you and guide you in the path of righteousness." He words were strong and convicting. I knew there was much more to the truth.

"Come with me, we're going to try something else, something more challenging." He clutched my arm and guided me toward the door. "Dress warmly, it's calling for snow again," he said tossing a sweater over his head and grabbing his coat.

In the elevator, I glanced at his emotionless face, so serious and beautiful, and tried hard to project into his mind. A strong metal wall blocked me out. I just wanted a glimpse into his thoughts. I chuckled when I heard the thoughts of the security guard when we walked out and I nodded a hello to the door attendant.

He looked back at me. "What's so funny?"

"Sorry; I guess they had bets on whether you were gay or not. They think we're *involved*." I laughed it off again.

"Really? They thought that?" He shook his head. "The lambs have nothing better to do than involve themselves in matters that don't concern them."

He dragged me across the street and turned into an alley, where he pulled me into his arms and flung me up against the side of the building. I glared at him as I climbed to my feet, brushing myself off.

"Watch very carefully: this is how you land." I hoped he was joking. I realized he was serious as his body flew up and came down fast. He landed in a crouch, knees bent position. "Now you try. Let the burn build up and use that energy to shoot you up, and then release it gradually when you come down."

His patience had become low and his frustration beyond clear in his facial expressions. Determined to figure it out, I worked for an hour and still no luck. Finally, he snatched me up and flung me over his back, where I held tightly. Like spider monkeys, we flew from building to building as the lights of traffic and shining neon signs shined below like watercolors.

My body connected to his rhythm, and at last we moved as if we were one unit, flowing perfectly together as the Lampir part of me embraced and locked into him. The brisk air pressing against my face and into my nostrils made me feel more alive than I'd ever felt. It was a completely new sensation, the Bruxa and the Lampir working as one, as all my instincts had joined in a holy union. My body revved up and tingled with exhilaration, ready to explode as we glided throughout the city.

I was disappointed when he slowed down, putting a stop to my high. He turned around to face me with a cunning grin, and I could not contain my excitement, which was written all over my face. The whole city seemed to fall silent as we stood there smiling awkwardly at one another. Looking at him, I wished I did not love Joey. *Alvero would never look at me the way Joey does*, I told myself firmly. I looked away, ashamed to have betrayed Joey in my thoughts.

"I need you to close your eyes and let the burning build up from your feet upward. Set it free by letting go," he told me.

Standing on the balls of my feet, I felt the burn surging up my spine. His fingers slid along my arms, lifting them up above my head. My body stretched upward as the mounting forces shot through me. With all that built-up pressure, I exploded into the air and jumped onto the next building. I landed gently and silently, crouching on the rooftop.

"Very good, my young apprentice," he said, suddenly standing right behind me. "How does it feel to release yourself?" He laughed. "Now catch up with me." His fangs flashed in the darkness as he smiled, then disappeared into the night.

I chased him, savoring this moment of complete self-freedom; he had given me my own personal salvation. He saved me from death, and now he showed me how to live. Tasting this little bit of the Lampir, I knew this is a strong part of who I am.

I focused on him as he paused on the next rooftop, I made my move. Misjudged my landing, I pounced right on top of him, knocking him down. "Oh my God, are you okay?" I asked concerned, wiping the snow off his face, scared of his temperament.

He smirked, threw me over, and pinned me down. "I'm fine, that is a good pounce." He chuckled as he released me, standing up and offering me his hand. "I think we'll call it a night; let's get down and reassume our facades of normal people. You may enlighten me about yourself." He smiled.

We stopped in front of a coffee shop, and he ran in while I waited outside. I stared at him through the window, knowing from this moment my life would never be the same. He was my angel regardless of his own demons; I saw a light in him I had never seen in anyone. I felt his touch rush through my veins like nothing I had ever felt before. I was admiring him as a woman, not as a high school girl with a crush. I watched him carry out my coffee, and we exchanged smiles as he handed it to me.

BRUXA

We laughed and talked about serious issues as we made our way back to his loft. I didn't understand how he could make me want to cry one moment and laugh the next second. When I told him about my gifts, he pointed out certain people and asked me to read them for him.

"Can you tell me why you love him?" he questioned, looking at me with deep concern.

"I don't know. He is the first boy I have cared about. I guess when I started my change he was my refuge, keeping my confusion at bay. I've never had someone care as much for me, except for my mother." I did not know if that was the right response.

"I watch you both and I see how you are together, and I wonder if he could ever love all of you, because I don't think you can love him with all your heart." He shrugged and grinned as if to take the sting out of the truth I feared.

"What do you know?" I hissed.

"I've been around for a long time, and I've seen firsthand how love changes when you change." His voice serious; I saw hidden pain behind his eyes as he patted my shoulder.

He changed the topic with, "Have you ever been to a hockey game?"

"Um no. But considering I was born and grew up mostly in Canada you think it would have been inbred in me. Why? Do you like hockey?"

Minutes later, thanking God that we were only a couple of blocks away from his loft, I had heard enough hockey talk for the night. A vampire who loved the Boston Bruins! It had never occurred to me that no matter what you are, we are all trying to survive and live in a complex world together.

I had not noticed how fast the time had passed until I washed up and got ready for bed, replaying my eventful night in my mind. I was disgruntled that my car would be fixed and I would be going back to my regular life. Now, knowing my abilities and not fearing them, I did not want to hide who I was.

Sinking back onto the couch, I wrapped the blanket around me and watched as he played his guitar.

"If you don't mind, tell me about Lampirs?" I asked, unsure if it was the right thing to ask. But I had the right to know.

"What do you want to know?" He immediately set his guitar down as if he had been waiting for me to ask.

"What is your diet, and will I ever have to kill?" I asked with deep concern, and then bit my lip, waiting for his answer.

"I was waiting for that. Yes, we do feed on blood when it comes to rejuvenation. We brethren feed on the wicked and unjust people who need to be exterminated, people society will not miss, — that is why we were created. We have secret blood banks we can go to as well. Most of us reside in places where there is war or corruption, so we can go undetected. We are Lampir; blood is what recharges our batteries. Without it, we become dormant and fall into hibernation. The fallen Lampir on the other hand will feed with no regard. "He picked up his guitar and resumed playing.

Mesmerized, I watched him with heavy eyes, admiring how truly beautiful his ability to make love to his music was. Regardless of his ignorance and past crimes, inside there was a deeply wounded soul capable of being virtuous. Listening to the guitar harmony, I drifted away in a peaceful sleep.

Chapter 15

UNDERSTANDING

Waking up knowing that this is my last day at the loft, I decided to snoop around and take in everything, trying to figure him out. I held his guitar and got an insight into his passion for music. I don't know why I felt such a strong bond with him as if he were a part of my destiny. Then what about Joey? I missed him and he was my world, but it was impossible to be what he wanted me to be — I would be living a lie. Even though Alvero can get under my skin, he still made me feel free — there was no over-thinking, and I did not have to hide any part of myself.

How could this be, that the one I despised was all I ever wanted and more? This had to be a moment of vulnerability; I had nearly died and had a wounded heart because Joey had not called or seemed to care. I pushed my feeling for Alvero deep inside me and wrapped it within a wall of pride. How could I betray Joey this way?

Circling the angel statue, I glided my fingertips over its surface, feeling all its details. I closed my eyes as my fingers traced its face. Something about it, I found so alluring. Its facial features resembled some of Alvero's, especially his full lips. I stopped and stood in front of the statue, wishing that I commanded his heart.

The mechanic called to convey that Mr. Vero had paid him a pretty penny to fix my car. I caught a cab over to pick up my car, knowing Alvero had taken care of me. Driving away, I realized how much I truly cared for him. A deep sadness plagued my mind as I drove to the house, and then guilt consumed me. How could I even think of anything but Joey?

I checked my computer to see if he had sent any messages. Still nothing. Why hadn't he sent anything for days? I understood his preparations for his eighteenth birthday ceremony coronation started tonight. Still... I told myself I was just looking for a reason to ease my guilt; then I changed my sheets and removed any traces of his scent from my room. The last thing I wanted was another tracker finding me here. Sitting on my bed, I wondered what would trigger such an attack.

A chill quivered in my bones as I remembered the look on Joey's face the day he told me what had happened. Everything about him that day rubbed me the wrong way, from the anger to the cold, empty look in his eyes. Alvero might be arrogant and hurtful, but his eyes told another story. Our eyes are the keys to our souls. Demons have no eyes to match their souls; they have only black pits.

My mother called after I had eaten. She was excited to hear my voice. She told me she would not be coming back until Tuesday night. Both of us upset that we wouldn't be spending Christmas Eve together. I called Allison in hopes for her company but her and Paul were going out tonight. She sounded surprised that Joey had never contacted me, for he had already called Paul.

I ran outside, frustrated and mad that he had forgotten me, after learning that Joey had called Paul a few times. I sprinted through the wooded area, releasing my anger. Suddenly I felt something flash before me. Standing my ground, I listened carefully for movement then flicked my finger, using my invisible force to knock it down. Crooking my finger, I pulled the figure up into the moonlight and immediately released my hold as Alvero hit the ground.

BRUXA

"Oh my God! Are you okay?" I yelled, running over to help him up.

"Let this be a lesson never to sneak up on you," he quipped while dusting the snow off him.

"What are you doing here? Oh, I forgot, you spy on me." I smirked at him.

"Well, you see, I thought if you were free you might need help finding a Christmas tree for Sunday. Or I can take you out on your first kill." He devilishly smiled back and lifted one eyebrow.

"Well, let's see—I will never kill and I don't want to get a tree. There is no need to celebrate by myself," I said in a bitter tone. I hated him for being so damn cute and worse, him acting as if he cared while flirting with my naive heart.

"Let's go," he commanded, throwing me over his shoulder.

As we flew through the trees, my arms clenched tight around his chest, I leaned my head against his back, aware of the growing desire that burned inside my soul. My hair blew recklessly around as we glided across the fields.

Seeing the Christmas lights that lit up the town dispelled my bitterness. Looking down from our perch high on the rooftop of Gloucester old city hall, we watched the unwary and unsuspecting lambs closing up their shops, the couples going out for dinner. I began to read the thoughts of the younger pedestrians for him. We laughed and joked like two best friends, enjoying our time together.

Everything about him felt natural, and those enchanting turquoise eyes lured me in. I was not sure if I was acting out of rebellion for being neglected by Joey. On the other hand, what if Alvero was my soul mate?

"Do you mind if I ask you a question about boys?" I looked toward the horizon, nervously fidgeting with my fingers.

"Yeah, sure. I don't know if I'll be much help." He looked at me.

"Why has Joey not bothered to call me?" Hearing myself, I realized how stupid I must have sounded. It wasn't at all what I wanted to ask. What I wanted to ask was if it were bad for me to have strong feelings for him, Alvero, or if I was rebounding from Joey. With him around, I couldn't think much about anything else. I was haunted by the notion that there might be a great love to gain with him. Gazing into his eyes, which took my breath away, I noticed their color changed with his mood.

"You know, I have no idea," he replied. "I know he's not what he seems. He has his own demons he fights. Let him figure things out. You bring out the good in him; I admit I hate how you and he…I guess

BRUXA

I hate the real male Bruxa in him. However, you are okay, youngling—at least, half okay. Wow, I have never understood this topic. How anyone can love anyone else—the thought is repulsive." He rolled his eyes and got to his feet.

"You know, I don't buy your fake 'I don't need anybody' attitude, and there is no way you can possess so much passion for your music if you don't believe in love," I retorted while also getting up. As he had coldly reminded me, there is no chance in hell he would ever love.

His eyes turned jade green as he stared me down. The wind whipped my hair across his face while I waited for him to dispute my comment. The fire within me buried wildly as we both stood there in silence. Finally, he broke the uncomfortable moment the coward's way—he took off. I chased after him as if playing a game of tag until I realized we were back at my house.

"You knew my father. What do you know of the Templar's connection to the Lampir?" I asked while bent over and holding onto my knees, still gasping for air. I had to remind myself to keep our relationship strictly teacher and student.

"It's a part of our history. When the spiritual war started, most of us served as soldiers for God, watching and protecting the lambs from the evils in the Holy Land until a certain French king, the Bruxa and the church betrayed us. It was a long time ago." He sighed with distaste, and then pressed his lips together.

I grabbed his arm and saw the mark of the Brethren. "Come—I want to show you something I'm hoping you can help me understand." I dragged him inside my house.

Lifting the lantern off the mantel, I lit it, and then ushered him with my head to follow me. He looked confused but smiled gamely and followed me into the study. Stalling for a moment, I reached in and pulled the latch. Hearing his faint intake of breath, a chill trickled down my spine. He stood right behind me, and I savored the moment.

"Please don't make me regret this," I said as I crouched down to duck inside.

"Oh, I didn't think you were that type of a girl. If I knew, I wouldn't have waited this long," he joked.

"You wish." I looked up at him with an evil eye and punched him in the thigh.

"Well, you don't have to be so sensitive." He enjoyed putting me on the spot. "Wait, there's another way." He reached into a shelf higher up and pulled another lever, and with a mechanical screech, a whole door opened. He inclined his head toward my shocked expression, grinning. "I've been around for a long time; I think I have seen it all. I don't know why you don't use your magic."

His face light up like that of a child as he stood in the entranceway. All night I watched and listened to his stories, his face and hand gestures animated. All his anger and hatred had disappeared.

"What is the story behind this?" I asked as I pulled down and opened the box containing the dagger.

His eyes turned a pale green as his face puckered in pain and started to hiss. I immediately slammed the box closed. "I'm sorry. I had no idea."

"It's the Dagger of God's Truth, made by angels and passed to King Solomon. With one slash, all your conviction crashes down on you as God's judgments. It is forged from rare metal and is lethal to whoever is not a lamb. Have you ever shown your boyfriend these things?" he asked, sounding worried.

"He has no idea what I am, and yes I've shown him this room briefly. Yes, I trust he would never do me any harm." I looked down in shame. "I had no idea at the time what I was."

"There is much for you to learn, my l—" He stopped and turned away. "There is something about shape-shifters I don't trust. You know they started this war, and so did your grandfather's bloodline. They were the day watchers, and we were the night raiders. They hated that we were immortal and began planting seeds of doubt in the lambs we swore to protect form the fallen angels and demons. They turned us into monsters, burning us alive and torturing our human families. They convinced the lambs we were the spawn of the devil.

"After that, we turned against the day watchers, now known as the Bruxa, and the foolish lambs. I remember your father, eager to kill your mother to end the Fragoso bloodline. Instead he ended up contributing to it." He spoke with passion as he rested his head back against the wall.

He went on to talk about his and my father's adventures, and about demons and angels, and the early Christians. Sitting as a child would, my body curled up on the floor. I listened to his voice, letting each story play in my head. I pictured the harsh beauty of ancient Jerusalem as he described it. He told me it was his birthplace and that his family had come from Spain. His mother was of Jewish blood and his father was one of the elite Knights Templar. From a young age, he had learned of angels and demons.

He told me my father's family had amassed great wealth and land in Jerusalem — his family's homeland. He was of Jewish descent. His family followed the old laws, his mother believed in Christian teachings; in fact, he told me, she was a descendant of one of the apostles, Matthew. It was a lot of information for me to process.

He continued rummaging through the books and laying around objects as he talked about his childhood. Content to sit and watch, my chin on my tucked-up knees, after a while I couldn't help but doze off. I remember vaguely being scooped up in his arms and carried to bed. Being nestled in his arms felt like heaven, with him as my angel. He set me down gently on the bed and tucked the covers around me. I held back any outward emotion, inwardly smiling and screaming with excitement.

"Good night," he whispered softly, tenderly stroking my face. In that moment, all the emotional walls I had built tumbled down. I felt him watching over me as I slept, and experienced the most peaceful sleep I had ever had since moving here.

Chapter 16

MERRY CHRISTMAS

Waking when daylight seeped in through my window, I sat up and looked around, feeling the cold breeze slipping through the bottom of the window, gently twirling the curtains. I flung myself back on the bed, frustrated that he was gone. Then I shook away my foolish desire — I had to remind myself that it could not be. I didn't care; I could not get enough of him. Joey had obviously forgotten about me, and I should do the same.

I turned over and pulled the covers over my shoulder, thinking about my life and what I would be leaving behind. What if Alvero hadn't been there to save me? I could have disappeared and no one would have known I was gone—except Alvero. He is the only one to see me for *me*, always watching from a distance and never judging me.

Deciding to show some Christmas spirit, I jumped out of bed in hopes of sharing the magic with him. An hour later, freshened and dressed, I hopped into my car and went to find a tree; unfortunately, the best I could find was a sad, Charlie Brown tree. I became a woman on mission: I would perk it up with decorations and ornaments. I drove to the mall and pushed my way through the crowds, snatching up decorations. With only a few hours left before dusk, I finally had everything I needed—and enough time— to transform Alvero's loft and surprise him.

Sammy the door attendant laughed at me as I came in, arms loaded with bags. "So he's like a big brother, huh," he commented as he held the door open. "You guys have undeniable chemistry."

"You're lucky my hands aren't free, or I'd slap you," I said, giggling. "We're just friends."

In his loft at last, I exhaled and dropped the bags beside the door, then peeked out and looked up and down the hall, making sure nobody had seen me use my magic to unlock his door. I went back down to bring in the tree.

A few hours later, my heart beating fast with excitement, I sat down on the couch and admired the tree beside the glass doors as I waited for sunset, second-guessing his reaction. Would he be pleased? Alternatively, annoyed?

"Merry Christmas," he said behind me.

I jumped, then sprang to my feet and whirled around to face him, smiling. My knees went weak as he took a step closer to me, his bare, sculpted chest just a hair's breadth from mine. Our eyes locked, drawn to each other like magnets; I fought hard against the pull. He looked down and lifted a strand of my hair to his lips. I turned away, needing to break the intensity.

"Thank you," he said into my hair.

I could feel the warmth of his breath against the back of my head. This was killing me. I wanted him with all my soul. I regretted my decision to come; it had been stupid to tempt fate.

"You're welcome," I managed, and then moved toward the table, saying, and "I know you don't eat, but I do."

He followed and sat down across from me. "This is amazing, Gabby. I've watched others over the years; I don't think I have ever celebrated Christmas with anyone." He paused and looked away, then looked at me again with a sly grin. "So, what do you say about being Santa's little helper tonight?"

"What do you mean?" I said before putting a forkful of food into my mouth.

"Every year I go out, handing out gifts to children who need a little help. It gives me peace to see a child smile."

"Yes, I would love to. I'm surprised—I mean, I would have never thought..."I bit my lip before something stupid came out of my mouth. I should have known, from the first moment I sensed him. He made me aware of who I am. It was different from being with Joey, where I had to suppress the Lampir in me.

I could not stop laughing at a vampire dressed as Santa Claus as we carried the two big bags of gifts down in the elevator. This seemed so surreal—something people feared was giving to the needy. "I still don't get it; this blows my mind." I shook my head in disbelief as we loaded his utility truck.

"The Brethren always help the good and kill the wicked," he told me. "Yes, we are killers, but we still feel, like any other man or woman, as long as we stay in the light."

"Have you every fallen into the dark side?" I immediately looked away, not sure, if I wanted to hear the truth.

"I'm not going to lie." He paused and looked down. "Yes, for a very long time…until — well, we're here." He sounded relieved as he quickly turned the truck into a fire hall parking lot and drove to the back. The conversation was forgotten as we snuck into the fire hall from the rear. Children screamed in glee as he came into the room and ran toward him, their innocent eyes full of hope and joy. Overwhelmed by the beauty of these tiny creatures, I felt a twinge of guilt at how selfish I could be. I always took for granted what God had blessed me with.

Noticing a tiny, chubby boy of around four or five hiding in the corner, I walked over and knelt down to his level. "Hi, my name is Gabby." I read his nametag as I held my hand out. "And your name is Zacchary."

He stared at me with wide eyes as his little hand grabbed mine. I saw into his thoughts and saw sadness — he had watched his father beat up his mother so badly that she been hospitalized and now is staying at a shelter. I pulled him into my arms and held him tight; assuring him that everything would be all right. When I released him and smiled down into his innocent eyes, I had to hold back my tears. "Don't worry, Zacchary, Santa Claus has something special for you," I whispered. I led him over to sit on Alvero's lap and selected one of the biggest gifts in the "boy" bag to give to him.

Knowing what he had endured; when I saw Zacchary smile it was by far one of the greatest gifts of my life. Now I understood the true meaning of Christmas spirit. I stood back and watched with admiration as Alvero smiled and let the children climb all over him. I had forgotten that he was a Lampir. Rather, he was someone who inspired me to become a better person.

As we were driving back to his loft, I told him about the little boy Zacchary — and about his father. Alvero's face glowed with happiness and animation, and he spoke of the child as if he had not heard all of what I said.

Sammy the door attendant was just getting off his shift as we entered; he smiled and shook his head, as if to say, "I told you so." I just smiled back didn't pause for banter. Finding it hard now to contain my feelings, I knew I had to get my stuff and leave. Alvero had me addicted to him. I had been awakened to him, and I wanted to give him all of me.

"How do I become like you?" I asked bluntly, as we entered his place.

He slammed the door, his face now transformed into anger. "What do you think — this is a joke because I've shown you a softer side? I do not ever want you to become like me. Can you kill a person?

Can you handle living on whenever someone you love dies? Yes, I know this is a part of you. It might not be you," he hissed, pushing me back against the door.

I cringed back from his heavy presence. "I don't want to wake up one day and become a monster out for blood. I want to change to be like you."

He sighed. "I keep forgetting—you look and act older than your actual age. Gabby, you are still young, and there's much for you to live for."

"I'm still aging," I agreed, leaning forward, standing my ground. "I haven't stopped. I walk in the light of day; I have the same cravings and desires as you." I felt the Lampir coming through as I stared him down. "I'm tired of everyone thinking I'm so fragile and weak. I have never had a normal life. Who are you to deny me of what I am, when it's clearly my instinct?"

Both of us were breathing heavily, locked in a deep stare, the air between us thick with tension. I told myself not to give in as I saw his pain. His hand came up and cupped my face, and passion replaced the pain in his eyes. I wanted nothing more than to kiss him, to claim him. I sensed his self-control crumbling, his resistance to his desire unraveling. Just as he was about to give in, he spun away with a growl.

BRUXA

He grabbed me by the arm. "You want to see what we really are?" He dragged me through the patio doors.

He took me to a filth-infested home on the other side of the city. Gagging on the polluting taste of sulfur, I felt the change in my body as the killer took over. I licked my fangs, wanting to savor something. Still in control of myself, I looked at him. His eyes were a glowing bright green. He grinned savagely, showing his fangs, and kicked open the door.

Inside, a man lay dozing on his couch in a darkened room, oblivious to what is about to happen. I looked at the man's face and realized it was the man from the alley—Carlos. Alvero tapped him on the shoulder; he pushed me back into the shadows with him. Carlos jerked upright and looked frantically around, cursing. I froze, not knowing if Alvero was going to kill him or not.

Carlos got to his feet as Alvero taunted him in the darkness. I heard the gibbering of Carlos's fear running through his mind. Sweat covered as his face turned pale. I wrinkled my nose as he soiled himself.

Alvero pounced onto the coffee table and crouched there as if preparing for the kill. "I think you were warned before to change your ways. Do you want to confess your sins before you die, you fat pig?" Alvero hissed, baring his teeth in an evil leer.

"Please — don't kill me!" Carlos blubbered. "I've done nothing wrong! I'll change, I swear it!"

"Do you have anything to confess to God?" Alvero shouted. Turning his back to me, he lunged for Carlos.

I watched, fighting the urge to participate. I looked away in shame as Alvero ripped his victim apart, telling myself that no matter how vile it seemed, Carlos deserved to be killed.

Everything happened so fast. My head started spinning, and I fell to my hands and knees. I sensed children crying in fear. Distressed, I tried looking for them, and sensed their energy coming from the basement.

I ran to the door and kicked it down, then glided down the stairs. Three little figures huddled in a corner, eyes wide with terror. They looked only five or six years old. They babbled hysterically in Spanish, straining at the ropes binding them.

"Don't be scared, I'm here to help you and take you away from this monster," I whispered in Spanish, gesturing reassuringly with my hands. I looked around to find something to cut them free, and saw a dirty bed with a tripod in front of it, off in a corner. Staring at the bed, assuming what was going to take place, my stomach turned with repugnance, my blood burned with fury like an uncontrollable fire. As the burning threatened to consume me, still staring at the bed, the force of my rage ignited the bed.

As the flames raced across the filthy sheets to the wall, I had no time to think. Turning away, my stomach twisting with revulsion, I ripped apart the bonds holding the children as if they were thread. Wrapping the children in blankets, I took them outside, where we huddled together in the snow, me comforting them as they cried.

"In the name of my God, may the blood of your son Christ shield and protect these innocent souls," I chanted, placing my hands on their heads. The smell of sulfur began to suffocate me, as a black distorted cloud started forming into a shape. I knew without a doubt it was a demon approaching. "May you always keep faith and trust in the Lord," I said to the children, my voice strong and firm, the demon slowly revealed itself through its dark shadow.

Keeping courage in my faith, knowing this was my duty as a Bruxa, what my mother had prepared me for, I yelled, "May the blood of the Gods lamb always protect us! In Christ's, name be gone."

The children looked at me and smiled, as if a great weight had fallen off their backs as it disintegrated.

Alvero came out of the house, wiping his mouth on his sleeve as another fire blazed to life in the living room, where Carlos's body lay. Relieved when I heard approaching police sirens, I knew the children would be safe. Alvero whispered to the children, and then quickly grabbed me, and we vanished into the night.

He did not speak one word to me as we entered his loft. My body trembling as I struggled to grasp what had just happened. Everything had transpired so incredibly fast that at the time I didn't think, just acted on instinct. As my nerves settled it dawned on me, *I am not of the lambs. Am I ready for this life?*

"Did you enjoy what just happened?" Alvero finally asked his voice harsh. "Trust me that was nothing; wait until you see evil face to face. This is what I am. Do you still want to be like me? If you had done what you should have that night in the alley, none of those children would have been harmed. Some people allow demons to consume them. This is why we exterminate the wicked."

"Are you trying to scare me away? I under-stand why you do the things you do, but there are other ways to deal out justice," I snapped, inside I felt guilty and confused. I could have stopped him before. Those children would not have been harmed. I curled up into a ball, arms around my knees, and cried.

"I'm sorry," he said, his tone softening. "This is the truth. This is what we are." He sat beside me and wrapped me in his arms, trying to comfort me and protect me from the painful truth we both knew one day I would have to face.

The Christmas Eve I had thought would be perfect had ended in a nightmare of reality. Maybe I did have a lot of growing up to do. I was clearly not ready to take this path yet.

I must have cried myself to sleep in his embrace. Waking up Later, washing the filth and blood off my face, I stared at my bleak reflection, wondering if there is anything left of the seventeen-year-old girl I once knew. Closing my eyes, I turned away, knowing I'm not yet prepared for this life; I had to walk away.

He had retired to his cubicle. I let my fingertips glide over his walls as I returned to the living area, feeling a love for him. Torn between my feelings for Alvero and my fear of becoming a Lampir, I would never be able to say what I need to. Therefore, I wrote him a note.

Alvero,

I never thought it was possible that you would be my angel. You brought all of me to life. I know there is still so much to learn. But I can't be around you right now. You have consumed my heart, body, and soul. I would give my life for you. Last night I realized you mean more to me than a high school crush. I know I am too young and I still have more to learn. As much as you tried to show me a monster in you, that isn't at all what I saw. I wanted to be that part of you. The only monster I saw was Carlos. It seems crazy to think it's been only one week and I already have strong emotions for you, I knew from the first time I felt your presence that you captivated the burning in my soul. This is why I have to stay away from you and figure things out. I am scared to let my feelings grow any stronger than they already are for you. I still need to figure out the other half of me.

Yours always,
Gabriella

I went up the stairs to the cubicle and gently pushed the door open. He sat perfectly still, as if in deep mediation, and seemed oblivious to my presence. I knelt and stared at him, wanting desperately to touch him. I waved my hand in front of his face, pretended to punch him. Absolutely no response. I reached out to brush his face and chest and pulled my hands back. I would not give in; it was already too painful. Burning his image into my mind, I placed the note in front of him for him to see and read. Then I walked away.

BRUXA

I held back my tears as I locked him in my memory. It felt like I lost a part of myself with each step I took. I closed the door to my heart as I walked out of his.

Chapter 17

FAMILY TIES

I sat there thinking as I waited for my car to warm up. Each thought fell like a grain of sand in an hourglass. Examining my remorseful decision, I was unsure if I had made the right choice. Surrendering my heart to chance, "God's will be done," a part of me hoped for the day we would be together. I pulled out, taking one last glance at his building.

Distracted, I contemplated my choice as I drove home; convincing myself, it only was infatuation. I could not shake an uncomfortable feeling that came over me, as if something bad was going to happen. My senses felt unhinged all over the place as I pulled up and stopped in front of my house.

BRUXA

As I walked up to the front door, a strong sting-ing sound ran through me. It surged when I turned the key to unlock the front door. The buzzing filled my ears and pain shot down my spine. I was con-fused. What if it was a warning? While placing my purse and keys on the foyer table, I smelled smoke. Not bothering to take off my boots, I immediately went to the kitchen to see if something was burning.

As I passed the front room, I caught a glimpse of a figure sitting in the armchair. My heart lurched in fear as I felt its powerful eyes probing me. It sat there watching, unmoving. Shivering with a new fear, I held my breath, not wanting to face it. My heart was beating so fast I thought it was going to explode right out of my ribcage.

What is this thing and why is it waiting for me? Paralyzed with fear, I could not even tell if I was breathing anymore. I kept telling myself I was a strong breed, but I was so unexpected and mentally unprepared. At any moment, it could kill me. If that were true, I told myself, I would be dead already. I turned my head toward it, forcing myself to look.

I regained some of my confidence when I saw an older, sophisticated-looking man sitting with his legs crossed. His salt and pepper hair shimmered above his smooth olive skin. I knew he was not a Lampir. Feeling his dark eyes scanning me, trying to read me, I immediately threw up my shield and prepared mentally to repel his attempts to get into my thoughts.

There was a moment of complete silence as his cold, dark eyes weighed heavily on me. Then he tilted his head side to side, as if cracking his neck. His aura unreadable, he looked like a powerful, extremely influential man.

"You are an interesting creature," he said. "Beautiful, yes, but you reek of death. Now I know why she kept you a secret. She was wise to block you from me." He spoke good English; I detected a Portuguese accent, though. He gracefully stood up.

Paralyzed by confusion and fear, I hid my fear deep in my subconscious and stood my ground as he walked toward me. I wanted to scream, but who would hear me? Most of all, I wanted to know what this stranger wanted with me. Was he here to kill or destroy me?

He walked around me, and turned to face me. "Please, sit down, daughter of Sonia."

I had no control over my body; he placed me in the chair. His mind powers were incredible. He moved me without lifting a finger. Now I knew for sure he was a Bruxa.

"What do you want with me?" I gasped, finding the courage to speak.

"You know, it's ironic, what life deals you. My blood has been infected with my enemies'. Still, blood is thicker than water." He placed his hands behind his back, reminding me of Father Remy, my fifth grade teacher who was always looking down his nose at his students. "You know, in my older years I realize the truth, as my time for judgment comes closer and someone will replace me. I see for the first time the lies and deceit that fill the halls of my domain. Nobody respects the old order. This generation of new leaders is only out for themselves." He sat back down.

I replayed what he had said in my mind, trying desperately to understand him and his intentions for me. "You still haven't answered my question. What do you want with me?" I whimpered.

"Nobody knows I'm here. I had to see you for myself. You remind me so much of her, but you have the eyes of a Lampir. She was around your age when she left. I have always known your father was not a lamb. I never wanted to believe that my flesh and blood could spawn you." He spoke with control I saw a deep sadness come into his eyes as he paused and pulled a silver cigarette case from his pocket.

He pulled out a cigarette and twirled it between his fingers before placing it gracefully in his mouth. He flipped a gold-encrusted Zippo and lit it up. He reminded me of an old Hollywood movie star—mysterious, angry, and calmly unpredictable.

He inhaled deeply then exhaled, saying, "You should not worry; if I wanted you dead, I would have already killed you. I'm not sure what to do. The man in me wants to welcome you warmly, however my pride refuses. I wish I could see into your future, but you have no future or even present—it is as if you never existed.

I had to look upon you with my own eyes before it was too late. You are the last hope of our bloodline, Gabriella." He took another deep drag of his cigarette.

I realized who he was and my fear vanished, replaced with resentment for my grandfather's hurtful neglect. "Why have you never come to see me before, and why are you here now?"

"Your mother never wanted me to meet you; she was scared of what I would do to you, and she never wanted anyone to find out the truth. This is why I am here now—to see for myself my granddaughter. You will have your coronation on your eighteenth birthday in a few more months. You have to prepare yourself to go undedicated, and with all the corruption now, you cannot trust anyone. If I can't get into your head, there is nobody except God with the power to do so."

BRUXA

After my fear had evaporated from my mind, I saw his good heart. He struggled with his own demons. He talked about his childhood and how he had been reckless and out of control until the day, my mother was born. He had worshipped her, giving her the best, and when she secretly married, he felt betrayed. Her returning home gave him a reason to live again and brought him hope.

"One thing I do see," he said. "There is a young man who'll do anything for you; his heart has been stained by a dark shadow. His love for you is half in vain, be careful for wolves in sheep's clothing. That is all I can tell you. You must learn for yourself.

Now we have a connection, I will be able to communicate in thought with you. I must go and catch my flight before suspicious minds wonder at my absence." He now spoke in a soft loving voice, and he smiled at me. He hesitated, as if unsure of his boundaries. He did not hug me or kiss me goodbye.

"Thank you for coming. I am glad to finally have the chance to meet you." I smiled and stood to wrap my arms around him, and asked for his blessing in Portuguese. He kissed my cheek and gave his blessing, an Old Portuguese tradition when greeting family.

I watched as he walked toward the chauffeur emerging from a black Rolls Royce that pulled up in front of the house. He turned and waved before disappearing into the car.

Lying in bed later, replaying everything he'd said, I tried to determine who was the wolf — Alvero or Joey. I wished he had never mentioned it. I shook my head. My life was nothing if not bizarre. I mean, I am half vampire and half witch — how much worse could it get?

Shifting my thoughts, I allowed myself to relive my night with Joey. It was as if nothing had changed as I pretended to look deep into his chocolate eyes while asking him why he had forgotten about me. His image disappeared, washed into obscurity.

I reminded myself how much Joey meant to me and how easily I'd let the thought of Alvero replace him. Was Alvero the wolf after all? He had a way of distracting me. Besides, he had a vain and arrogant side to him. Then again, I had a taste of Joey's cold temperament. One thing was for certain, without doubt, Alvero had more human empathy and sense of right and wrong. What I saw in those children's faces on Christmas Eve was the purest magic of all.

****

Never have I been happier to see my mother as she emerged from the terminal. Her adoring smile was like the sun peeking through a dark haze. Overloaded with excitement, I ran to her and held onto her, acting like a child again. I felt desperate for her affection, hoping somehow she'd be able to lift or diminish my inner conflicts.

"I missed you so much. Did you sort things out?" I asked, brushing away a tear trickling down my cheek. I was relieved that I wouldn't have to run to Alvero anymore.

"You have no idea how much I missed you," she said, smiling and taking a step back and resting her hands on my shoulders to look at me. "We have a lot to talk about when we get home."

If I heard her say one more time how things had changed in Portugal on the drive home, I would have pulled over the car and screamed. I was glad when we pulled up to the house, but also dreading our talk, knowing I had to tell her everything that had happened, especially the information about mentally starting a fire on that bed.

I could feel her tensing up beside me as we opened the front door. Then she walked in slowly, and turned her head toward me, her lips parted. "He was here, I smell his smoke," she promptly proclaimed. "What happened?" She took a step toward me and her fingers dug into my shoulders.

"He wanted to meet me. He told me he always knew what I am. He talked about how much he loves you," I said casually, shrugging my shoulders out of her grip and hoping she'd relax.

Her eyebrows crunched together. She didn't sound surprised. "It's funny; I think until you're a parent, you never understand why they do the things they do."

"So you didn't happen to see Joey at all?" It was a long shot, so I threw out the question anyway.

"As a matter of fact, I did. I was there with your grandfather when Joey presented himself to the council." She avoided eye contract.

"He didn't happen to mention me at all? Why didn't you tell me you saw him?" I blurted, dodging around, trying to making eye contact with her. She turned away, desperately trying to look busy. I knew she was hiding something.

"Look, Gabby, I had to do what any mother would have done. I had someone pick him and his family up from the airport. I blocked you out of their minds until their return. I could not take the chance of the elders prying into his head when he faced them. I am sorry, I had no choice; things are different. No one is to be trusted." Her voice fell, and she bowed her head in shame.

"Why didn't you tell me?" I exclaimed, not believing she would do that to me. I turned and walked away, disappointed that my own mother would have kept me in the dark. I didn't even want to waste my energy or time with her. I locked myself in my room. Joey had no memory of me, and God knew what he was doing. I was mature enough to know that she honestly was looking out for me, but I could no longer tolerate her dishonesty and secrets.

I didn't even bother to call my friends—I couldn't vent all the dirty secrets piling up in my head to them. I wished I had Alvero to talk to. I regretted writing that note revealing my feelings. I would be an idiot to go running back to him now—what if he didn't share the same feelings for me? No, I did not care—I needed to be heard and not lied to. Still, I stared out my window watching as it started to snow, deciding whether to go or stay. I abruptly grabbed my things and left before the snow got worse.

"Where are you going?" Mom asked as I walked past her. "Gabriella, you can't just run away and not hear me out, I'm your mother."

"I need to get out and gather myself. I'm not going far," I muttered, standing in the doorway with my back to her.

"Be careful. And Gabby—I do love you, and all I do, I do for you." She reached for me, I stepped forward, out of her reach.

"You have to stop leaving me in the dark," I said in a flat voice. "You have no idea what your deceit is doing to me." I left, though it hurt to close the door behind me. How could she expect me to tell her everything when she kept running behind my back with her own dirty secrets?

With no thought of consequences, I jumped into my car and took off, music blaring in hope of filling the emptiness I felt. The past few months flashed in my mind like a slide show as I tried to understand my life's purpose. Alvero's face right now was the one thing that gave me comfort.

I reminded myself of my grandfather's warning as I pulled off the highway onto the shoulder and parked. I sat there, realizing how stupid it would be to run back to Alvero. I dropped my head onto the steering wheel, regretting my poor decision. What was I going to say to him without sounding like a reckless juvenile? I threw my head back against my seat, in frustration. Then, I gripped the steering wheel tightly, turned the car around, and drove toward the lighthouse. I had to find the courage to face my own guilt.

BRUXA

I got out of my car, my thoughts were as heavy as the falling snow. The moon's light reflected off the snow to light up the night sky, and to me it seemed like the calm before the storm. My blood burned as the Lampir flared in me. I entered the cold building, my catlike eyes making it effortless for me to see my way around in the dark. I glided up the stairs.

I clutched the railing around the catwalk at the top as a tidal wave of memories rushed through my head. I thought of Joey, knowing now that he hadn't forgotten about me; he had no idea that I existed. "Why?" I screamed, falling to my knees. I cried, all too aware of my feelings for Alvero and knowing I had betrayed Joey in my heart and mind. Nothing made sense anymore. In fact, nothing about my life made much sense right now.

I stared out into the never-ending ocean, not even registering that I was no longer alone. Closing my eyes, I wrapped my arms around myself in hopes of comforting my pain. Joey and I could never be; it would be impossible for him to love the real me. Too much had changed in these past few days.

My blood flared up as a dark shadow fell over the railing beside me from behind. Startled, I jumped back and turned around.

His green eyes darted out of the darkness as he came forward. "Well, that isn't quite the reaction I anticipated from you." Alvero grinned.

"What are you doing here?" I muttered, wiping my face clean of tears.

"I felt you were in distress and I thought maybe you were in need of aid." He smirked, arrogant.

"Wow, you feel my distress?" I replied sarcastically, though relieved to see him.

"Isn't that scary? You're one messed-up girl," he teased as he leaned against the wall. "So let's hear it." He folded his arms and look at me expectantly.

I told him everything about my grandfather, careful to leave out the part about the wolf in sheep's clothing. I told him about my mother and what she had done to Joey. My mouth went dry and pasty from all the talking. I had never been able to get everything off my chest; it was heavenly to have someone to tell everything to — and he had a way of dulling the serious facts of the matter.

"This is what I hate about the Bruxa, especially your lineage," he growled. "They go into others' minds and switch it all up. Do you have any idea how many wars were caused by their meddling? Slavery — they abused their powers for wealth crushing those with strong spirits. Look what they turned us into — feared demons! I have lived long enough to see firsthand how the Bruxa and the church have enslaved people to religion. They enslaved those who opposed conversion, because they had only a basic understanding of the truth. Do not get me wrong, there have been as many great Bruxa and great men of the church who found their faith in God. Just like us, look how many have turned against humans, and built a strong hatred, becoming the fallen forever damned."

He sighed. "Yes, I was almost one of them. I was lost for so long, until your father saved my soul again. I would never want to go back to be what I was before. And it was your mother who saved his soul from the brink of turning." His voice had grown sad. He pushed off the wall to pace and clear his mind—of painful memories, I assumed.

He broke it down for me. I had often wondered how we survived the witch hunts and why Christian holidays followed old pagan holidays, and how the countries where the Bruxa were strong—Spain, Portugal, France , and some areas in the U.K where nobility had married into the Bruxa bloodline—were all guilty of slave trading.

Nothing is worse than a lamb that is able to see into our world. Not all of the witch-hunts were intended to kill the real witches like us; they also targeted the lambs that God blessed with the gifts of discernment or healing. They used the name of God to hide their shameful actions.

"What is wrong with me? I hate this! It's as if I'm torn in two inside—I have no idea who or what I am anymore," I cried, turning away to look out to the sea. "How did you become what you are and handle all these changes?"

"It's been too long. I hardly remember all the details. All I remember is dying protecting this family crossing into Jerusalem. Your father and I were outnumbered but we still managed to get them out of harm's way. We fought at least twenty men, and we were badly wounded. Your father never gave up. He fought until his last breath, taking them all out. He prayed as he dragged himself and my dying body across the dry, barren ground.

A bright light fell upon us as if from heaven. An angelic being asked if we would devote our lives to defending others in exchange for eternal life. We were dying, of course. Your father and I were too weak to understand the implications. I wasn't ready to die. I had much to live for—I was young and ambitious."

He leaned against the wall, hands in his pockets, and looked away as if haunted by his choice. I heard the pain in his voice, and it made me comprehend that an eternity is never-ending. "No matter what, Gabriella, always be true yourself. Trust in God. You are the first to be born of mixed blood and the last female of your lineage—you are a special creature. Your mother is right to protect you." He sighed.

"You're right. I need to talk to her."

He turned and approached me. "Gabby, are you going to tell your mother about me?"

"Yeah, I have to—I expect her to be honest, so I must be honest with her." I did not understand his concern. After all, my father was his friend—what was the big deal?

"Wait—I need to be honest with you." He grabbed my hand and pulled me back toward him. "Please be patient." He seemed scared and confused. He paced back to the wall and stood there. He dropped his head to pinch the bridge of his nose.

"Oh my God, are you okay?" I asked, frowning with concern and placing my hand on his shoulder, wanting to ease his pain. "You're scaring me."

He grabbed my hand and squeezed it, gazing deep into my eyes. "It has been a lifetime since I felt like a real man. I want to thank you for making me feel alive again," he whispered before looking away.

Unsure if this was our last goodbye or a dark secret he wanted to hide from me. I did not want to hear his confession. Whatever it was, he had a hard time telling it. Obvious that it left me with a bad impression, he had the power to crush my heart.

"I've desired you from the first time I sensed you walking in the woods," he murmured. "That burning is our bond, connecting us. I hated every moment as I watched Joey capture your heart. This week just past, you had me fighting every burning desire to make you mine. I have never craved anything more. I...lo—" He stood up straight and began pressing himself closer, avoiding any meeting of our eyes.

"I must have read your note at least a hundred times," he continued. "I feel as if I've lost the light that shone through my darkness." He ran his hands through my hair as our eyes danced a dangerous tango.

My blood pumped hard, as if my heart was about to explode. I felt my back hit the wall. Finally, it was happening, or I was fantasizing it all. My body trembled with excitement.

"I felt you standing there that day as you set the note down. You have managed to crush all the walls I have built up over the years, with one look. You are everything I need and more; I am addicted to your light. I never thought it possible for me to love again. You're my angel," he whispered, resting his forehead against mine.

I felt the intensity of both of us fighting our instinctive bond. I tipped his face up and stared right into his icy green eyes, though his full lips tempted me. "You have always had me," I told him. "I've never had a choice, gravity has pulled me into your soul." I knew without a doubt that I loved him.

"As much as I want you, I know that right now I'm another complication you don't need. You were right to leave me that note. You need to find out who you are and deal with this Joey situation. I will always be watching you from a distance, unless he comes around. I cannot bear to see you with him. He is all about Bruxa, not like your mother. She was right to have blocked his thoughts. He knows I watch you, but he has never seen me. Be careful of your dog boyfriend, he has a shady family."

"Can't I run away with you, and we can go to Brazil where nobody can find us?" I suggested, desperate to have him.

"I wish. We have to figure out what is going to happen to you. You need your mother's protection, too. I can't imagine the idea of losing you. You're an angel who sings to me in thought." His breath brushed my skin and a chill ran up my spine.

The chemistry between us was undeniable, we craved one other. My heart pumping like a piston as we stood fighting our instincts. My eyes closed as I waited for him to take me in his arms and kiss me.

Instead, he pushed away and stepped back a few paces from me.

"I don't understand—why?" I blurted. "You know its right; we were designed for one another. Why do you fight it?"

"You know, it's time you went and talked to your mother. Soon enough, you will know why. There is one thing you do need to know. My past is something I am not proud of and it was your father's love for you that saved me. It was you who brought me back into the light." His voice sounded weak and lost as he turned away from me. He vanished into the night.

Walking back to my car, I felt even more lost and confused, and my body and mind felt as if they were going through withdrawal. I didn't know how to feel. I didn't understand anything except how much he meant to me. One thing was right—I had to set things straight with Joey. How could I go back to pretending and denying who I am?

I saw the lights on in the living room when I pulled in our driveway—Mom was waiting there for me. I sat in the car a moment, finding the strength to face her wrath, putting myself together again and pushing back my emotions. With each step I took, my mind became a little clearer.

BRUXA

I held my breath as I entered the house, immediately feeling tension in the air. I dragged myself into the living room and sat down on the opposite end of the couch, not looking at her.

She stared at me then looked away. Silence hung between us. Neither of us knew where to start. I bit my lip, waiting for her to make the first move. It was as if we were playing a vicious mind game of chess.

"Where did you go?" she asked in her firm mother voice.

I sat straight up and looked at her. "Look, I don't want to fight and I don't want anymore lies from you. I want to know the whole truth. In exchange, I'll tell you my truths."

I went on to tell her everything about Alvero from our first moment, and how he had saved me and showed me how to control myself. I told her about the whole Carlos thing. I confessed it all to her, from the beginning to the end. She sat and absorbed everything. She did not have one thing to say. Even after I told her everything, she sat there in a deep moment of silence, her face empty of everything but disappointment. Her reaction confused me; I mean, after all, she had slept with the "enemy"—I was proof of that. My eyes drifted away from her face as I waited for her to say something. The silence killed me.

"I'm finished—I came clean about everything. Now it's your turn," I said my voice beseeching. "I wish we had normal family problems. You have to remember that I cannot be what you are—I will always be part Lampir. I cannot help my instincts. Please, Mom, say something to me! I need you to talk to me and guide me by telling me everything." Tears ran unnoticed down my face.

She rounded on me. "You know, you have been acting like a selfish brat. All I do is for you, and you walk out on me. I have been worried about you all this time while you were running about like a floozy. What are you becoming? I did not raise you to throw yourself around. I've been wasting time and my energy to protect you from Joey's family in hopes that you kids have a chance, and now you're running around with the thing that—" Her voice had risen as she spoke. Now she stopped, speechless with bottled-up anger, and launched herself off the couch, flinging her arms around.

"I'm sorry, Mom, I can't help how I feel. I didn't plan for any of this to happen to me. When I almost died, I knew I didn't want to hide who I am. He saved me and took care of me when nobody else was around. If it weren't for him, who knows what would have happened to me? He is the only one who understands my burning and teaches me how to control myself. I can't even tell Joey what I am. I had no idea you had blocked the memory of me from his mind. I didn't know what to think." I fell down on my knees in front of her, crying for her forgiveness.

Her big brown eyes watered. Cupping her palm under my chin, she tipped my head up, shaking her head in disbelief. Her reactions puzzled me. I did not know if she forgave me or not. "Gabriella, I love you so much…you have no idea what you've unleashed upon yourself. It will be almost impossible to present you before the council. You have created a completely new problem. Once Joey boards the plane home, all his memories of you will re-emerge. And now you are going to have to deal with this problem on your own." She released my chin and walked away.

My mind and body shut down. I stared into space. What I was going to do? She was right—how I could be this selfish and not think of consequences? She had no idea how hard it was to deny my feelings for Alvero. We'd done nothing except confess our true feelings and deny our instincts.

A good while passed before I snapped out of my daze and dragged myself to my room. I lay in bed and cried myself to sleep, feeling as if my heart were being torn apart.

When I woke I just lay in bed most of the morning, searching for the motivation to get up. I stared out my window, for some strange reason having a flashback of my father chasing me around as we played in the greenhouse. The sky had been cloaked in a thick overcast, only filtered light being the only thing making its way through the glass roof. I heard a pot shattering. I ran over, and froze. His face had changed into something cold, and he yelled at me to find my mother. The fear I felt from him terrified me. I ran back into the house. It was the first time I had heard him yell—and the last time. All turned into black fog; I couldn't remember what had happened.

I jumped out of bed, thinking it was strange that I'd have remembered that now. It seemed so real. Assuming my mother had gone to the shop, I moped down the stairs and walked into the kitchen for a glass of water. Turning away from the sink to drink it, I choked on the water, startled to see my mother sitting in the nook, still wrapped in her white fluffy house robe.

"What are you doing home? I thought for sure you would be at the shop," I exclaimed, hoping she would talk to me today.

She lifted her cup to her lips and took a moment to savor her morning coffee. Then she patted the seat next to her. "Come."

BRUXA

When I sat down, she began with, "I know I was tough on you last night, and no, you're not a floozy. We do have to talk about everything. Why don't you go upstairs and freshen up then get comfortable? Because you're not going to like what I'm about to tell you." Her lips pressed together.

I complied, taking more time than usual in the shower and in drying myself off, extending the moments I had to myself. I tried mentally preparing myself while drying my hair, expecting more confusion and wondering if I had any more space in my mind to process it all.

Pushing myself every step of the way, I re-entered the kitchen. She hadn't moved. My throat tightened. Now is the decisive moment I had been dying to hear. Now that the cards were all laid out, I was not sure if I was ready to play.

"Where do I start?" She paused and rubbed her face while finding her courage again. "First we'll talk about Joey and the Bruxa. You already know about us, we are the last of our lineage. Your grandmother is from the Conjures clan; her great-grandmother carried the Malicus bloodline. Her gifts were similar to ours. Against her will, she was forced by the elders to marry my grandfather and produce a female heir. She loved another man named Laruen, from the Lougaro clan. His hatred grew for the elders and their decisions. He swore an oath to destroy your grandfather and our code. He has been successful in his alliances and is strong.

"Joey is a part of the Lougaro lineage; that is why I had to see into Joey the first time, to know where his faith stood. Because it is the Lougaro shape-shifters who are our soldiers, they can kill Lampir instantly. Since I have been gone, a lot has changed. They have become strong, practically in power. Your grandmother has betrayed your grandfather all these years." Her voiced cracked and she broke down in tears, covering her face.

"I had no idea," I whispered. "I'm sorry."

She lifted her head to look at me. "My own mother! Do you have any idea what it was like to learn you were created for breeding purposes, like an animal? To know that…I am a mother, I see now the lengths my father went to protect me at the time—everything he did was out of love. My running away with your father killed him—I was all he ever loved, and I was selfish all those years because of my mother's lies." Her voice hardened on that last word, and she stood up in anger.

I do not think I had ever seen my mother as anything else but a mother—until now. My heart broke for her. Unable to speak, I was too scared of saying the wrong thing.

BRUXA

I rose too and guided her to the living room, where I sat her down on the couch and grabbed a throw to cover her shivering body. Then I ran back into the kitchen and made her a fresh cup of tea.

I saw things a lot clearer now, I realized as I stood in the kitchen, waiting for the kettle to boil. The missing pieces of the puzzle had all come together. I vividly saw my grandmother, though before I had never known the truth. Now I knew how my grandfather knew about me without ever meeting me; he had been protecting me all along. "I am the key!" I said aloud in sudden realization, and ran back to my mother.

"What?" She looked at me, confused, shaking her head. "What are you talking about?"

"Mom, they can never destroy me because I'm half vampire—I have powers they have never seen. I'll protect you, both the Lampir and our kind." Suddenly sure of myself, I ran back to take the steaming kettle off the burner. How had I not seen that God's purpose for me is to restore balance to both sides and keep everything stable somehow?

"Gabby," she said as I returned with the steaming cup, "You are only one. I love you. I wish that... there is much more." Still, she chuckled. At least I'd made her smile.

"I am going to teach you to project into my mind and your grandfather's, no matter where you are," she said. "There are only us three left of the Malicus, so nobody else will be able to see in, other than God. This will be a network — no matter where we are, we will be able to communicate clearly in thought, even if we're out of range of each other — I will see through your eyes, and vice versa. Only you, a Malicus, will hear the sharp, piercing sound of our call." Her spirits had lifted. She seemed relieved and excited for me, eager to make me part of this game.

She took me to the washroom and showed me how to call my grandfather. Filling the sink, she pricked her finger as she made the sign of the cross. Then she laid her palms flat on the surface of the water as she channeled her thoughts. I heard her clearly in my mind and saw through her eyes.

She told me to tap three times before pressing the tips of my fingers against my temples, and I would be able to communicate my thoughts back to her. She would also see my surroundings from my perspective. This was freaky! I loved this newfound trick. She told me that this was her and her father's secret and that they did it when she was a child. It was a way to protect oneself while communicating with another, even across oceans.

"Wow, I can't believe I did this," I exclaimed, jumping around. I kissed her on the cheek. "Are you going to show me more?" For the first time that day, I felt excited.

"One thing at a time, sweetheart, we have a lot more to conceal."

"Is it possible for others — besides those in our lineage — to read our needs or be able to look into our thoughts?" I asked while following her back into the living room.

"That's a good question," she replied. "Only if your soul has chosen its mate for life. It is not common amongst us; it is with the Lampirs. It happens with the joining of souls, when one becomes one with another. Why do you ask?" She went slightly pale.

I sat back down, unaware of the chaos that was going to be unleashed upon me. I knew now that whatever she told me wouldn't be good. Sure enough, she kept repeating her words, trying to sugar-coat something about Alvero. Clenching my teeth, I stopped paying attention to her gibbering about how I didn't know Alvero, and that I should never see him ever again. I thought it was hypocritical of her, considering her relationship with my father. What did catch my attention was that she kept mentioning the night my father died.

"What do you mean? He was murdered in our own backyard?" I asked.

"You were young. I blocked everything from that night out of your mind. Last night while you were sleeping, I reopened your memory, allowing you to see for yourself what had happened — because you would not believe me. Now, at least, you'll witness the truth," she said in a voice full of pity for me.

I had no idea what she was talking about, and from the sound of it, I did not want to know either. I remembered what had happened upstairs, the vision of my father, and realized it must have been a part of that memory.

She rose from the couch and kissed my forehead before leaving. I heard her climbing the stairs. Now, more than ever, I wanted to know what happened that night.

Chapter 18

CONFLICT

Girls' night out was exactly what I needed. Allison called me this morning to let me know she and the girls were taking me out. I was shocked that my mother had actually wanted me to leave, to clear my thoughts, and have a good time with my friends from school. God knows, I was in need of some normal people therapy.

Hearing Ana's car horn from the driveway, I pulled together a cool façade and scurried outside, gratefully leaving all my problems at home. I felt renewed and excited to be free and reckless with my friends. Cindy rolled down her window as I approached, and they all welcomed me with howls as I got into the car, as if I were the quarterback playing the final game in the playoffs.

"Are we going to have fun tonight, girls, or what?" I asked, putting on a poker face. Then I tipped back my head and howled, feeding off their energy and hiding my inner apprehension.

We sang and acted like seventeen-year-old idiots. The sad thing was I enjoyed it.

"Oh my God, did you guys hear about the other college student who disappeared last night in Salem. I heard they found the body of the first boy who went missing two days ago in Boston harbor. Actually, my cousin met this really hot guy who said he had classes with a couple of the missing guys.

You have to see this guy she met he's on her profile pictures." Cindy killed my buzz when she talked about the college students who had gone missing. Another one had gone missing in this area the night before. Watching the news earlier, the reports linked it to some gang related link since they all were college frat brothers. Very typical of Cindy, to change the topic from meeting this sexy, dark, mysterious person while with her cousin last weekend to missing persons.

"Have you heard from Joey yet?" Ana asked changing the topic. Allison glared at her in surprise.

"I'm sorry, Gabby. Forget I asked," Ana apologized quickly.

"No, it's okay Ana. Actually, he hasn't called. I'm sure there is a good reason." I bit my lip and looked out the back window, knowing the truth — my feelings had changed.

"You know what? Screw him! You don't need him," Cindy declared. "We're going to find you someone better tonight." She giggled and threw her hands up, waving them around to the music. I think it was her attempt to make me feel better.

Allison tilted her head to share a look of disbelief at what popped out of Cindy's mouth. I knew this had to be uncomfortable. After all, Allison is dating Joey's best friend. I gave her a smile and a reassuring nod because I knew she was perplexed with Joey's behavior, too. I'd felt the same way, until finding out the truth — poor guy, clueless of what's happening.

"So, where are we going again?" I asked Ana, leaning forward over the front seat as the car bounced over the bumpy road, jerking me back against the seat.

"My big brother Sal is throwing a party. My parents left yesterday for Italy, so except for Allison, we will have our pick of college hotties — as long as my brother isn't paying attention. You know how brothers are, never mind Italian ones." Ana laughed while pulling her car into the long driveway, already lined with cars and strolling partygoers.

I could already hear the music and mayhem seeping out of the house. It was a good thing the house was on the outskirts of town, with no neighbors to call and complain about the noise. *Wow, this is lambs gone wild,* I thought, laughing to myself and thinking this is the last place I wanted to be. *Hey, I'll only live once,* I told myself. *If I have to baby-sit; at least it will occupy my mind.*

I refused to consume alcohol—trust me, the last thing I wanted to do is lose control of myself. Besides, it was a lot more entertaining watching everyone else. Damn, if some of them only knew my problems, they would not be crying about an ex-boyfriend from two years ago.

Allison joined me on the sidelines. We watched and laughed at the drunks for a few minutes. "Tell me, how are you really doing?" Allison tone went serious as she peered with concerned eyes. "And don't tell me 'fine,'" she warned quickly, holding up her hand.

"It's been quite the adventure. One thing for sure, I've had time to find myself." I smirked and cocked an eyebrow. "How is Paul doing? He doesn't mind that you're out with us?" I asked, trying to push the spotlight onto her instead of me.

"He had important family business to take care of the last few days. I still haven't met his family. I don't like the secretive thing; it's starting to bother me, as if he's ashamed to bring me around." She sighed, and then quickly smiled to hide her true pain.

"Trust me, he's not ashamed of you," I said. "His family is very traditional. Believe me when I say you're probably better off not knowing them right now." I laughed it off as a joke. In truth, I couldn't be any more serious.

Feeling a strong hand grip my shoulder, I turned to look up at a tall, dark, *beautiful* male, hovering above me, drunk out of his mind. "Well, aren't you the prettiest thing," he slurred. "Do you know who I am?"

His breath alone could have made me drunk. I rolled my eyes and looked away, knowing his intentions. I would be the first girl in a long time to reject him, I knew. He was full of pride and would harass me all night. I turned my head to shoot Allison that famous female in distress look. Nobody had to be psychic to read my facial expressions. She laughed at me — while this beast of man hovered around me.

"I couldn't help but notice such a sexy little thing like you," he continued. "I can have any one of these girls, but I chose you. I even think I could possibly be in love."

I truly felt sorry for him, knowing he would never act this way if he were in the right frame of mind. "You..."I paused as I felt Alvero slide past me.

He tapped the other man's shoulder. "She's with me. Sorry, man, you are out of luck here. There's another hottie over there," Alvero shouted over the noise, and I felt him using the power of suggestion as he pointed the boy in the opposite direction.

"Thanks, man. I'm sorry, I didn't know — you're a lucky bastard." He patted Alvero's back and staggered off.

I looked at Allison and saw shock on her face. I looked at Alvero as if to say, "What the hell are you doing here?" I wondered how he had the ability to influence the college boy's mind. Pressing my lips tightly together, trying desperately to maintain my composure, I stared at him, unsure whether to be mad or excited.

"Thanks," I muttered between clenched teeth, glaring at him. "What other magic tricks do you possess?"

"Hey, if I hadn't come over, he would have kept bothering you. By the way, I am Alvero. And you are?" He smiled at us both, then winked at me and held out his hand to Allison.

"My name is Gabby, and this is Allison," I said, hiding a smirk and playing along. Allison sat there with her mouth hitting the floor.

"I'm going to get something to drink. Do you ladies want anything to drink?" Alvero asked. I shook my head; Allison still sat frozen.

As he walked away, Allison sprang to life and tugged hard on my arm. "Gabby — oh my…! Gabby, what the hell just happened? I can't believe he did that! Oh my…I say forget Joey. If you can have that — I mean, Joey practically forgot you. I would not think twice; I'd be all over that."

"Allison! Where is your loyalty?" I teased.

"Forget that, Gabby — he's a man, and a good one, at that." We both looked at each other, and then broke into hysterical laughter.

"What's so funny, guys?" Cindy yelled as she and Ana approached us. Looking at them, we laughed harder. Cindy and Ana exchanged a confused glance.

"Hey ladies, I'm back." Alvero squeezed between them. Their confused expressions stretched into gap-mouthed looks of awe.

"Alvero, this is Cindy and Ana, our other friends," I gasped amidst my laughter. If my friends only knew the whole truth!

Alvero shot me his cunning smirk, and I knew he was laughing inside. Allison nudged Cindy and

BRUXA

Ana off to the side. They looked like two manne-
quins. For the first time since I had known her, Cindy
could not talk. If I had known that would happen, I
thought, I would have convinced Alvero to join us
at lunch breaks.

"What the hell are you doing here?" I muttered
under my breath, thrilled to see him but nervous
about the outcome. "What the hell is up with your
mind influencing ability?"

He turned his back to the others. "I told you I'll
always be watching out for you. Plus I wanted to
make your night a little more interesting. Did you
think your kind were the only ones to have power
over the weak?" he whispered.

"You can't do this to me. You have to stay away,"
I muttered in annoyance, glaring at him.

"I can't, I have to talk to you about something
important tonight." I felt his breath tickle down the
side of my neck. "Besides, you heard your friend say
to forget Joey. I like your friend already." Before I
could retort, he walked away.

There would be no escape from my friends as
they surrounded me eagerly. Feeling trapped in
a movie playing in slow motion, I instantly tried
thinking of what to say to counter their impressions.
It bothered me how quick they were to dismiss Joey
without knowing his reasoning.

"Sorry to disappoint you, I told him I had a boy-friend," I told them, then looked away wishing that had been the truth.

"Are you stupid, Gabby?" Cindy cried in disbelief. "You turned him away for a loser boyfriend who can't even call you? God knows what he's doing." She tossed her head back in disapproval. The others nodded.

I shrugged and paused for a moment as I felt my heart race and my blood burn with an incredible sensation that made me quiver and want to fall to my knees. "Maybe you guys are right—I was too quick to dismiss him." Putting on a smile, I turned away from them, pretending to look for Alvero when truly I was looking for a place to conceal myself. Within that second, Alvero returned, realizing something was wrong with me.

"Wait, give me a moment with my friends so they don't worry," I whispered to him.

Regaining my strength, I turned to my friends. "You know what, guys, I think you're right. I am going to take my chances. Please don't wait for me, he's already offered me a ride home." I was glad that I sounded confident in my decision. Everything was playing out perfectly; they had no idea what was really going on.

"Whoa, whoa, Gabby! Are you crazy?" Allison leaned over to hiss in my ear. "You just met him. You're running off with a complete stranger."

"Allison, relax. We all know his name and where he performs," Ana spoke up.

"All right, Gabby, take my mace and call if anything happens. I don't know—I still don't like this at all." Allison pressed her lips together, shaking her head while digging the mace out of her purse. "You call me, all right?" she demanded with a concerned look in her eyes as she handed it over.

"Yes, Mom," I quipped, before hugging her good night. *Now that is a true friend,* I thought, respecting her more than ever and wishing she knew the truth—that he wasn't a stranger.

We slipped out of the party and walked awhile. I had the same feeling as that day I had been attacked. Usually I smelled sulfur remembering that night at Carlos's, I knew this to be different scent. We were in a dark, open field surrounded by trees, at least a mile from the party.

"I need to get you home now, there are other Lampirs coming for you," he said with a trace of urgency. He seemed panicked and distracted, looking around.

I grabbed his face to focus him on me—his reaction was making me nervous. For the first time, I saw fear behind his eyes. "What are you talking about? I'm not going anywhere," I said sternly.

Alvero closed his eye as if to ignore me. Then his eyes whipped open and his fangs emerged as anger hardened his face. "I told you, we have to leave now! Don't deny me, your blood is mine!" he yelled, and I felt my heart flutter with fear.

Chapter 19

SURVIVAL

Turning around, angry, I tried to leave. Something that made me feel strange and uneasy was approaching rapidly through the shadows. As if in slow motion, I turned my head. Glaring eyes pinned me down like daggers of light in the darkness. I glanced at Alvero. As our thoughts became one, we both nodded in agreement, knowing we were surrounded, just out of sight amongst the trees.

My blood pumped violently through my body as the Lampir came to the force within me. Survival mode kicked in. I heard their thoughts dancing around me and was aware that they wanted my blood. "They intend to kill and destroy me," I whispered fearfully. "One of them wants me badly. The other four are followers and will do anything she tells them. If we can take out the leader, the rest hopefully will leave in peace."

Taking a step away from Alvero, I stared toward their locations one by one, trying to determine where the leader was. Sensing strong, vindictive thoughts, I turned in that direction. "If it's my blood you want, then come out from hiding and let me look upon you with my own eyes," I yelled with confidence, though deep down, panic consumed my mind.

She leisurely stepped into the open. The moonlight reflected off her long, golden blond hair. She looked angelic. I was amazed that such a beautiful creature could possess so much hatred. The breeze caught her mane and blew it around her striking features as she smiled coldly at me. I tried reading deeper into her thoughts, too unfocused by the thought of living another day. "What have I done to offend you?" I yelled to her hiding my true fear behind brave stance.

Alvero abruptly stood protectively at my side as she glided closer. She licked her lips as she circled around us, like a lion keeping at a safe distance while figuring out her strategy of attack. It couldn't be any clearer that she wanted blood—my blood.

"Isn't this funny, Alvero," she said. "The angry renegade prince of darkness who thrives on killing the very thing he's protecting." She smiled with satisfaction, tapping her index finger against her mouth. Slowing to face me, she rubbed her hands together. "And a Bruxa princess running around with the enemy — this is a lot better than I thought." She devilishly chuckled.

She darted forward until face to face with me. "What about the little shape-shifter who tracks down and walks away like a coward as his friends tore apart my sister like a science experiment? Tearing her apart and laughing as if it's some joke? Well, they won't be laughing anymore." She pushed the words through her teeth, glaring deep into my eyes studying me like a hawk.

She stepped back as a new emotion overtook her. "Isn't this ironic, this little witch processes some of our qualities. You are an interesting creature. Now I know why Alvero has taken interest in you. What would your boyfriend do if he knew the one he loves is the running around with his enemy?" Her cruel, heartless laughter ate at me.

Slithering around me like a snake to approach Alvero, she caressed his face with her hand, as if they knew one another intimately. "It's a shame, you could have the world." She teased him with her lips. "If the others only knew you were protecting this thing...well I guess they will never know." She hissed devilishly.

"Silva, Silva, that was the old me! I would think about the mistake you will be making. Your sister's death was wrong, the way they killed her...she was a fallen and fair game and you know that," he said calmly and smiled in a threatening way.

She pulled back and stepped away with darting eyes, and then retreated to the safety of her followers, glaring at us while investigating possibilities. There was something familiar about her name, but I couldn't put my figure on it.

I looked at Alvero and whispered, "She will never stop until she has blood." She might not stop with us, but I knew she would be after Joey and all his college friends—by the sounds of it, she had already dealt with them, assuming she had been involved with the college students who had gone missing. The sad truth is I would do the same if I had a sister. Nevertheless, I would never let her hurt Joey.

"Are you ready to do this?" Alvero whispered. His eyes were bright as slivers of jade as he slid his hand into mine and squeezed tight. I felt his concern as his chill aura embraced my soul and we became one. He lifted his other hand to trace his imprint around my face, and then brushed his finger lightly over my lips.

"Yeah, I'm ready," I whispered. "You are my raven." I squeezed his hand back.

I felt myself suffocating with fear, but put on a fearless facade hoping that somehow this would end peacefully. I observed as they assumed their positions to strike. I felt for Silva; her thoughts were full of anger, hurt, and hunger for revenge. Then I saw a glimpse into Silva's mind, there had been something more fueling her attack. She wanted to break the truce and restart the war.

"This has nothing to do with your sister, does it?" I said suddenly. "Why bother with us?"

"This has everything to do with you, my pretty," Silvia screeched, catching me off guard and flying in closer for the kill. "Alvero killed my mate to protect you—he took something dear to me and I will do the same to him!" She charged closer toward me and then I remembered the night of my accident I kept hearing the other Lampir saying her name.

I squeezed my eyes tight and prayed. Pulling my necklace out from my jacket, I began to rub the charm. I drew a deep breath and channeled deep into myself for my inner gift, embracing both instincts of the two bloodlines surging through me, as if I had become one with the earth.

BRUXA

I opened my eyes. She was within seconds of killing me. I raised my hands up wielding my power I tossed her away with my powers. Alvero charged the other ones coming at us from the side. Inspecting him for that second, I paid no attention to my own danger, until I heard him scream my name.

Instantly I turned to see Silva just before she knocked me down. It felt as if each nerve and muscle vibrated from the impact as I hit the ground and the wind gusted out of me. Scrambling back onto my feet, I blocked her next attempt using my inner force, and then flung her across the field this time. Relentless, she charged back. Again, I blocked her before she could strike me. She was incredibly fast, making it difficult for me to keep up.

She slid behind me, got a hold of me, and kicked me behind my knees. The echo of bone crackling rippled through my body. My legs buckled, and I fell to my knees. She dragged me by the hair and threw my body against a tree trunk. I fell to the ground, and she tossed me around like a rag doll.

Finding my strength, I raised my hand, pulling the force from deep within myself. It flowed through me and shot her right in the gut, knocking her over. Sighing in relief, I thought it was over. I let my guard down trying to get back up to my feet.

Within seconds, she had pounced on me and put me in an arm lock. She started head butting me.

Everything went muffled and hazy as I felt my body weaken and tasted warm blood in my mouth. Trying desperately to regain my strength, I heard her laughing at my defeat.

I struggled to remain conscious. She slowly approached, savoring my fear. "How does it feel to know you're going to die tonight?" she purred, raising my head up by pulling on my hair.

I grabbed my necklace and squeezed with all my strength, grasping for my father's strength. I began to chant, trying to call out to angels for help. She pulled the chain from my neck, and the charm ripped out of my hand. I felt defeated and lost my courage, finding it harder to breathe.

"What is this…? Oh my God — not you! Where did you get this?" she hissed, kneeling to look at my face.

"My…fath…er," I cried choking on my blood.

"It's true — the daughter of Matthias." She released her hold, and my head hit the cold ground.

"Silva, this ends now," Alvero growled, wasting no time as he approached us.

"This is getting more interesting by the moment, I'm just getting started," she said with an acid laugh. She lifted my head up to Alvero and hissed while her face pressed against mine. "Take a good look at your father's killer," she whispered in my ear. She lifted me up, tossing me against another tree, freeing herself to fight Alvero.

My body and mind shut down as her words ripped apart my heart. Hearing them wrestling violently with one another, my eye caught the glimpse of Alvero deliver one lethal blow to her chest, ripping her heart out, instantly destroying her. Her body hit the ground and disintegrated into ashes.

Seeing him approach, my locked away memory unfolded. Seeing the little girl running as her father yelled at her to leave and find her mother. She ran into the house, stopping inside the glass doors curious of the stranger. She looked back, watching as the two men exchanged angry words. He had turned his back to look at me — my father to his daughter — as his body gave away. I had turned my back, screaming for my mother.

Scared for my father, I had pushed the glass doors open and ran back to him, too young to comprehend events. I heard a bone-chilling cry of anguish from the stranger as I approached. The stranger's face was still a blur. My father looked up and smiled, reaching for my hand, and holding his hand, I felt a calming peace as I knelt beside him. As the stranger hung his head, my father grabbed his hand looking at the stranger and placed my hand in his, and the blurriness faded.

Alvero.

My world came crashing down.

Alvero looked at me as tears of blood ran down his face. "Gabriella, it's all over now." His voice sounded angelic as his lips brushed my forehead while he pulled me into his arms.

I flinched away in disgust. An angry flame of betrayal consumed me. "You killed him," I whimpered.

My body's pain was nothing in comparison to the pain that tore at my heart, to know that the one person I loved was my father's killer. Looking at him, I hit him with what strength I had left. He wrapped me up in his arms. I was too weak to move, I tried pushing him away.

"I know you hate me right now. I have to take you to your mother," he murmured, easily overcoming my attempts to push him away.

My body shut down. I fought to stay conscious, my vision darkened. I just felt the cold air whipping across my face as he raced to my house.

"What have you done to her?" I heard my mother's voice scream. I felt more at ease knowing I made it home alive.

I felt him push past her, then climb the stairs to place me on my bed. "That night, I should have told you the truth," he whispered into my soul. "I am guilty for what happened, and it is my greatest shame. Believe me, I did not kill him. Never did I lie about how I feel for you; no matter what, my feelings for you will never stop. No matter how much you might hate me." I felt his cool lips against my cheek. I cringed, trapped inside my mind unable to push him away.

Then I heard him leave. My room filled with silence. I found it hard to breathe. I vaguely heard my mother arguing with him in the hall. Their voices faded in and out until they faded completely as I passed out.

Chapter 20

HEALING

The mild daylight burned my eyelids. I tried desperately to open them as my body screamed in pain. I squinted against the sting of the sunlight until my eyes adjusted, anxious to see where I was. A stale smell of formaldehyde hung in the air. I heard faint breathing; someone had to be nearby, watching over me. My body constricted in pain as I tried to move.

Footsteps quickly approached and I sensed someone else hovering over me. Now there were two bodies observing me. Panicking, I forced my eyes open, my vision still unfocused.

"She's moving, her eyes are opening!" someone shouted. The voice sounded like Joey's.

BRUXA

I vigorously blinked my eyes to clear them. *Was that Joey's voice, or was I delusional?* How could that be, and what had happened to me? My eyes finally focused. Looking up, I saw my mother and Joey looking down at me, both with loving eyes. Looking around, I saw bouquets of flowers everywhere. An IV drip attached to my arm. I definitely wasn't home then. I knew I had been in the hospital.

"Where...am...I?" I croaked as I tried to sit up.

"I've been so worried about you," Joey whispered as he adjusted pillows behind my back. "I came home as soon as I heard the news."

My mother held the straw in a cup of water to my mouth. "Oh, Gabriella, I've been so worried. You've been out for so long. The doctors were worried you might fall into a coma." She smiled with relieved excitement and kissed my forehead.

"What are you talking about?" I asked, feeling disconnected from myself. "I'm fine, just a little sore, that's all." What had happened? Had all this been one messed-up dream, or had it really happened?

No, I knew I did not dream this entire thing. What was going on here? Why did I get the impression that something was wrong with this picture? I could not even remember what I thought I should remember. As if everything had slipped from my memory. *Wow, I must have had a blow to my head,* I thought as fragments played out in my mind, as if teasing me about what was fact or fiction.

I saw flashes of what I remembered happening as if it were all a dream. I held on tight to the idea of Alvero and my experiences with him. Everything else seemed like a blur. I heard Joey and my mother talking to me. I could not process what they were saying. I tuned them out, trying desperately to remember what had taken place.

"What day is it?" I asked, trying to put the pieces in my mind together. I watched both of them closely.

"It's Friday—two more days to New Year's Eve. You've been out for a couple of days," my mother told me. "You had some crazy car accident. The doctors have been monitoring you closely. You had some vivid dreams going on in your head." Her voice sounded comforting but not genuine at all. "All right, I'm going to leave you kids alone." She kissed me again before leaving.

Joey sat on the edge of my bed, smiling at me. Something about Joey did not feel right anymore. His face looked older and a little empty. I still saw his love for me beneath it all. He caressed my face and smiled. Guilt filled my mind, since I knew that I had allowed my heart to betray him. I felt ashamed forever doubting him, knowing that he left Europe to come to my aid.

"How was your trip, and why didn't you call me?" I asked, not letting on that I knew what had happened—I mean, he did not even know himself.

"Sorry, I don't know. Everything seemed to slip my mind. I was so busy with strict training and observations, I wasn't allowed to communicate with the outside world while training with Laruen." He pressed his lips together and looked away, knowing he had forgotten about me until my mother called him.

Laruen. That name sounded familiar, I could not quite put my finger on it. I thought he would have been more passionate when talking about his trip. He always spoke strongly of the Bruxa. Every time he mentioned our kind, his face usually lit up. Now he sat slightly turned away, looking subdued.

"Who is Laruen? Why do you seem distant when you mention his name? Did something happen there that you want to talk about?"

"Gabby, right now it's not about me. I am mad at myself—I cannot believe I never thought to call or see how you were doing. I don't understand it. It was as if I were in another world, one that did not include you. The guilt is killing me. I had forgotten all that I was before I left. I don't know what I would have done if I'd lost you." Still he avoided eye contract. I knew he was hiding a lot more.

We sat there in awkward silence, looking at one another as if guilt were forcing us together. I think he somehow felt responsible for what happened to me. Something definitely was missing in him. Maybe the Lougaro in him had taken over. His inner battle was readable in his eyes.

"Joey, none of this is your fault. Things happen. Indulge me—tell me about your training." I was very interested to know.

He told me about a huge estate that belonged to Laruen, and at first, he seemed excited. He told me he ran around as a Lougaro freely, and that it had taken its shape. He learned to track properly, to hunt, and to destroy evil spirits. He did not agree with some of Laruen's ideas. He confided, they had bumped heads a lot. There were five in the group, and he blushed as he admitted he was one of the strongest in the group.

The door opened slowly, and my mother peeked in. "Are you hungry yet?" She came in bearing food, and Joey left my side and sat back down, giving my mother some time with me.

"He hasn't left your side since he came back," she whispered as she spoon-fed me homemade soup. "He's been worried about you, and so have I."

I had many questions that I wanted to ask my mother, and I wished we could have time alone. I didn't understand anything. My mind felt lost, distorted, and unable to shake Alvero out of my head. What was going on? I turned my head away, refusing to eat anymore. I knew she had probably blocked my thoughts, as she had with Joey.

The doctor entered, smiling at me. He picked up my chart and read it, his expression first puzzled, then shocked. He came to my bedside and held his hand out to introduce himself. "Hello, Gabriella, I'm Dr. Jeffery. You gave us quite a scare, young lady — or I should say bionic woman? Your body has healed with remarkable speed, and frankly, I am surprised to see you awake and sitting up. I would like to keep you for another night, for observation."

As he shone his penlight in my eyes, I could not wait for him to finish. "It's amazing, how you didn't break a bone," he said in disbelief as he made notes on my chart. "And as for you two, you need to go home and relax," he said to Mom and Joey. "Give her some time to breathe, that's the doctor's orders."

When I awoke next, it must have been early afternoon. I saw a bouquet of red and white balloons coming through the open door and heard my girlfriends whispering amongst themselves, not knowing if I was awake or not. They all squealed with excitement when they saw me sit up.

"Hey, guys," I said, equally excited to see them.

They ran up with lots of love—I had to admit, I loved the friends I was blessed with. Allison seemed a little off, and I knew something was troubling her behind her cheerful façade. She kept glancing at my mother and Joey.

They all told me about their holidays and how they wished I'd get better soon. Nothing seemed right at all about this picture. I could have sworn I was just with them. I could not remember the details of my night.

I sensed Joey's discomfort at being surrounded by my friends as he came up and kissed my forehead, telling me he would come back later in the evening. He flashed my friends a fake smile as he walked away, glancing at me before opening the door to leave. I knew something other than me lay deep in his soul. My mom followed in his tracks, leaving shortly after him.

"Allison, is everything okay with you? You seem off," I said. Noticing that they all turned a bit pale before looking away, I knew I had asked the wrong question. "I'm sorry, if you don't want to talk, we won't,—that's fine." I patted her hand and gently squeezed it.

"No, it's okay, Gabby. Paul and I got into a fight a couple of nights ago," she said, looking down at the floor. Then she looked up, smiled, and squeezed my hand back. "Hey, this isn't about me! I'm glad to see you recovering."

They stayed for about an hour. I continued to sense that Allison was not telling the truth. This is one lamb I wished I could read. My other friends were clueless about what was really going on with Allison. I wasn't going to push—after all, I needed to figure some things out for myself.

After my friends left and I lay in the room by myself, I stared out the hospital window, watching as night consumed the sun. Scenes from the past week played out in my mind while I tried desperately to figure out what had happened to me.

I heard the door open so I looked over, saw my mother, and looked away again. She knew I was struggling with my thoughts and emotions. "What did you do to me?" I muttered. "I'm not crazy. Why is my memory of that night gone? Why does this week keep fading on me? And who is Laruen?" Holding back tears, I looked deep into her eyes.

"You are getting stronger," she observed. "I wanted you to heal first, before your heartache kicked in. Your thoughts for him are powerful. I promise, when you are strong again, everything will come back. I had to block your friends' memories of that night to protect who you are. Joey must never know. He is Laruen's new protégé. His strength and ability to transform are remarkable. He will be next in line if anything should happen to Laruen." Her expression saddened as she placed her palms on my temples and pressed gently, reopening my mind.

It felt as if her fingers sent an electric shock through my brain. Everything replayed in my head—except what had happened that night. I remembered everything about the family feud with the Lougaro, and my grandmother's betrayal of my grandfather and mother.

My mother helped me get up and go into bathroom, where she helped me wash. I felt my mother's pain. She was all alone with no help, dealing with my problems and the problems of her parents. I smiled at her. "I do love you, Mom, and I'm sorry for how selfish I have been this year—it's been one hell of a year for me and you both. I do wish you could find someone to love again."

She helped me back into bed and tucked me in, and I saw how much she loved me. I knew that she had her reasons for what she had done. She always had my best interests at heart. Her tender smile eased my mind as she told me in strictest confidence that the Lampir in me was growing just as strong as the Bruxa in me.

"I have a few more months to enjoy you before I have to let you go. And maybe I will find somebody to love." She chuckled, but I knew she was serious. She kissed me good night and left.

A cold breeze drifting into my room sent shivers down my spine and reawakened my soul. Looking around, I saw nothing—wishful thinking. I sighed in disappointment, wishing Alvero had been here. Whispering his name, I reached out, pretending he was present. His song hummed in my mind as I fell into a deep sleep.

A short time later, I quickly awoke feeling his cool fingers tracing over my face. I sat up abruptly, excited to see him. He disappeared back into the shadows, waiting to see my reaction. I was confused by his timid behavior. He slowly re-emerged into the soft city light that poured in through the hospital window. I felt the fire rekindle within my veins as he stood in front of me. He looked conflicted, his expression full of pain. I desperately wanted to comfort him.

He whispered, and I tried to focus on his words and make out what he was saying. "The truth... um, you know." He turned away, pulling his hair back, frustrated with himself. Then he spoke in riddles, as if he could not tell me the truth. Anxiously, I searched his face for clues, his face unclear. He paused and stood there calmly, looking into space. Then he approached slowly, locking his stare on my face, focusing his eyes directly onto mine. "My words keep getting in the way. There are things I should have said or told you. I have to do the right thing, even if it is not fair to either one of us. I cannot take anymore of this, I am falling apart. I just want to bury myself in your precious heart and forget all the things I have ever done wrong, and be who I really am. You brought out the man in me who always runs and hides, and I will always love you for that. Things are never what they seem. I can't let you become..."He grimaced in pain as a red tear fell from his eye.

"What are you trying to say?" I cried, hurt and confused.

"Gabriella, after tonight you'll never have to worry about seeing me. I can't bare to have you hate me for something that was out of my hands, not my crime. Yes, I have done many bad things and lied about who I am. Believe me when I say...my soul... is forever yours." His voice cracked.

I closed my eyes. I could not bare to look at him or listen to what he said. It was tearing me apart. When I opened my eyes again, he had vanished. I sat there by myself, mystified by what had happened and feeling lost.

Then my memories of everything that happened that night flooded in and replayed in my head. I heard again Silva telling me, "Look at your father's killer." I sat up straight and screamed, "*No!*"

Joey burst into the room and rushed over to calm me. "It's all right, I'm here now — there is nothing to worry about," he consoled me as I held onto him, sobbing. I had coerced my heart into thinking I loved the one who had killed my father. All of this was unfair to Joey. I wanted to tell him the truth, but there was no easy way; I would have to confess what I was. Clutching him tighter, I cried uncontrollably, releasing my pain.

He settled me back onto my pillow and looked at me uncertainly. I felt so guilty, I didn't deserve his love. I wanted to be alone or run as far as I could from all this chaos.

When I finally left the hospital, I couldn't believe how excited I was to be going home. My body felt amazing, as if nothing had happened besides the wounds to my heart. I tried to smile at my mother as she helped me out of the car.

"You're still young," she assured me. "Your heart will heal and mend itself. Try to live your life as if it never happened." Her words of encouragement were no use to me. In fact, they bothered me. I am only seventeen years old. Torn between two completely different worlds and I almost gave everything with Joey up to follow my instincts and give my heart to my father's killer. Yeah, I think I am allowed to be messed up.

I was tired of living a lie, tired of all the secrets and pretending. I hated my life right now; it felt as if darkness held me tightly. I was angry, hurt, and feeling my love for life slipping from my grasp. I went straight to my room. I did not want to see or talk to anyone.

I woke up in the darkest hour of night. The house lay in silence. I pushed out of bed and walked over to sit on my window seat, staring out into the night, lost in my thoughts. I realized I was waiting for Alvero to show up and beg for my forgiveness. What would I say—"I hate you but I can't remove you from my soul"? Time passed.

As if lightning struck me, I realized he was not coming. My heart ached. I cried uncontrollably, yearning to see him or feel him again. Wishing I never let him into my heart, I crawled back into bed, wrapping myself in my sheets, trying to calm my sobs before I hyperventilated. I could not control my emotions. The more I tried, the harder I cried. My agony flowed out of me like water from a broken dam, leaving me drained and directionless. I cried myself to sleep.

There was no way to hide my feelings from my mother when I joined her for brunch the next day. I kept my head down and avoided looking at her to hide my bloodshot, swollen eyes, staring down at my plate. It held a mouth-watering homemade waffle smothered with fresh berries and cream, I was not hungry. I cut apiece off, knowing I would not be able to digest anything.

"It's for the better," my mother said as if reading my thoughts. She came over and cradled me in her arms. "You know the truth, I know you can't stop how you feel right now. The strange thing is I know he loves you, too."

I reached up and held onto her arms, beginning to cry again. "Thanks, Mom," I sobbed, knowing she meant well, but that was the last thing I needed to know.

New Year's Eve was going to be uneventful. My mother prepared my favorite dishes. Otherwise, I would celebrate at home—I was still recovering, and this was the second time in a month that my body had been battered. My heart was in so much pain that I hardly noticed my body, though. Reflecting back on Alvero, I had a difficult time fathoming the idea that I had been in love with the man who killed my father. True, I didn't see him actually killing my father in my dream. I shook my head. Regardless, I had to teach myself to let go of him.

My mother invited Joey over to spend the evening with us, since his family was still in Europe. On the last day of the year, I looked back and assessed my holidays, trying to accept the facts. I still felt disconnected from whatever normalcy I had left as a person.

My mother was off conjuring up a dinner feast, while I laid on the couch, emotionless, watching TV. I was still trying to grasp the concept of Alvero killing my father. None of it made any sense. I told myself I shouldn't believe him innocent. Why did my father tell him to protect me? Who in their right mind would tell his killer as he is dying to watch out for his only daughter?

My ancestors howled in my blood, vindictive thoughts teasing my pain. I forced myself to push the darkness away. One part of me wanted to blame him for taking my father away. I hated him more for making me love and want him. Finally, I had enough. I locked away the memory of Alvero and envisioned sealing the vault in my mind. I had to disconnect the fact of loving him from my memory. I had to try to surrender myself to Joey and focus on my family honor, I was the last of my bloodline.

I got off the couch and went upstairs to have a shower, refusing to let my hurt drag me down anymore. I had to show a confident front, had to feel good about myself and take pride in remembering who I was. After drying my hair, I grabbed my makeup bag and went to work concealing the puffy eyelids and dark circles under my eyes, then brushed on some bronzer in hopes that it would brighten up my face. Taking a good look at my reflection when I finished, I smiled. I did indeed feel a bit more confident.

As I strolled down the stairs, I heard my mother welcoming Joey into the house. Pulling my hair back with my hands to reveal my face, I smiled down at him. His face lit up, glad to see the old me back.

"It's good to see you up on your feet again," he said as we met at the bottom of the stairs.

"I'm going to finish setting up while you two kids get caught up," my mother said, sounding relieved. She disappeared back into the kitchen.

Maybe I was feeling a little too confident. Teasing him with my eyes, I adjusted his collar over his wool polo sweater. "I'm glad you came back," I whispered.

"Trust me, so am I."

He leaned in to kiss me. I blocked his attempt by putting my index finger over my lips and widening my eyes, looking toward the kitchen to remind him of my mother. In truth, I couldn't escape the shame of falling for someone else.

Joey made me laugh. He told me crazy stories of the old men back home in Europe. He avoided talk about Laruen and his training. Something was missing in him, though, and it definitely had nothing to do with me. Something must have happened to him there, I decided. Well, whatever happened, I had no right to judge.

He mentioned our night together before he left, and told me that one night in the home country he was daydreaming about me asking him why he never called. At the time, he thought I was a figment of his imagination. He leaned in to kiss me again and I turned my head, still ashamed.

"My mother—you." I pointed to the kitchen, then to him, giggling to hide my guilt.

"Damn, I keep forgetting, my parents are coming back in a couple of days," he moaned throwing his head back. Then he laughed and invaded my space as he cuddled right up to me. He grabbed my hand and rubbed it lightly. "Why is it that we have so many rules and codes we have to obey?" He sighed, looking away.

"Well, I don't follow anybody's code and rules. I follow the laws of God," I said, with a shrug. "That's how my mother raised me. Yes, I am learning Bruxa are taught differently. We were once the day Watchers and our enemies were the night Watchers.

I don't understand how we all became enemies and lost our true paths," I mused.

He turned to look at me in disbelief. "They hunt us. Who told you about day and night Watchers? I refuse to believe we shared anything with them. To me, they are the same as demons that feed off the weak. I would die before I ever believed that. Do you have any idea what they did to our kind? You are living proof — you are the last of your bloodline. Do you know why they kill all the females? So we no longer reproduce and be a head of the game."

His words stung me. Slowly pulling my hand from his, I remembered why I had fought with Silva. If he only knew the other half of me...

"Why do you care about our enemies? You are always so quick to defend them. They hunt us, and we hunt back." He pulled away disappointed in me.

"Doesn't Christ teach us to love our enemies, and to never judge? Why do you hate them so much when you don't even know them? You hate because that is what you are taught. Isn't that just like the lambs, weak in their flesh and easily manipulated by what they are taught? We have been blessed, with our powers to keep balance within the realm of good and evil and protect the lambs. Maybe I'm glad I was never brainwashed into hating something I don't understand." I was breathless by the time I finished my zealous comeback. I was tired of his judgments against my other half when I knew the truth — that there is good and bad in everything, including us.

His looked at me in surprise, his brows drawn down at my bold statement, which mystified him. I could see in his face how he struggled to understand what I said. He reached out, recaptured my hand, and pulled it to his chest. "I love your compassionate heart; I wish I saw things through your eyes. You are right — unfortunately, that is not how it is. Gabriella, do you not understand what I am designed for? The Lougaro purify the world of all monsters. We are the only thing strong enough to destroy the Lampirs. And you're right, there is good and bad in everything," he whispered as he placed his head on my lap.

I hesitated, then gave in and traced my fingertips gently over his hair, allowing myself to open my heart to him again. I did care deeply for him. Nevertheless, it's completely different from the way I felt about Alvero.

I did realize that with Joey I had a chance to have a somewhat normal life, to walk freely in the daylight and never have to hide in the shadows. No matter how much I loved the Lampir in me, I never wanted to live forever. I would hate the fact of watching everyone I loved die when I remained the same, unchanged by time.

My mother called us over to her seafood feast. We ate and laughed, enjoying both the food and my mother's company for the remainder of the night. Together we counted down the seconds to the new year, shouting, "…three, two, one—happy new year!" before kissing one another.

The warmth of his lips on mine again brought my old feelings rushing back. My heart connected with his once more, and I smiled, wanting more of him. I giggled with excitement as he danced around my mother, even making her laugh. I laughed, too—glad the nightmare year was over.

Chapter 21

A NEW YEAR

I felt refreshed and welcomed the new day, jumping out of bed and feeling glad to be alive. I had the rest of the week to get myself together before returning to school. As I got dressed, I thought about the last two weeks, which had been a crazy roller coaster ride. Looking out my window, I sighed in relief. It was all over for now.

My mother had invited Joey over for our traditional New Year's Day brunch. When I heard the doorbell ring, I rushed downstairs to let him in, but my mother beat me to it.

"Good afternoon, Mrs. Fragoso," he greeted my mother as she welcomed him in.

BRUXA

"Hey Joey, did you sleep well last night? Please, don't be shy—there's lots of food." She smiled warmly, ushering him to sit down as she passed him a glass of freshly squeezed juice.

"So, do you two have plans tonight?" Joey politely directed the question toward my mother. "I know Gabby just came home from the hospital, but I was wondering if Gabby would be allowed to come over to my house. I want to make dinner for her if that's okay with you, Mrs. Fragoso?" He bit his lower lip with uncertainty.

"I don't know," she replied. "You'll have to ask Gabby yourself." She raised her brow at me.

After eating, I insisted it would be better if we walk to Joey's house. I needed to feel the fresh, crisp air and marvel at God's winter land artistry. With my strength back, my pent-up energy needed release.

We stepped outside, and I paused to inhale the cool, fresh air. Then he grabbed my hand, and I looked at him, feeling strangely unsure and odd as we began to walk.

"Look, Gabby, I know there is a part of you that hates me right now and that is uncertain about our relationship," Joey earnestly spoke. "Trust me when I say I never meant to hurt you in any way. I cannot forgive myself for the last two weeks. I don't understand what came over me."

I put my finger on his mouth to silence him before guilt consumed me again. "Shh, please...I just want to forget these past two weeks. Whatever happened between the both of us can remain locked away in the past. Maybe this is a fresh start for both of us."

"So whatever happened, you're willing to forgive me and move forward?" His concern faded, into a smile. Letting go of my hand, he bolted ahead in excitement, disappearing as he turned a corner.

I reached that point and looked around, confused. Where had he disappeared? Then he jumped out from behind a tree. "Ha!" He grinned and raised his hands up, cupping a snowball. Recognizing his intentions, I swooped down and collected my ammo, dodging his first throw as I formed an icy ball of my own. I pitched it like a curve ball, aiming for his chest missing and hitting him dead center in the head.

His eyes bulged, and I made a run for it, laughing, as he darted after me. His speed was incredible. Within seconds, he had grabbed me, carefully tossing me over his shoulder, exclaiming that he was going to snow-wash me. Pounding his back, I shrieked, "Don't you dare, Joey!" I was still weak. I managed to squirm, trying to get out of his hold.

"What — you think you can get away from me?" he roared, tightening his grip. We both broke out in laughter.

Finally, he placed me back down on my feet, and without waste, I ran off. He caught up to me and knocked me over into a soft bank of snow. He then stood over me, gloating at his touch down victory as I lay in a snow bank. I sat up, laughing, and threw snow in his face. Sputtering, he fell to his knees in defeat and stared at me. I sat there, unsure if he was mad or about to retaliate.

He lunged forward and the weight of his body pinned me down. Looking down at me with the most cunning smirk, he shook his head. I could not escape if I wanted to. All my feelings for him came rushing back as we gazed at each other, the warmth of his breath brushing my lips. His eyes hungered for me. He hesitated for a brief moment then, without warning, he lunged in for the kill and kissed me.

My body shivered with joy. I felt I had been lost and found again. My settler had returned. I felt my Lampir half curl up inside me, allowing it to become dormant again. I looked into his eyes. Everything that had happened while he was gone seemed like a distant memory or a dream.

He picked me up, and we walked to his house. Finally feeling comfortable with him again, I nestled my head into his shoulder and held him tightly, never wanting to let go.

"I can't believe I'd forgotten how good it feels to have you beside me again," he sheepishly admitted as he unlocked his door.

I watched Joey struggle around the kitchen while he prepared dinner for us, Silva's voice echoed in my mind: "Look at your father's killer." Those words kept scratching at me like a cat sharpening its claws on a post. Building a hatred for Alvero allowed me to deny me the fact that a part of me still cared for him. I tried replacing my feelings with disgust, still haunted by my guilt as I watched Joey dicing onions and garlic.

"Damn it!" he shouted as the knife sliced his finger.

My heart raced as I approached him grabbing his hand. I pulled his arm up, the smell of his blood made me feel ill. Trying not to gag, I turned on the tap and ran the cold water over his finger. "Where is your first aid kit?" I asked, anxious to leave the smell of blood that still lingered in the air.

"Don't worry Gabby, the wound is already closing. Don't you know we Lougaro heal fast?" He looked at my face and frowned, then turned me to face him. "Why do you look sick? Are you okay?"

"Yeah, I'm fine. I guess I can't handle the sight of blood. It brought flashbacks of the accident." I avoided meeting his eye.

"What did happen to you that night?" he asked, lifting my face up.

My mind froze. What should I say? I didn't have a clue as to what my mother had told everyone, and there would be no way in hell I could tell him the truth. "Can we please just not talk about it right now? I want to forget. Besides, I'm not one hundred percent sure myself." I tried looking innocently at him, I could not keep my eyes from watering.

"Sorry." He released his hold on my chin, and then smiled. "So, are you ready to be surprised by my cooking ability?" He swept one arm dramatically toward the door to the living room and said with mock sternness, "Now, young lady, you have to get out of my kitchen, so go sit down, and relax."

"Actually, if you'll excuse me, I need to use your washroom," I said.

Making sure I locked the washroom door, I filled up the sink with water and used the tip of the angel wing charm to prick my finger. I called out to my mother as the drop of blood fell remembering what my mother taught me. I waited impatiently for her response, sighing in relief when I saw her image in the mirror. Mentally rewinding my thoughts and replaying them for her to see. "What did you say?" I asked when I was done.

"That night I went to each of your friends and planted new memories of that night in their minds. I told them that you had driven yourself to the party and you were not feeling good so you left early and lost control of your car and hit a tree. We had to stage the accident. Alvero was there when the police and ambulance arrived, manipulating their minds as well. We could not take the risk of anybody being curious or having any loose ends. Go back and enjoy your time with Joey— no messing around." She smiled and blew me a kiss as her image faded away.

I took a good look at myself in the mirror, making sure I looked composed before I went back to the living room and sat down on the couch. I was scanning through the channels, hoping to find a distraction. When Joey came up behind me and hung over the back of the couch to rest his head on my shoulder, "Do you trust me?" he whispered in my ear.

Uncertain of the reason for this random question, I felt my throat closing. "Why do you ask?" I finally managed. "I wouldn't be here if I didn't." I turned my head to look at him, smiling but deep down I felt a bit uneasy.

"Good." He stood back up and moved directly behind me. A silky red scarf came down over my face covering my eyes.

"What are you doing?" I exclaimed, feeling panic. I struggled to remain open-minded as he directed me to stand.

"Do you trust me?" he asked again, grabbing my hand and pulling me toward him.

I mentally probed his intentions and relaxed. He had a surprise for me. "I guess I have to," I whispered, and he led me down the hall, then slowly down the basement stairs. The fresh smell of summer filled my senses as he continued guiding me. We stopped and he turned me slightly to the right before loosening the blindfold.

The soft silk slipped from my face and fluttered to the floor, my heart dropped to my stomach in dismay. I stood speechless, gazing at the Indian garden oasis he had created for me. A carpet of cushions and flower petals dusted the floor. All within a canopy of a sheer, burnt orange material complete with lit candles casting a warm glow.

"You shouldn't have." I wept, looking away, ashamed at myself for ever doubting him, and for the secrets I had to keep from him. "It's amazing— I don't deserve all of this." A tear rolled down my face.

"Trust me, you do. I am the one who doesn't deserve you. I have been a horrible boyfriend. When I saw you lying in that hospital bed, my world shattered and I realized how much you mean to me. We agreed to start fresh and that is exactly what I want to do. Consider this our first date. After all, I'm not the same person—I'm full Lougaro now." He pulled me under the canopy.

After we were finished our meal, which included much laughter and teasing him about his impressive cooking ability, I rose to clean up our mess. He grabbed me around the waist and pulled me down. "You're not going anywhere," he said against the back of my hair.

"What do you think you're doing?" Snickering, I turned my head. He brushed my hair off the back of my neck and I fell still, absorbing the warmth of his breath against my exposed skin. Tingles ran through me.

Everything about him seemed familiar, yet different. I still couldn't place my finger on it. I wanted to enjoy the innocence of our relationship regardless. My feelings for him were deep, but still I felt unsure what being in love was. I turned my body around and looked at him in amazement.

"What? Is something wrong?" he asked perplexed.

"No, nothing. I was just thinking I have never seen you in your new Lougaro form. I'm sure you're still a cute dog," I teased.

"I don't think I want you to see me in my form. It's not a cute dog anymore." He brushed it off as a joke I sensed he felt no humor. "I have to be triggered by something. It's not like the movies where with a snap of a finger I turn into a creature." He lowered his head and massaged his eyelids with his fingertips.

"I think it's important that I know what you are, I don't want to see you in your animal form unexpected." I begged because if one day he has to hunt me down I will know it's him.

He nodded and nudged me away bolting towards his room, holding his head as if in pain. I followed him. The bedroom door opened by a crack. Gathering myself, I pushed it open then stood paralyzed, witnessing his transformation. His body elongating, his muscles bulking out as his body stretched unnaturally; within seconds, this massive black wolf consumed his body.

I had heard stories and it was a strong part of our culture, nothing could have prepared me for this. The sleek dark fur hid any human form. He crouched on all fours like a real wolf, but twice the size. His ears pointed back, and then he turned his head my way and his lips rolled back as if to smile, baring his strong white fangs. Terrified, I covered my mouth. He had come a long way from a cute dog. I didn't recognize anything of Joey in him until I looked into his eyes.

He spun and fled, pushing against his French doors and leaped out into the night as the doors flew open. The cold winter air gusted in and whipped around me. I could not move. Minutes must have passed before I broke out of my trance and ran outside, screaming, "Joey!"

Nowhere in sight, and then I felt a rush of air as something was charging me from behind. I slowly turned to face him.

"You wanted to see, now you've seen it!" he roared. "You're looking at me like I'm a monster," he moaned circling around me.

I did not know what to expect. I did not feel his warm soul. My pulse raced to the burn, pushing my Lampir blood through my veins. Clenching my teeth, I channeled deep inside to restrain the Lampir within me. My body started to quiver, not out of fear. I shut my eye's holding back my tears, but one managed to escape.

I took a deep breath as I opened my eyes; He stood in front of me, his head hanging in shame. As if in slow motion, he turned away and scampered back into the house. I stood there for a minute feeling lost, before following him back inside the house. I closed the doors to find him curled up into a ball in a shadowy corner of his room. I felt his pain as I went to console him, approaching with caution. He had transformed back to his normal form. He huddled in the dark like a terrified child, shivering in shame.

I held my hand out towards him, knowing I made him feel that way. "I'm not scared of you, and there is nothing to be ashamed of. You are still beautiful to me," I whispered as I cradled him in my arms and helped him to his feet. "I've never seen you transform and I had no idea how much of a change it would be. Yes, I was shocked, not disgusted."

"I saw you trembling, and I saw something completely different in your eyes," he said. "I have never seen it before. It was if it was a — I can't even describe it," he groaned, looking away from me.

I grabbed a blanket and wrapped it around him, rubbing it against his body to warm and calm him, helping him on to his bed. I laid down beside him. His back turned away from me, lost to the world. I sat up and brushed his hair off of his face. I hated this, coming to another obstacle. I take three steps forward, and get knocked back three steps. I found it hard to keep my faith, but I am not about to give up, no matter how hard the journey will get.

I must have dozed off. I woke up to the feel of something tickling my nose. Then I remembered I was at Joey's house. He was twirling a feather over my nose. He smiled when I looked up at him, embarrassed I couldn't help but giggle.

"I've been watching you this whole time. I am sorry you didn't like what you saw, It killed me, that look in your eyes. Something about it hit a nerve in me. I think you sensed it in me as well. Back home with Laruen, everything about it felt right." He sighed as he dropped back down beside me.

"The Lougaro carry the animal spirit guides of our ancestors," he continued. "The animal that best suits your personality and that best suits your life's purpose, becomes a part of you. It can be a wolf, a wildcat, even a bird. The wolves are loyal, strong, and are leaders. Wildcats are strong and are controlling and cunning—Laruen is a mix between wildcat and wolf. The birds are usually the women who are free spirits. They are always guarding the children and are the masters of the sky. Each animal possesses its own traits, as does its master. And we become one with it." He turned on his side to look at me with adoring eyes.

BRUXA

I was curious to know what was going to become of me on my own eighteenth birthday. I looked away feeling ashamed, and unsure if the embrace of the Lampir would come out as my gift? Only time would tell. "I've never really had much—or any—experience with the Bruxa. I had grown up with stories and teachings, but now everything has become so real. Until meeting you, I never understood how complex our world is. I've never met others my age, or the Lougaro, before." Sighing, I turned to face him.

"Now that I am getting closer to eighteen, there is still much for me to learn of our own kind and the differences in our lines. I am of noble blood and you are of Lougaro blood. We have two completely different functions. You are a shape-shifter and I manipulate matter and thoughts. And to top it off, I'm the last of my kind." I sighed heavily, distressed as I grasped our situation and its effects.

"You worry too much." He said as we both sat up. "Besides, those were the old laws. Now it does not matter what kind of lineage you choose to be with—you are the last hope to carry on the Malicus lineage. Your grandmother is a Conjure, and your mother still came out as a Malicus. Once you have your ceremony, you'll understand our laws and way of life more. It's different for each linage and individual. "He rested his head on my shoulder and I found comfort in his reassuring voice as it pressed against my hair.

He wrapped his arms around me and pulled me back down, then rolled over to hover above me. Our eyes locked in a fixed stare, as we silently smiled at one another. Lifting my hand up to pull away his hair that hung on his face. I sighed in relief with a smile, knowing I had my shelter back.

"Oh my God, my mother is going to kill me! I was so supposed to be home already," I wailed noticing the clock on the wall, pushing him off me and straightening my clothes, I quickly kissed his forehead and then brushed my hand across his face. "I will call you later. Thank you for tonight—it was beautiful." I grazed him with a kiss.

"Gabby." He grabbed my arm and pulled me back to cup my face in his hands. "Sorry."

"No, I'm glad to have been able to see all of you. I just wish I had been more prepared." I smiled, taken by surprise as he plunged in for another kiss. His hand slid down to my waist and pulled me down as our kiss became passionate.

My body tingled and I ran my hand through his hair and pulled him closer. I had forgotten the warmth of his mouth and his touch. As his hands caressed my back, the tension of last night evaporated as our desires took over. My blood burned like a wild fire. I wanted to devour him. Knowing I had to stop, I pushed him away. "This is getting a little too much," I gasped, pushing to my feet. "I really have to go home before my mother kills me."

"Sorry, you're right," he muttered, looking at me with pouting eyes.

We did not say much to one another as he dropped me off at home. "Wait," he called, stopping me before getting out of the car. "I didn't mean for things to get out of hand. It is crazy, how much I feel for you. I can't wait for the day I can take claim of you."

"Mr. Davale, be careful of what you hope for," I teased, and got out of the car.

I waved to him as I entered the house, hoping my mother would not be waiting up for me. The house was quiet and I assumed my mother had already gone to bed. I ran upstairs to wash up and change, enjoying the little time I had to myself.

Towel drying my hair as I walked back into my room it hit me like an ignited match; I felt the burn flare up within me. I dropped the towel and ran to my window. Reaching to pull back my curtains, I dropped my hand stopping myself. Within the moment of hesitation, I felt the fire with in burn out and I knew he was gone.

A New Year

I sat myself down in front of the bay window, pulled back the curtains feeling disappoint. I looked out to the ocean, watching the waves as they crashed heavily against the frozen shore. I connected myself with the tides as they engulfed the pieces of broken ice knowing I am just as broken inside.

A part of me would miss Alvero and his guidance I realized how foolish and reckless he had made me. With Joey, being back things almost felt somewhat normal again. Leaving the past few weeks behind and hoping to start a fresh new year. I know my life will always be upside down no matter what. I am the last Malicus bloodline of Bruxa and will always be Bruxa first but I'm also my father's daughter. My last near death experience had been enough to open my eyes and make me realize the responsibility of caring on my bloodline. I will have to find away to balance the Bruxa and the Lampir within me, and trust in God my future.

Continue to follow Gabriella in Blood Ties
Coming 2013

A.F. Costa has been creating vivid, imaginary worlds before she could even pick up a book, so it was only natural for her to put a pen to paper the moment she learned to write. Growing up with rich Latin superstitions and strong spiritual beliefs sparked her interests for the paranormal world. Captivating small audiences with her campfire stories resurrected her passion for writing, but seeing her same passions for reading and writing developing in her son has inspired her the most.

Toronto, Ontario-based stylist A.F.Costa has been showcasing her creative abilities for over sixteen years, working with some of the best in the industry. As it is with her visual creativity, A.F. Costa brings the same passion to her writing. In Bruxa: the Secret Within, you'll discover an innovative world of witches and vampires like no other, blending Latin, Portuguese and Hebrew folklore into a modern day love story with an unforgettable twist.